For Brooke

("Don't spray your shots!")

Sweetspot

Confessions of a Golfaholic

Hope you like it.

John O'Hern

John O'

THE
EDITING
COMPANY

Westport, CT

The Editing Company

252 Post Road East

Westport, CT 06880

ISBN 978-0615760483

Cover design by Seth Johnson

www.SweetspotTheBook.com

THIRD EDITION

This book is dedicated to Lisa,

my never fail rescue club

Acknowledgments

The secret to my survival has been to surround myself with people smarter than me. In the three years it has taken me to learn how to stitch this story together from its theatrical beginnings I have many, many friends and acquaintances who volunteered their time to read and critique as I stumbled my way forward: Mark and Brandon Graham who got me started, my class mates at *Write Yourself Free*, everyone at the *Westport Theatre Artist Workshop* who put up with me and my scribbling for so long, Sari Bodi, Brian Meehl, Dick Siderowf, Tom Gordon, Gary McCann, Rusty Ford, Tom Fordiani, Tom Torti and anyone else who read a page and got back to me, I thank you.

A special thanks to Kevin McMullen for going the extra mile and to Dan Meyer for reaching out to a stranger.

All my friends at Longshore: Cooper and Tyler, Mark, Bud, Tom and all the rest who supported me by coming to the show and cheering me on. Especially John Cooper and Chris Carriero, my fountains of inspiration, and then they had to listen to everything.

Max and Declan, my two angels who dared to ask me, "How's the writing going, Dad?" Then they'd stand still and grit their teeth, knowing full well I was going to tell them.

There are no coincidences. My newest neighbor Svea Vocke, a screenplay writer and teacher who offered sympathy over our shared fence then volunteered to take a peek. After a month's long meticulous read, copious notes and a two hour, page for page critique at my kitchen table, I found myself deeply in her debt.

The last smart one to come my way was Beth Kallman Werner who I met while dragging this mangled beast across the finish line. She administered a lifesaving injection of wisdom.

In the end though, it came down to Tish Fried and Patrick McCord of *Write Yourself Free*. They gave me their time and ultimately their friendship. Patrick's knowledge of writing was essential in helping me to clarify my vision and turn it into words. Thanks Pat.

Smarter than me, all of them.

Chapter One
The Sickness

Fuck me.

His father-in-law's plump, whisker-shrouded lips, reeking of Lo Mein and garlic, hovered close to Tom's face. The old man was over enunciating his words, almost hissing them to drive home his point. Normally, lunch with Larry was an easy affair, a few minutes of shoptalk and the rest about whatever shenanigans his twin grandsons had been up to.

But not today. "Learn to play the game of golf, Tom…" A sliver of pork was lodged in the corner of Larry's mouth, held there by an orange gob of duck sauce. "…or find another line of work."

Someone at the office, or a client maybe, had whispered in Larry's ear that Tom had once again turned down an invitation to play in the Annual Statewide Medical Supply Industry Golf Tournament sponsored by their firm's largest orthopedics supplier. Tom had hardly given it a thought. He'd hated golf ever since his own father had tried to cram it down his throat as a teenager. Not to mention the couple of times he'd gone to a driving range with college buddies on a lark and made a complete ass of himself; that memory didn't hit his joy button either. But lately he'd been struggling to make his monthly sales numbers, so Larry was going ballistic.

For the benefit of everyone else in the office Larry shouted the next bit. "Not knowing how to play golf in this business—any business for that matter, is making a cripple out of you." The silence of the hushed eavesdroppers on the other side of Larry's door was deafening. "I won't work with cripples, Tom, I can't afford it."

Something clenched in Tom's bowels. His face flushed with such intensity that he could feel the heat coming off his cheeks in waves.

For God's sake, don't sweat in front of him.

In all the years since Carol had dragged him home for a meet-the-parents dinner on their second date, this was the first time his father-in-law had raised his voice to him in anger. The fact that Larry was yelling had only one meaning. Tom was being "red flagged" in front of the staff, a punishment reserved for those unfortunates in Larry's domain whose misbehavior put them a heartbeat away from being pink-slipped.

"Larry," Tom responded quietly, trying to ratchet the tone back down to an intimate level while simultaneously dabbing at specks of Larry's spittle resting just below his right eye, "I know you used to play in all these events…until your…" he flapped a hand at the two hundred and thirty pound frame standing before him, "…back went out. From what I hear you were a laugh-riot to play with."

"Wrote a lot of business out there too, Tom," Larry replied. With one hand Larry was rattling a mass of keys and coins in a front pants pocket and furiously man-handling his salt and pepper beard with the other.

I'm going to have to lay it out for him! Tom swallowed hard, then, threw himself over the cliff.

"You see the thing is…as much as I enjoy spending time watching golf with you on the weekends, the whole thing just…bores me to death." He watched the flesh around Larry's eyes pucker as the realization hit home that Tom had been play-acting enjoyment over the years whenever they'd watched tournaments on television together. "The idea of me playing golf is just stupid," he added for good measure.

Tom was in total free-fall now, saying reckless things, almost giddy with it.

"It's a game populated by fat-cats and snobs. The guys I know who are into golf get all glassy-eyed when they blather on about it, and if you let them, they'll talk you through their last eighteen holes, shot for fucking shot. They're total jerks."

In place of Larry's usual open-faced grin, his lips were now frozen in a truncated sneer. A shudder passed through the older man's massive body and Tom guessed he was suppressing an urge to deliver a ham-hock-slap to the side of his son-in-law's head.

Did I just call Larry, Stupid, a fat cat and a total jerk?

A short film—Tom might have titled it "Carol Hears Her Husband Got Fired,"—started playing somewhere in his frontal lobes. The flickering drama behind his eyes, full of tears and screaming recriminations, climaxed with Tom sitting at the kitchen table, head hung low, and a puffy-eyed Carol screaming, "You idiot, you total idiot!"

Tom sagged, held his hands up in surrender and was about to apologize for his suicidal outburst when Larry switched gears, flashed an "all-is-forgiven" high-beam smile and graced him with a gentle punch in the shoulder.

"Tough shit, Tom," Larry barked out a laugh, "you're going to learn how to play anyway." He slung an arm over Tom's shoulder, guided him to the door, opened it, and with a public slap on the back, pushed him out with a parting thought. "It's just golf for God's sake. What's not to like?"

The following weekend Larry all but frog marched Tom down to his garage—the place overflowing with a life's worth of collected crap—where, after a good deal of exploring, he uncovered his old set of clubs. He handed Tom a rag, a can of Pledge, and together, they dusted off the enormous, mildewed, lipstick-red, leather golf bag. When they'd buffed it to a lustrous sheen,

Larry pulled out the set of decrepit clubs and lined them up against stacks of cardboard boxes full of god-knew-what.

"I didn't give up the game because of my bad back, Tom, although that was bound to happen sooner or later," Larry confessed while massaging a rust spotted shaft with a handful of steel wool, "it was that I'd gotten so fat, I couldn't bend over far enough to see the damn ball at my feet."

The old man let out a howl of delight at his own expense. "I was never that good at it anyway, Tom. You might hear a story or two about how I won a lot of tournaments but that's all hogwash. The fact is I played just enough to maintain a twenty-six handicap. You can't lose with a handicap like that."

In a funk, Tom refused to oblige Larry with eye contact. Instead, he kept his focus on scraping away at a fossil-hard chunk of dirt from the face of one of the decades old persimmon headed drivers. When he finally spoke though, he did his best to keep from sounding bitchy. "Where am I supposed to do all this golf ball hitting? Any suggestions on that?"

Larry had all the answers. "Connecticut is full of driving ranges Tom. Rocky Shores is the public course where you live in Westwater. It's an easy track and it's got a driving range, too, if I remember."

"Oh yeah," Tom shrugged. "I've heard of it."

"It's a five minute drive from your house, Tom." Larry was oozing enthusiasm. "You'll have fun, I guarantee it."

Even though he felt like a brat in the process, Tom went mute again, letting his unhappiness marinate the mood. *Can't you see I don't want to do this?*

"The trick to the whole business…" Larry elbowed Tom in the ribs and leaned in close to share the secret, "…is to just get yourself a really high handicap and exploit the hell out of it."

Tom remained impassive until Larry threw in a sweetener.

"I'll let you out of work a little early to practice if you like." Then Larry gave him the old "big wink" and added, "At the very least it'll give you an excuse to get out of the house."

Tom lifted an eyebrow and tilted his head in Larry's direction.

"Come on, Tommy," the old fart added, digging in with another elbow of fellowship, "what's not to like?"

* * *

"What's not to like?" Tom wished he had a nickel for every time he'd heard his father-in-law say that. Using the toe of his shoe, he teased another ball onto the mat, set up and swung at it. "Jesus Christ Almighty!" he said and almost threw the god-forsaken 7-iron out onto the range.

There's a secret to this stupid fucking game and I'm not getting it!

In an effort to distance himself from the other golfers on the driving range—people who looked like they knew what they were doing—Tom had taken the farthest open slot down the line of hitting stalls. But there was no hiding his swing. Dressed in his business attire, highly polished Cole Haan loafers, pressed slacks, and an open collar button-down white shirt, Tom stood slumped over his pile of practice balls. His arms hanging limp at his sides, mouth agape, he was breathing hard and beads of sweat were popping out on his face. He'd just hit twenty shots, one after another, and each one had flown about four feet off the ground—and dead right.

Looking up he noticed that the other golfers, protected only by a knee-high plastic guard separating each stall, had all stopped hitting. In fact—*holy shit*—

they'd backed away from their mats and were clustered in a protective herd at the other end of the range. They were all giving him the evil eye and muttering amongst themselves. *Did someone just say "douche-bag?"*

You need to take lessons. That's what he'd been telling himself with every bucket he'd flailed his way through in the two months since Larry had laid down his command, but he'd resisted. It wasn't just the money. Yes, Carol would let out a roar if she thought he was dropping a hundred dollars an hour on something as frivolous as golf lessons, but there was more to it than that. He *was* athletic. He'd been on the track and soccer teams in high school, and fairly competitive too. *But you're not getting it,* the voice boomed in his head, *you're clueless, just-take-a-fucking- lesson.*

What was wrong with him? It wasn't rocket science after all. Everyone around him seemed to be deriving great pleasure from their buckets of balls. Now and then he'd hear a soft moan, "Oh yeah baby… nailed it!" from someone down the line. A few days back the guy next to him had hit a tremendous blast with his driver and while holding his finish pose whispered under his breath, "Oh…yes, Jesus, yes," like he was having a religious experience. *Christ, it sounded like the guy was getting a hard on.*

For Tom however, each swing was a lesson in humility. It was time to crawl back to Larry and admit defeat.

Bending over to pick up the half bucket of unused balls, he was aghast to see Marty, the Head Pro, striding toward the range and staring directly at him. *Shit, shit, shit.* Butterflies pinged in his stomach and Tom felt his face go flush. Someone must have gone into the clubhouse and complained that there was a psycho on the range. From all the buckets of balls Tom had purchased in the pro-shop over the past few months, he knew Marty well enough to say hello to, but never, not once, had he ever seen the tanned and handsome Pro make an appearance on the driving range.

As Marty marched forward in pressed, pleated sports slacks and a snug fitting polo shirt that accentuated his muscular physique, the group of golfers parted, allowing him to pass like royalty cutting a path through scruffy peasants. Marty came to a stop directly behind Tom's hitting station and looked straight at him. With his arms folded across his chest and topped off in a black golf cap with reflector sunglasses, Marty looked like a cop. He nodded once and then demanded, "Let me see your swing."

Like one of his toddler sons on the verge of tears and about to be sent to his room for a time-out, Tom's breathing became shallow with a little hitch in it. He felt like he'd been pulled over by a State Trooper for reckless driving, and with other golfers rubbernecking, he was being forced to take a field sobriety test. Surprising himself, he pulled a fundamental tenet of Carol's spiritual beliefs out of thin air, something she had said to him many, many times. "When encountering a difficult task, take a deep cleansing breath, concentrate, and find the Zen of the moment."

Focusing as hard as he could, Tom took a deep inhale, swung, and promptly skittered another ball low and forty five degrees to the right. *Christ, it almost went backwards.*

Marty winced. "Oh, my God," he sighed and walked toward Tom, shrugging his shoulders and holding his palms up to the sky as if to ask, "What?" What the hell was Tom doing? What was he trying to do? What the fuck?

The Head Pro stepped in close and spoke in a low, professional manner, close enough for Tom to get a whiff of Tic-Tacs and a pungent men's cologne. "I'm going to take mercy on you. I've been watching you out my window for the past fifteen minutes and I can't take it anymore."

He gently pried Larry's ancient 7-iron out of Tom's white knuckle grip and guided him backward, off the mat and out of harm's way. For a moment Marty held the iron in front of him examining the nicked clubface and worn out grip. He twirled the shaft in his finger tips a few times, then, with a delicate flick of the club-head, culled a ball from the half-empty basket at his feet and positioned it in the center of the mat.

His practice swing was so slow and smooth, it looked like a motion someone might make while under the influence of a healthy dose of valium. Marty set his feet apart in a deliberate stance and set the club head behind the dented and scuffed skin of the range ball. Then, as if motored by a gentle breeze he turned and lifted the iron behind him.

The downswing appeared to be powered by gravity alone.

Like a rocket, the ball left the clubface arcing high to the right and then drawing back in toward the left. It seemed to hang in the air forever…then landed a foot from a small flag in the center of a target green about 140 yards away.

Marty turned to Tom and as he handed him back the iron he said, "Well, it's not the club, we know that much."

For the next ten minutes Marty made "a few adjustments." He began by changing Tom's grip and stance, then went on to demonstrate in a curt but professional manner that Tom's takeaway was completely wrong and his swing plane was non-existent. Marty ended his instruction with, "There's no point in my showing you the follow-through 'til you learn how to take it back."

"Thanks, Marty," Tom gushed, "I appreciate it."

Marty looked at Tom and raised an eyebrow. "What have you learned?"

Tom thought about it for a moment then smiled. "I need to take some lessons."

Marty gave the slightest of nods, "That, and you need new clubs. I'll take the ones you have on a trade-in if you like. Those are real antiques you know." He made a start towards the clubhouse, but then stopped and looked back at Tom over his shoulder. "Saturday, ten a.m. Don't be late."

By the time Marty had returned to the shop and closed the door behind him, Tom was already at work on his new grip and swing motion, trying to memorize what Marty had shown him. After a few minutes, he summoned the courage to give his new skills a try and for the first time ever—yes, the first time ever in his life—he made solid contact. His timing of stepping through the shot and releasing the club-head was perfect and something clicked deep inside. It felt fantastic and resonated through his hands and arms, his entire torso flexed with pride. Tom wouldn't be able to admit it to himself just yet, but the sensation of resonance went much deeper. The physical after-buzz of flush contact pulsing through his mid section had an almost sensual tingle to it. The very place—Carol would insist it was one of his chakras—that had shrunk when Larry threatened him, was now warm and glowing.

As he admired the flight of the ball soaring into the twilight he heard the distinct sound of a wooden match striking and flaring, followed by a gravelly voice. "That's the ticket." The voice sounded as if it was right in his ear and it made him jump. "What have I been telling you?" the voice spoke again.

Tom spun around to see who it was, and sitting on a bench behind the mats, on a slight rise of turf overlooking the range, was a dapper, gray-haired gentleman. He was wearing a collared light brown shirt that shone like silk under an exquisite white cardigan sweater, topped off with a classic short-brim, Herringbone golf cap that matched his attire. Normally, Tom was not one to pay much attention to the way men dressed, but this guy looked sharp right down to his lustrous brown golf shoes. The look was way retro, his father's idea of cool, but sharp nonetheless.

Sitting and facing the soft amber light of the evening sun, the gentleman seemed to have a golden aura coming off him. His head was shrouded in a faint haze of tobacco smoke from the non-filter cigarette he held, and as an ex-smoker himself, Tom felt a momentary tug of the nicotine urge. The man was nodding his approval at Tom while twin jet streams of blue smoke poured from his nostrils.

Tom looked up and down the driving range and saw that it had cleared out. He and the gentleman on the bench had the place to themselves. Although Tom did not know the man, there was something familiar about his features; and that voice, that too seemed to ring a distant bell. The man spoke slowly with a slight southern twang, Texan perhaps.

Thrilled with the dramatic improvement of his swing, Tom's natural inclination to hit his balls and hurry home before Carol made a stink abandoned him. Instead he felt the urge to talk to someone, to share his excitement. He strolled over to the bench and sat down next to the gentleman, then stuck out his hand and introduced himself. "Hi, I'm Tom."

The gentleman shooed Tom's hand away with a dismissive flick of his cigarette. "I've been telling you to take lessons and now you have. I think you'll be quite surprised at what happens next." Then he smiled and wisps of smoke filtered through big, yellow teeth.

Tom felt immediately off balance and his heart began to race. *What does he mean he's been advising me?* Tom's whole body twitched hard for an instant. It was like what happened to him sometimes in bed at night just before drifting off; the sensation of falling, then a jolt of panic, and catching himself at the last second. In that moment something fell into place. He almost recognized the face, the voice, the outfit. *I don't know this guy*, he thought, *but I'm supposed to.*

Tom let his eyes pass over the gentleman's face repeatedly and watched, envious, as he sucked in a deep puff from his cigarette and blew another cloud of smoke out of the corner of his mouth. The man continued to smile but said nothing. There was a smear of magenta sky on the horizon and Tom could see maroon specks reflected in the old man's eyes. "Hey," he said suddenly, "you're somebody famous, aren't you?"

The old man nudged his head toward the remaining pile of balls in Tom's stall and spoke, his words punctuated by puffs of smoke. "Let me see you hit a few more, fella."

"How'd you make out?" Marty asked.

After finishing the last of his balls Tom strolled through the golf shop towards the parking lot as Marty was closing up.

"That was great Marty, just great; I can't thank you enough for the help."

"Don't mention it," Marty said, pulling the last of the window shades.

Tom was about to leave the shop, but then hovered by the front entrance. "Marty? Did you see the old guy I was talking to on the range? Any idea who he is?"

"Can't say as I did," Marty was at the register now, pulling out wads of cash and wrapping the bills in a rubber band. "What'd he look like?"

Tom described the man as best he could; hat, clothes, cigarette, but Marty shook his head.

"To be honest, I have no idea. I don't know anyone like that."

Tom glanced around, hoping to offer Marty some further clue. *There was just something so familiar*...Tom's eyes flicked around the shop.

In an attempt to make the cramped space more festive, Marty had antique golf equipment mounted on the walls: a hickory shafted set of irons, a small glass encasement of weird looking golf balls from the distant past, a framed sweater vest once worn by someone named Gary Casper. Each exhibit was individually lit by special track lights in the ceiling. There were half a dozen black and white photographs of old time professional golfers: Arnold Palmer, Jack Nicklaus, and a few others Tom didn't know. One wall had a poster-size picture all to itself. It was a blown-up photograph of a golfer who looked—snazzy was the word that came to mind—a cigarette dangling from his mouth, adoring fans lining the fairway, a dead ringer for the old man Tom had spoken to down on the range.

"He looked exactly like that guy." Tom said, pointing to the picture. "In fact, I'm pretty sure it was that guy."

Marty looked over his shoulder at the picture and when he turned back to Tom he was laughing. "Jesus," he said, "I don't think so, Tom. That's Ben Hogan."

* * *

Carol was sitting up in bed, her back resting on a triangular pillow, a book in her lap by John Edward, a popular psychic she'd become intrigued with. Tom was sitting next to her Indian-style, a phone tucked under one ear while he sorted through a stack of product brochures and order forms he needed for the next day's sales calls.

"Just a heads up, Larry," Tom garbled through a yawn, "I'm driving straight up to Kent in the morning to introduce our website to the retailers up there, so I won't be in the office 'til noonish at the earliest." Tom nodded a few times while listening to his father-in-law on the other end. He raised his eyebrows at Carol and made a *he won't stop talking gesture* with his hand. Carol swatted his hand and Tom stuck his tongue out at her in response.

Larry must have asked Tom something important then, because Tom sat up straight and when he spoke Carol noticed a distinct change in his tone. "Holy shit, Larry, you're not going to believe what happened. I got a quickie lesson from the club Pro this evening and in five minutes he had me really hitting the ball. He wants me to start taking lessons," Tom pointed an accusing finger at Carol, "which Carol says you should pay for because it was all your idea."

Carol punched Tom in the arm and tried to grab the phone. "I did not say that," she shrieked.

Tom laughed and tossed the phone to Carol. "Hi Daddy... I never said that." Carol slapped Tom's shoulder while she spoke. "No, no, I'm sure we can afford it, but I'm warning you. If Tom goes over the edge with this golfing business I'm going to blame you for it." She eased back into her pillow while she listened to her father's reassurance. "Well, he may not be hooked on it, but it's all he would talk about at dinner and I didn't like the look in his eye." Carol wagged a finger at Tom now. "You know what look I'm talking about, he looked like one of the twins, like a five-year-old with a new toy at Christmas."

Tom grabbed Carol's hand and started kissing it, lightly at first and then threw in some nibbles as he began moving up her arm.

"I can't stay on Daddy, Tom's misbehaving. All right, love you too. Love to mom." She tossed the phone down and pushed Tom back to his side of the bed. "Cut it out," she said. "I just need to finish this chapter, then its lights out." Tom sighed and went back to his briefcase. He pulled out some spreadsheets and started checking off numbers with a pen. Carol picked up her book but kept one eye on Tom as she read. She wanted to talk a little bit more about this golf business, but instinct told her to wait and see if it didn't fizzle out on its own. After a few minutes she closed her book.

"It turns out the kitten we got at the shelter may be more damaged than we thought," she said.

Tom patted Carol's leg but his eyes never left the pile of papers in front of him. While she spoke she studied Tom, who seemed lost in thought. *Was he still sulking because I rebuffed him?* "I took him to the vet today and he said the infection has blinded one eye and will probably have some serious effect on his aural nerves."

Tom lifted his head an inch, acknowledging the sound of her voice.

Carol folded her arms across her chest and sharpened her tone. "What did I just say?"

That got his attention. "What?"

"You didn't hear a thing I said, did you?"

Tom nodded. "Of course I did. We got ourselves a one-eyed pirate cat that's also hearing impaired. Carol, every word you say is like gold to me, you know that."

Carol lifted a foot and dug her heel into his back. "You're so full of it," she said, putting her book on the night table and dropping the reading pillow to the floor. "You're sure you locked it in the laundry room? I don't want to find a mess all over the downstairs in the morning."

Tom swept up his papers, crammed them into the briefcase that rested on his night-table and rolled himself up next to Carol. "Yes, the cat is locked up for the night." He got under the covers and tried to slip a hand up her pajama top, but she swatted him away.

When the lights were out, she turned to Tom in the darkness. "Get home in time for dinner with your family mister, and I might be more responsive. It's not a play night anyway."

Tom turned away and mumbled some dark thing into his pillow.

He was going to sulk for sure now, but Carol was not about to give in. Tom had an addictive nature; she'd learned that even before they were married. When Tom found something that gave him physical pleasure, like tobacco *or* alcohol *or* sex, he couldn't get enough. But his love for Carol was far greater than his lust for idle pleasure. When she'd thrown down an ultimatum, forcing him to choose between cigarettes and guzzling six packs *or* their relationship, he'd dropped his vices overnight for her. As for his insane sex drive, that had to be dealt with more firmly after they had the twins. They settled on a maximum of three nights a week and no more daytime surprise attacks.

Once settled into their routine positions under the blankets, Carol spoke out in the darkness. "You'll never guess what the boys named the kitten."

Tom lifted himself up on one elbow and pounded his pillow into submission. "Helen Keller."

"Fluffer."

"Oh my God, Carol, it's a male cat, isn't it? You can't name a male cat something like that. Blind, deaf, and *gay*? The Christian thing would be to take it in the back yard and hit it with a shovel."

She gave Tom a sharp elbow. "Quiet. I told the boys it was a wonderful name and I won't have you making fun of it."

Tom did as he was told. He got quiet for a while but then rolled on his side, facing her in the dark.

"Carol, what's channeling?"

"What?"

"Channeling, what is that exactly?"

She reached up and snapped on the light, then glared at Tom's face, scrutinizing his expression, scanning for a hint of sarcasm. "After all the time that I've been exploring spiritual phenomena, this is the first time you've ever asked a single question without laughing in my face. May I ask why?"

"I was trying to explain your hobby to a couple of clients of mine. All the meditation, the psychics, past lives, all that stuff you're into, but I couldn't explain to them what channeling is. Is it like possession, a ghost or something?"

Carol felt herself being boxed into a trap. Was he baiting her? Normally, whenever she tried to share her spiritual life with Tom he launched into a five-minute comedy monologue that included comments about how cruel psychics were for not using their intuitive talents to warn Lincoln away from the theatre or Kennedy from Dallas. And why weren't psychics all rich from the stock market? "I assume horse whisperers must really clean up at the race track," was his usual vein, all of it childish digs at her presumed gullibility. He always got smug about it, forcing her to tap into her deep well of compassion for him.

"No, it's not like possession. Possession is when a spirit has entered your physical being against your will in an attempt to take over. In that case it is not a friendly spirit but a demon trying to relegate your true spirit to a secondary position or even replace it completely. A person who channels incarnations from the Other Side usually does so through a personal spirit guide, a spirit that we have unconsciously chosen to help guide us through our present physical incarnation on earth."

Carol bit her cheek and waited for the customary sarcastic bombshell.

"Do you have a spirit guide?" Tom's tone was anything but comical. He seemed almost on edge. If he was setting her up for a joke of some kind she was going to get very angry.

Pushing aside her better judgment, Carol plunged ahead. "I do. *Ung-Gah* is my spirit guide. In her prior incarnation she was an ancient Incan medicine woman. When I meditate in the morning I open myself to her and listen for any messages she has for me."

"And what exactly do you hear? I mean actual thoughts, words?"

Carol sat up, dumbfounded by what was happening. Tom was up on one elbow, his eyes unblinking and focused.

"No, not words, not really, just ideas that sometimes pop into my head. I'll meditate and come away with a notion to let go of a lingering resentment that's disturbing my energy field, or perhaps I'll feel the suggestion that "staying in the now" is something I need to work on more diligently."

"But no actual conversations, back and forth dialogue, nothing like that?"

"No, Tom, nothing like that. I've seen some people do it though, people who are more practiced, more fully evolved than me." Carol was wide awake now, invigorated by the positive energy Tom was emitting.

"Do any of your friends, the more evolved ones, do they claim to actually see the spirit guide physically, or is it all just a conversation taking place in their heads?"

"As far as I know it's all in their heads. The words are communicated by vibrations we know virtually nothing about." Carol lay down and pulled close to Tom. She drew a leg over his hips—her knee coming to rest on a patch of warmth—and looked into his eyes. "Wow, you really seem gripped by this." Carol reached over and stroked a tuft of reddish-brown hair behind Tom's ear and snuggled in close. "Would you like me to dig out some books on the subject?"

"Yeah, I would actually."

Carol turned out her light and pressed herself against him, thrilled that Tom had shown such an interest. She had written him off as spiritually blocked, his male ego standing in the way of a real awakening, and had come to believe that only an earthshaking event, a near-death experience or the loss of a loved one, would bring him anywhere close to a state of enlightened consciousness. Could it be? Was he reaching out from the darkness? For the first time in years Carol was able to envision the two of them meditating as one, pounding out the throb of the universal heartbeat in a harmonious drum circle of love.

Tom lifted his head and gave Carol a dry-lipped peck on the forehead and she responded by lifting an open mouth to his, signaling an abrupt change of plans.

Carol lay close, her breath coming in warm gusts on his neck, their legs entwined. After lovemaking, Tom usually liked nothing better than burrowing into the delicious, almost narcotic aroma of his pillow and passing right out, but not tonight.

What a wonderful day.

As hard as he tried to get his mind to go blank, he kept drifting back to the exhilaration he'd felt that evening on the driving range. Each time the memory surfaced, it registered its presence with a ping of adrenalin blooming in his gut.

Carol was asleep now, he could tell by the sound of her breathing. Since the twins were born she'd developed a timid snore that signaled she was really out. As for Tom, he was wide awake, his heart pounding.

He lay on his back in the darkness, staring at the ceiling, thinking about what Carol had said about channeling, and marveling at it. "More evolved," he mouthed the words silently to himself, again and again. "More evolved."

Chapter Two
An Opening

"Come on Jerry…just hit the fucking thing, would you?" Tank flicked his cigarette butt off to the side and glared at the pain-in-the-ass in the tee box.

Jerry wheeled out of his stance and took a menacing step towards the three men waiting for him to hit. He was holding his club out in front of him like a sword. "Fuck you, Tank. I don't rush you with your shots…do I?" Jerry paused for a second, looking each of his three partners in the eye, then shouted another "…do I?" When none of his companions responded, Jerry bent over and re-teed his ball while mumbling loud enough for the three men behind him to hear. "You wouldn't pull that shit if your best buddy Tommy was here instead of me…no siree…not in front of Marty's new golden boy…no fucking way."

The 17th hole at Shinacockle was a beast, and Jerry, who was doubling up on his already endless pre-shot routine, had every reason for caution. It was the signature hole of the course, offering a magnificent view of Long Island Sound from a dramatically elevated green, but it was a blind shot from the tee with a two-hundred-and-thirty-four yard uphill carry. Today, with the pin placed in the back you could see the tip of the flag from the tee box, but that's all. Shinacockle wasn't their home course but they'd played this track often enough to know that you could go left or right of the hole and still have a chance at par, but going long on 17 wasn't an option. A few yards just off the back of the green, the land fell away to a sheer one-hundred-and-thirty foot drop to craggy rocks and thunderous surf.

Father Charlie and Doctor Silverstein had hit, and although their shots were long enough not to roll back down the imposing hill the hole was situated on, both were well short of the green. Jack, known by his friends as Tank or The Tankster due to his short and corpulent frame, had hit a solid three-wood straight at the flag and with any luck had landed just short of the green and bounced on.

Jerry Mahoney was the last to shoot. He hadn't held honors since he'd won the toss on the first hole, and his mood was a perfect reflection of the state of his swing.

Tank grinned at Jerry, fighting the urge to laugh at his club choice. Desperate to find some advantage, Jerry had over-clubbed and chosen driver and after teeing his ball up once again began his exaggerated pre-shot routine of waving it back and forth and then thumping the enormous head of the club on the ground. Anyone who played with Jerry knew this process could go on for a full minute and by the end of a round it was exasperating to watch. He slowed his action and gently rested the head of his club behind his ball.

While Jerry settled himself with a final shuffle of his feet, Tank let out a wet, phlegm-clearing cough.

Jerry's hands dropped to his sides, his head sunk low and "Jesus Christ Almighty," came out of his mouth in a low growl. "

"Sorry," Tank held up a hand in apology while trading raised eyebrows with Silverstein and Father Charlie. "I must be coming down with something."

Jerry muttered some unintelligible foulness in the direction of his golf ball, then shot a final glance at Tank. "It's the cigarettes, you fucking idiot. You're coming down with something alright, lung cancer."

Tank winked at his two friends and grinned back at Jerry. "Thanks for the cheery thought, pal," he said, and pulled out a thin metal flask from the pocket of his windbreaker, unscrewed the cap and took a mouthful.

Jerry took his backswing and the three men gritted their teeth, waiting for Mahoney's customary rage-filled spew of filth, but to the surprise of everyone, Mahoney hit his first decent drive of the day; too good by the looks of it — straight at the pin but still hanging high in the air as it sailed over the top of the hill.

"Too much club?" Silverstein asked, marching past Jerry and shoving his hand cart towards the steep incline to the green.

Tank hoped the sensation of a flush golf shot would cheer Mahoney's desultory mood and brighten the dark cloud that had hung over the foursome all day long. But no. Jerry raised a fist to the heavens and wailed, "It's long. Fuck me, I can't believe I hit it long."

Back in the day, when they'd all enjoyed playing with each other, before Jerry's game went south and he turned into an asshole, Tank would have jumped all over his old friend with a good natured ribbing. "You're already down thirty bucks Jerry and if you've gone over the cliff, you're correct. You're completely fucked. I hope you brought enough cash with you." But now, after years of awful golf—which had turned Jerry into a mass of raw nerves and left him full of resentments—that kind of spirited language was out of the question. *One wrong word and he'll come at me with a pitching wedge.* Instead, picturing Jerry's ball trickling over the edge of the precipice and disappearing into the void stamped a shit-eating grin on Tank's face.

It was a hard climb to the top of the hill, and although there was a chilly spring breeze blowing, Tank was wiping sweat out of his eyes and panting like a race horse when he reached the edge of the green. When he could get his eyes to focus, he was thrilled by what he saw. As he'd hoped, his ball had landed short and run up onto the green. It had drifted left of the hole, but it was a makeable birdie putt. Charlie and

Silverstein were both short, each having difficult chips to get close. Best of all, Mahoney had clearly driven through the green and Tank prayed that Jerry's ball now slept with the fishes.

"Fuck me," Jerry said. He began foraging for his ball in deep grass in front of a calf high guard rail that represented the hazard line. DANGER signs were posted at either end of the rail, reading "No Shots From Beyond This Point."

Tank marked his ball and after Charlie and Silverstein chipped on, the foursome gathered at the rail looking into the thick grass just beyond.

Charlie spoke up. "There it is," he pointed towards a white dot just visible beneath the last foot of rough before the precipice.

Jerry went to his bag and pulled out a wedge. His playing partners glanced at each other but said nothing until Jerry slipped a leg over the guardrail and headed in careful mincing steps towards his ball.

"Hey, Jerry…" Silverstein and Tank said in tandem.

"Oh for heaven's sake, Jerry," the priest cried out, "just take a drop, okay?"

In full prick mode, Jerry shouted, "Take a drop, my ass." He was red in the face now, distended veins clutching at his temples. "I'm already down at least thirty bucks. If that fat bastard," Jerry jabbed an index finger in Tank's direction, "sinks his putt, I'll be down God knows how much."

Tank remained impassive. As much as he'd come to hate playing with Jerry, he'd begun to take a perverse pleasure from Jerry's payout at the end of each round. Watching the hump on the brink of tears with shaking hands as he pried open his wallet was a delicious spectacle.

There was a great silence now as the three men watched their long time partner struggle to get a stance. It was downright windy at this elevation and after each practice swing Jerry was forced to grab his bright yellow cap before it flew off his head. Then he would grab his belt and cinch up his pants. He had to lean forward a bit to counter the breeze and then he'd take another swing and start all over again; cap—pants—stance—swing.

Jesus, it looks like a Charlie Chaplin routine. Tank took out his flask and began unscrewing the cap. He felt time come to a standstill. Were his friends as frightened as he was? Anyone could see that Jerry's swing motion was terribly flawed. He had a classic double pivot. He leaned forward and dropped his left shoulder straight down on his takeaway, then fell backward onto his right leg on his downswing, throwing his center of gravity completely off kilter. It was ugly to watch under any circumstances, doubly so here on the edge of such a precipitous drop. Even Tank, who wished the man nothing but pain and suffering, was stirred to action.

"Not a good idea, Jerry," he shouted, "Come away from…!"

Tank, Silverstein and Father Charlie stood as close to the edge as they dared, staring into the abyss. For a long time the only sounds were the whistle of the wind, the crashing surf below and the occasional squawk of a seagull flying over head.

Charlie made a flamboyant sign of the cross over the bluff and then began fingering a set of rosary beads he'd pulled out of his pants pocket.

"You know," Silverstein said, pointing to a yellow dot that appeared to be Jerry's cap being tossed by the foam and spray below, "I bet there's a ton of lost balls down there."

"Don't be an idiot," Tank said, "how would you even get to them?"

"You'd have to get a boat I guess…a long pole with a net…" Silverstein mused.

No one spoke or moved for another minute at least.

It was Father Charlie who broke the silence. "What are we going to do, fellas? We have the club opener this weekend. It's a four-ball event, isn't it?"

Tank held a hand out to Silverstein. "Gimme your phone," he said. "We'd better call Tommy…we need him now."

In the moments before his life changed forever, before his cell phone broke in with Lynyrd Skynyrd's "Free Bird" and lit up with Silverstein's number, Tom had been driving towards the golf course chewing on his lower lip. He was regretting his clumsy three p.m. exit out of the office where he'd startled everyone in earshot by jumping up from his desk and shouting out, "Oh Jesus, the dentist, I forgot the dentist."

It wasn't a complete lie. Truth was he did have a touchy molar that was sensitive to hot and cold, but the words root canal and extraction terrified him so he just lived with the occasional shriek of pain. On the plus side the decaying tooth came in as a handy excuse to run out of the office, even though by now everyone knew where he was really going. This time however, as he was breezing through the office doors he'd heard Larry's sniping bark chasing after him, "How long have they been practicing dentistry at the golf course?"

Would he call Tom at home later and chew him out about it? "Christ, I hope not," Tom muttered at his reflection in the rear-view mirror. If Larry called and got a hold of Carol first there was going to be an extended frost delay in the house tonight for sure.

Just the other day he'd walked in the back door from a lovely afternoon round and Carol ambushed him with credit card receipts from the pro-shop. "How many golf balls are there in a practice bucket?" She was waving the receipts at him from her seat at the kitchen table where she'd been tabulating their monthly expenses.

"About forty," Tom said. He pulled a beer from the fridge and cracked it.

Carol's eyes narrowed for a moment then she flipped through some back pages of her account book. There was an explosion of fingernails clickity-clacking on the calculator keys, then another pause while math was being checked. "Oh my God," she gasped, "do you know how many practice balls you've hit over the last decade? Do you have any idea?"

Tom gave her a benign smile, feigning interest.

"At least fifty thousand balls by my count, Tom, minimum." Then she laughed and got all snide, "If you haven't found the swing by now Buster, maybe you should just give it up."

There was no point trying to explain to her that he was close, so very close to realizing his dream of possessing the secret, of breaking the code. Over the past few years he'd been triangulating his approach to the swing. That's how he saw it, triangulating. His first task was all about balance, perfecting his stance over the ball. After that came a solid year's effort working solely on his takeaway. Lastly, he'd focused all his practice buckets on a relaxed but forceful downswing. All he had to do now was to combine the three elements into one fluid motion and the swing would be his. And there Carol was, suggesting he was a spazzoid; that he should quit. *Fuck me. Between the anxiety I get from Larry and the guilt from Carol, it's a wonder I can hit the ball at all!* "Guilt and worry," Tom nodded and wagged a finger towards the mirror again, "are the two greatest toxins to a golfers swing."

But he was beyond all that now. The lyric, "I'm as free as a bird now," kept repeating in his head, held aloft by the impact of the Tankster's magical message.

"Jerry was dead." Any negative feelings cramping Tom's imagination flew right out the window.

He snapped his cell phone shut as he pulled into a parking space at the town golf club and let out a war whoop. Yanking the keys out of the ignition, Tom sat back in his seat and closed his eyes. "Yes..." he whispered, stretching the word out under his breath, the same way he would after hitting a really good shot. The full and amazing implications of Jerry's death began to take shape in his imagination. Unable to contain his excitement, he snapped his fingers then pounded out a drum roll on the dash. *Jerry's dead. Incredible. Tournament play with the boys this weekend. Fantastic. Told Carol I'd go antiquing with her on Sunday, but that's out. She'll understand. I'll get her some flowers to soften the blow. This changes everything. Good old Jerry! I'm in! I'm in!*

Too excited to play the course, he decided to calm himself by plowing through a large bucket. He needed to work on getting some extra sizzle out of his low irons, hitting one after another until his stroke was strong and smooth. *Compression, I need more compression.* He popped the trunk of his Volvo sedan and got out, glancing towards the front of the clubhouse just as Marty, his golf instructor, his mentor, was escorting a female student down to the private teaching area for a lesson. He almost yelled the news to him, but shouting gleefully across the parking lot that Jerry Mahoney was dead would turn heads, no doubt, and interrupting the golf pro in the company of a female student was strictly taboo. He'd catch Marty before he went home.

"Don't get carried away," a familiar voice in his head told him, "self control is essential in golf." He sorted through a mental list of emotions, trying to pick one most suitable for a man approaching middle age. Any attempt at expressing grief for Jerry's demise would strike a false note even if he had a day or two to practice a frown-full of condolence in front of a mirror. He discarded elation and rapture as greedy and childish. Even Tank, who'd hated Jerry, had been able to sound dignified and solemn on the phone, so Tom finally settled on gratitude. Under the circumstances, gratitude was probably most appropriate. He was sorry for Jerry; Jerry's family would certainly suffer from the pain of this catastrophe, but he was also grateful for Jerry's sacrifice. *Did it qualify as martyrdom? He'd ask Father Charlie.* In fact, as the joy of the moment crystallized, Tom was grateful for everything in his life.

Despite her grousing, he was grateful for Carol, for her patience, for her strength, and his children of course; twin boys, healthy and happy. He was especially grateful to Carol's father, Larry, the founder of the feast. Without Larry, Tom realized long ago, he wouldn't have golf in his life at all.

As he continued to feed his gratitude with warm thoughts the emotion ballooned inside him. Lugging his bag behind the clubhouse and taking in the glory of his surroundings he felt gorged with it. He looked down towards the driving range, watching other golfers diligently working on their swings. Then he saw a couple of high school students on the practice green struggling to get a posse of eight year olds in the after-school junior clinic to stop gripping their putters like baseball bats; and finally he gazed at the sun sitting low above the gray water of the harbor, nestling into a thick quilt of purple haze.

Unless he was mistaken it was ten years ago, almost to the day, that he'd been on the verge of quitting golf completely when Marty marched down to the range and interceded. Now Jerry was dead and the coveted slot in the foursome of his dreams had been laid at his feet. It was nothing short of a miracle. Half turning, Tom glanced over his shoulder to the empty bench on the rise of turf just behind the hitting stations on the range, and his heart warmed with a sense of community, of being at home. He jabbed a brass token into the slit at the top of the ball machine. There was a loud crash and when the balls cascaded down, banging like a machinegun into the empty bucket below, a shiver of anticipation ran through him.

Chapter Three
Breathe in…Sooo…Breathe out…Humm

"You mus' check pocket! You mus' check pocket!" Mr. Kim, the Korean dry cleaner, jabbed his finger and shouted at Carol, then held up a zip-lock baggie full of multi-colored golf tees he'd collected from Tom's suit pockets over the past few weeks. "You no check pockets, you no come dis place!" he raged at Carol while waving the bulging baggie for Carol and the line of grumbling customers standing behind her to see. "If you break my presser," Mr. Kim wailed, eyes wide, veins popping, and pointing to a variety of machinery in the rear of the shop, "You pay or I sue. I sue you!"

Years ago, she had laughed right along with Mr. Kim when he'd handed her the first batch of tees he'd collected from Tom's pockets. Nobody was laughing now.

That evening, with the boys fed and the dishes cleared, Carol sat at the kitchen table glaring at the baggie of golf tees before her. She glanced to the clock on the stove; an hour and a half past dinner and not even a phone call. She shut her eyes, focusing her energy away from the negative, and practicing the Art of Mindfulness, concentrated on the harmony of sounds in the house around her—the hum of the refrigerator, the tick of the clock on the wall, the flush of a toilet upstairs, the rhythmic drip in the sink. *It's not working…* she was distracted, her concentration lapsed, the monkey chatter in her mind tugged her thoughts back to Tom.

What bothered her most was that his devotion, no, it was more than that—his obsession over golf had turned her into a nag. She was careful not to speak harshly to him in front of the twins, but she'd do it quietly with her eyes. Seven days a week he'd walk in the door and she'd pointedly look at the clock on the stove, then back at Tom, letting him know he was late or he'd been gone too long and she was not happy about it. She nagged with her nose, too. In fact it was her ultra sensitive nose that made her begin to red flag—that's what her father called it when he smelled trouble brewing around the house or at the office—Tom's behavior with golf. As an adult, not long after she began to devote herself to becoming a spiritual seeker, she visited a psychic who specialized in past life experiences. The psychic told her that she'd lived a prior incarnation as a timber wolf, an Alpha female the psychic had said, and Carol believed it.

When she asked Tom if he'd been hitting balls or sneaking in a few holes and he dared to say no, she'd start sniffing at him like a dog. Sunscreen, yes, always that. She had no qualms about taking his left hand and bringing it to her nose. If he'd been at the golf course or on the range the hand smelled of the leather golf glove he'd been wearing. Sometimes she caught a faint hint of a men's after-shave. Not Tom's—she would never allow a cheap, pungent aroma like that in the house— but whose then? Is that what his golf instructor wore?

Carol shook her head, straining to pull away from negativity. She took a breath and felt a vibration in her feet telling her the hot water heater had kicked on in the basement. When she cocked her head she could just make out the boys' playing a video game in their room upstairs. A woodpecker hammered at a tree in the backyard and she conjured a vivid image of the piercing beak of the bird boring a blood splattered hole in the bald spot on the top of Tom's head. *God damn it!*

Carol sighed. Finding a spiritual balance tonight was impossible. After leaving Mr. Kim's shop that afternoon she'd decided that she would have to put her foot down. Even though her horoscope indicated this was not a good time for a "successful resolution of conflict," she'd have to risk it. The winter months were behind them and the grass was turning green. Could she withstand another six or seven months of nothing but golf? Golf books and magazines lying all over the house, golf tournaments on the television every Thursday, Friday, Saturday and Sunday—God knows how much money being frittered away on golf shoes, clubs, lessons, and nothing coming out of Tom's mouth but golf, golf, golf? Carol noticed she was tapping her foot in time with the ticking of her inner clock, the beating of her heart.

The irony was that it was her father who had insisted Tom learn how to play the game for business reasons, and now Tom was driving Larry crazy with it too. Over the years her father had put together a pretty good impression of Tom barging into Larry's office at work––just about every morning according to Larry— launching into a breathless five minute monologue about the advances he'd made in his golf swing. "I'm really getting great compression right now by letting my hands lead the club head—lag they call it—and when I hit the ball you can really hear it zip off the club-face and then, if I get my follow through to come up high like this…" Larry was hilarious when he did the imitation and never failed to get a laugh, but underneath the laughter, the last couple of performances had seemed more angry than funny.

Something had to be done. She should have nipped it in the bud years ago, when he first came home all pink in the face and yammering on about his magical golf instructor, and how this Marty something or other was showing Tom the deepest secrets of the golf swing. Whenever he talked about Marty his eyes would sparkle and he'd get dry mouth, running his tongue over his lips like he was hyperventilating. Now worry had crept into her life and this persistent worry was keeping her from accomplishing one of the most basic of daily spiritual tasks, "staying in the now." Instead of reveling in the day's smell of spring, of rebirth, she found herself grieving in advance over the diminishing presence of her husband in the months ahead. Negative thoughts were draining her life force.

Her eyes drifted to the basement door. Beyond the endless hours Tom spent on the driving range and the golf course, that's where Tom was disappearing to. She'd attempted to dissuade Tom from building a private room just for himself in the basement, but in the end had to relent. Years back, as she became increasingly serious in her personal search of a Higher Spiritual Plane, she had taken over the upstairs guest room and turned it into a meditation sanctuary, a holistic healing center just for her. If Tom insisted on a space of his own, how could she argue against it?

What bothered her most about Tom's room was that he kept the door padlocked so she couldn't even sneak a peek at what he was up to. She only knew what he shared with her, that he was building golf clubs from scratch and keeping notes about the progress of his swing. Even with the television on in the den, she could hear him talking to himself down there. Sometimes it sounded like he was having a back and forth argument with himself...or someone, and it made the hair on the back of her neck stand up. She'd asked Tom what it was he wrote to himself down in his basement hideaway, but his answer was always the same snarky joke. "It's the secret of the golf swing, Carol. I could tell you, but then I'd have to kill you."

Within minutes Tom would walk through the door. With any luck he wouldn't be wearing the latest addition to his golf attire, a white straw cowboy hat, emblazoned with some kind of shark logo. The hat, along with the bright red fu-Manchu mustache and sideburns he'd let grow in—his "gunslinger look" as he put it—made her feel embarrassed for him. Sometimes he accessorized with a leather vest and it was like watching one of her sons get on the school bus with an outfit she was sure the other kids would make fun of.

She'd ask him about his late arrival and he'd lie. "Traffic," he'd offer with a shrug, or "late meeting," with a work-weary expression. As soon as he gave her a hug, one sniff would reveal the truth. They both knew he was lying, but after nearly a decade of this behavior Carol had become almost numb to it.

Instead of letting anger consume her she decided to let it go, banished it and turned to the spiritual path. "Focus on the positive," she whispered on an inhalation, "Stay in the now," softly, on the exhale. They had been blessed with two wonderful children, both of them healthy and happy. Tom's job seemed to be going well and they had a roof over their heads. They were well fed and clothed, college accounts grew steadily. *What's not to like?* The only intrusion on their serenity over the years was the tragic mauling death of Fluffer, the family cat, whose body parts had been found scattered around the back yard, a victim of an ever-growing population of coyotes. In recent years coyotes had begun to plague the suburbs; in the past year alone several children in nearby Westchester had been attacked. Under the umbrella of their overall blessedness Carol had allowed herself to live with white lies about golf, but no more.

She took Tom's plate of roast beef, mashed potatoes and asparagus from the table and put it in the microwave, ready to be reheated when he came home. She rinsed the boys' and her own dinner plates and was putting them in the dishwasher when she saw Tom's car lights flash across the kitchen window as he pulled into the driveway. Glancing at the baggie of golf tees, she made a decision. She would not confront Tom with them the very instant he walked in the door, but use them later for ammunition in the fight she knew was coming. As she heard Tom's car door shut, she slipped the damning evidence into the silverware drawer.

The doorway from the garage entrance into the house opened and Tom, singing half-remembered lyrics to an old Beatles song, *Help*, breezed into the kitchen as if arriving home from work at this hour was perfectly normal. Carol flared her nostrils and sniffed as he hummed his way past her to deposit his briefcase on the kitchen table: sunscreen, cut grass, but no Marty smell. Did he only hit a bucket? Did he play? *Whatever... That makes three times this week!*

"What's with all the sunscreen?" Carol sniffed, while wagging a finger at Tom's briefcase.

"When the boys are grown," Tom grinned as he removed his briefcase from the table and put it on one of the chairs, "you should try and get a job as a police dog sniffing out hidden drug caches or explosives. I bet there's money in that."

Carol wiped her hands at the sink and gave her man a hug. No matter what she said he almost always came back with something clever that took the edge off her irritation. He was good at making people laugh and when she had the time to give it some thought, she remembered that's what she loved about him most. "Fifteen years and two children later you've come to see me as a dog—is that it?" She grabbed the dishtowel by the sink and swatted his backside. "Thanks a lot."

Tom hung his jacket over the back of a chair and began to unknot his already loosened necktie. There were no perspiration stains under the armpits of his shirt. *Jesus, he's changing in and out of golf clothes before he comes home.*

I'm not saying you wouldn't be a pretty dog." Tom continued. "You'd be lean and sexy, with a beautiful soft coat of fur." Tom let out a low growl and started to stalk Carol around the kitchen table while snapping his jaws, like some kind of lunatic, sex-crazed beast. "And you'd know how to wag that tail of yours, I bet."

"Stop that right now." Carol protested but she let him catch her and while he wrapped his arms around her, growling and giving her little love bites on her neck and cheek, she laughed out loud, only half struggling to get away. Tom worked his lips across her cheek and gave her a big kiss on the mouth, and though the smell of sunscreen was so strong she had to hold her breath, she felt her anger melt a bit in his arms. "I made roast beef. You want a salad with that or not?" she said as he lifted his mouth from her face.

"No thanks, Sweetie."

He pecked Carol on the forehead, grabbed his jacket and started to head upstairs to change and say hello to his boys, but the embarrassing sting of her experience at the hands of Mr. Kim was still fresh.

"I take it you were hitting balls today." Carol said as she peeled the Saran Wrap off his dinner plate. She said it without anger but there was no warmth in it either. Tom was at the door leading to the upstairs hall and when he turned back his face had gone blank. He was going to tell her a fib now, she could tell. Ever since she had known Tom, whenever her nose told her he had sneaked a cigarette or had a beer or two with lunch and she confronted him about it, he would more often than not tell a little white lie or a sneaky blend of fact and fiction, trying to throw her off the scent. What he failed to realize was that he wasn't very good at it. His face would drain of expression, she could almost see his brain shut down for a second, and then he would rapidly blink for another beat while the computer in his head rebooted itself. Then the animation would come back into his face and right behind it, the lie.

"One of my clients has his business right across the street from a driving range. He and I went over and did our business while we hit a few. Your father was right," he grinned. "Golf opens a lot of doors."

"You're in an awfully good mood this evening. I take it you're hitting the ball well… or did we win the lottery?"

Not only did Tom miss the sarcasm but his face lit up again. He slapped his forehead and came back into the kitchen.

"I completely forgot to tell you. You won't believe my luck."

Carol was setting the timer on the microwave, her finger on the start button when she turned and looked at Tom. Even with that overgrown mustache with its twin sidebars that ran down on either side of his mouth like thick red fangs, his adolescent excitement made him irresistible."Well?"

Tom rubbed his hands together then interlocked his fingers and cracked his knuckles. "Sit down," he said, "I've got a fantastic story for you."

Carol lunged for the dish towel on the counter and snapped it at him. "Come on, out with it." Tom's eyes were bright now, beaming, and he was starting somehow to expand before her, to swell with victory, accomplishment. It was the same look he had when he came home after making a significant sale for her father's company. Carol felt a lump grow in her throat. For a second she started to believe that he actually had gone and won the lottery.

Tom raised his hands in the air and danced a tight pirouette, like a prize fighter after throwing a knockout punch. "Jerry Mahoney's dead," he sang out in a taunting school yard melody.

For the next ten minutes Carol stood next to the sink using the counter for support while she drifted in and out of a state of numbness. As Tom recounted the story of how this poor Jerry fellow fell to his death, he struggled to keep his emotions in check, but she could tell by his glassy eyes and an occasional deep breath that he was thrilled about it. *Fantastic*, he'd said, *lucky*.

She focused on her alignment and counted her breaths in repeated series of twenties to maintain her composure and keep centered. But, when Tom got to the part of the story where Jerry's lifelong golfing companions had called Tom from the 18th fairway to ask him to become the new permanent member of their foursome—all this while poor Jerry's body was going out with the tide—she snapped to attention. "Are you telling me that your friends continued to play after their friend went over the cliff? Is that what you're telling me?"

Tom shook his head side to side, gently, like a parent disappointed with a dense child. "C'mon Carol, I told you they were in the middle of a match. It was the seventeenth hole! I'm sure they called it in before they finished up, I'm sure of it. Anyway, what would have been gained by not finishing?"

Carol clapped her hands to the side of her head. "My God, Tom, it's probably against the law, like leaving the scene of an accident. Secondly, it's about respect, human dignity," she almost shouted. Then she dropped her tone, trying to set the table for a serious talk. "What kind of people are you associating with?" She spoke with a shrill coldness that normally stopped Tom in his tracks, but instead he started waving his hands at her in protest, as if she was completely off base.

"He was gone, Carol, he was gone. There was nothing anyone could do." A benign expression came over Tom's face and he came close and took her hand in his. With an index finger he lifted her chin and smiled down at her. "Carol, what are you always saying to me when bad things happen to people? Jerry chose his fate, right? His transition from this life to the next was his karma - isn't that what you say? The truth is that if they'd stayed on the seventeenth hole until the

Coast Guard had fished Jerry out of the drink, it would have been well after sundown. Christ Almighty, they'd still be there now trying to putt-out in darkness!"

Carol was bone tired all of a sudden, confused too. Tom was beguiling her with his warmth and sincerity. There was a response to Tom's ridiculous line of logic, but she was too exhausted to come up with it. . Instead she got up, walked over to the hall leading upstairs and shouted, "Come down for dessert, boys." Then she went to the kitchen drawer, pulled out the bag of tees and tossed them across the kitchen table where they slid off and landed at Tom's feet. "We have to find a new dry-cleaner," she said. "Those are a parting gift from Mr. Kim."

Chapter Four
Secrets Down Below

"You're sophomores, for Christ's sake, you can't tell me nothing interesting happened at school all day." Tom sat at the dinner table wolfing down his plate of beef and potatoes while his sons polished off their bowls of ice cream. "Don't make me..." Tom said in a low voice, "...tell you about the nine holes I played this afternoon." Both boys groaned, laid their heads on the table and began exaggerated snoring. After years of trying his hardest, too hard probably, to get the boys interested in golf, Tom knew better than to try and engage them on the topic. They had less patience than Carol. Whenever he asked them to watch a tournament on television with him or started talking about an interesting course he'd played, they became expressionless drones with slack, vacant eyes, reminding him of the desperate droids who worked at the Department of Motor Vehicles.

Tom ruffled Max's hair. "Surely some thread of knowledge was exchanged?"

The two boys popped their heads up, shared a look, shrugged and continued eating.

"Really," Tom wiped his mouth with a napkin, "nothing at all?"

Zach dropped his spoon into his empty bowl and gave his brother a quick smirk out of the side of his mouth. "Well, if you must know Dad, in homeroom this morning we discussed the topic of sharing."

"No kidding."

"Yeah," Zachary held up a hand and gave Tom the peace sign with his index and middle finger. "You see this?"

From his seat Max started sputtering laughter and Tom knew he had set himself up for some kind of mischief. "This is my half," Zach said wiggling his index finger. Then he bravely held Tom's eyes while he folded his index finger leaving Tom the one-finger salute.

"And this is your half."

After Tom chased the boys back up to their room, snapping the wet dishtowel at their backsides as he went, he rinsed the last of the dishes and dried his hands, then walked into the hallway and leaned against the banister, listening for any sign of movement from upstairs. He could hear the light tapping of his boys' fingers on the keyboards of their computers, but not a sound from Carol. Somehow the exhilarating story of Jerry Mahoney's passing had put him in the dog house with her yet again, so there was no point in going up and trying to engage. Certainly she was in no mood to hear that he wouldn't be available for antiquing over the weekend. That would have to be dealt with later. Hopefully she was in a deep meditation or better yet, asleep. Tom went back into the kitchen, took a club soda from the fridge, opened the basement door and went down.

As a boy, Tom's favorite superhero was Superman. He envied Superman's strength and invulnerability. As a child he'd often dreamed he could fly and his first sexual stirrings involved fantasies of seeing through his pretty fifth-grade teacher's clothing with x-ray vision; but what he envied most was that Superman had a private, far off, secret place in the Arctic, his Fortress of Solitude. It was there that Superman went to be alone and think great thoughts.

With help from Tank, Tom had put up some drywall and sealed off a ten-by-eight-foot cell in the basement. Then he and his friend fit a door into the wall that could lock from the inside. On the door he hung a brass plaque that Tank had given him. The plaque was inscribed with the words, "The Bunker."

Once inside his private workspace he turned and locked the door behind him, then bent down and pulled out a gray metal lock box from under his bench. It was about twice the size of a cigar box, secured with a small luggage lock. Then Tom turned over a framed photograph of Ben Hogan that had been taken at the moment of a ferocious ball strike, and peeled off a small key that was taped to the back. Tom opened the box, lifted the object from inside and laid it on the workbench.

What seemed like a lifetime ago, on the day Tom handed over the first of many, many crisp hundred dollar bills for an hour of Marty's wisdom, Marty had favored Tom with a present - a blank, beautifully embossed, leather-bound journal. "Write down what we're working on," Marty had advised him, "it'll help keep you focused on what I want you to practice."

Under Marty's tutelage Tom had gotten into the habit of writing down exact details of each lesson along with Marty's swing thoughts and what he should be practicing on the range. Brought up as a Catholic, Tom found a satisfying release while writing in the journal, not unlike confession, a place where he could unburden himself. When Tom came home from a disappointing round or frustrating time on the range, he would retreat into the bunker and vent his frustration or search for inspiration. *The Word According to Marty,* Tom had scrawled on the title page.

From a series of small cubbies constructed against the wall behind the bench where he kept extra grips, tape, solvent along with a few hard won trophies he retrieved a pen—a fountain pen that gave his writing a sense of permanence, he was writing scripture after all—and unscrewed the cap. Tom sat at the bar stool in front of the bench and bent to his task. After writing for over an hour, he stood up and stretched. In the stark light of the single overhanging lamp, Tom surveyed his cramped man-cave.

At first the sanctuary had been just a place to re-grip clubs and store his equipment; golf shoes, old putters and the like. But over the years it had become much more than that. He'd decorated the place with posters of his favorite players, and as many grainy black-and-white photos of Ben Hogan as he could lay his hands on. He put down green Astro-Turf in place of carpeting so he could practice putting on rainy days. Eventually he installed several vice grips on the table and began buying top-grade shafts and club heads. With instructional help from a golf-club-building magazine he delighted himself by assembling his own clubs, knock-offs of popular and exorbitantly priced brands. Most of all, it was here in his monk-like cell where he could keep his musings under lock and key, Tom wrote in his journal.

"What the fuck is wrong with you?!!" many of the entries began. Less often, after an exceptional lesson with Marty or a well-played round, an entry would open with, *"You're taking divots like a man now. Keep up the good work. Marty is a God!"*

It was in the journal that Tom first began to articulate his dream of finding the perfect golf swing, *Being in the Hogan Zone*, he called it. It was only here that he dared express his thoughts about his secret friendship with the great man himself.

At first Mr. Hogan only presented himself to Tom infrequently, usually when Tom was alone on the range in the evening, or when he was the last man on the course at twilight, getting in some practice holes alone. Sometimes he would merely glimpse a familiar figure watching him from a distance, smoking in the shadow of a tree, and they would acknowledge each other with a simple wave of the hand. Other times he would look up and be startled to find his Spirit Guide walking next to him and offering a welcome grin. Often as Tom approached a difficult shot, they would talk it out. Within a few years, Hogan was showing up in the car on long rides to distant sales calls, until finally all Tom had to do was think of the great man and instantly he would hear the rasp of a match being lit, smell the delicious aroma of a burning cigarette, and know that Hogan was with him.

The golf swing can be found in the dirt, Tom had written in his journal more than once. Hogan had told him that. Or had he read it? No matter.

Hogan means you find the swing through work and practice, Tom wrote. In the margin he'd scribbled in bold print, *let's start hitting more lunchtime buckets!!*

Early in their friendship, a hint of doubt entered Tom's mind about his relationship with Hogan. Was he really channeling the spirit of the golfing genius or, as Tom sometimes worried, was it all just a fantasy in his head? Was it unhealthy? Now and then, when he and Carol were having a wonderful time together, laughing over a lazy Saturday breakfast or snuggling at night, legs entwined, in bed reading, he was tempted to tell Carol about his breakthrough spiritual experience. She was better equipped to sort out what it might mean, but in the end he thought better of it. She would either think he was crazy, or worse, she'd be jealous of his vastly superior spiritual connection and make him stop. It was a no-win situation either way; better to work it out in the journal.

Journal Entry #122

I love having Hogan's company on road trips and on the course, but lately he's been popping up at work and at home, and it's distracting. Saturday I was mowing the lawn while Hogan was yelling in my ear trying to

*persuade me to stop the "bullshit" and get my
lazy ass to the practice range. As far as I can
tell, that's when I ran over the cat. What a
horror show. I told Carol and the kids the cat
must have been attacked by coyotes, and
thankfully they bought it. The funeral service in
the backyard was pathetic.*

Sometimes Hogan would delight Tom and visit him
in the bunker. To accommodate Hogan's tobacco habit,
Tom had been forced to put a fan in the basement
window. If Carol ever thought someone was smoking
in the house there'd be hell to pay. Together, Tom and
his friend would build clubs from scratch, make journal
entries and talk about all things golf.

The journal also allowed Tom a place to work out
his conflicting emotions about Carol.

Journal Entry #11
*Carol's been pestering me to build a sand box for
the boys in the backyard; like I have time for that. I
know what I'll do. I'll make it big enough so I can
practice bunker shots out of it. Ha! Perfect - like she'll
know the difference.*

Journal Entry #27
*The door to the bunker was ajar when I came
down this eve. I'm getting a vibe that Carol's been
down here sniffing around. I don't go barging into her
meditation room, do I? She complains about how much
money I'm dropping on golf, but Jesus! The stuff she's
got in her 'sanctuary' must have cost a fortune. The
stereo alone set us back a grand. A hundred CD's of
nothing but nature sounds, waves crashing, owls
hooting, a whole hour of nothing but the sound of rain
falling. OMG! What about the 'healing crystals', the*

candles, the incense? Christ, the whole upstairs reeks of it.

Sometimes Hogan would snatch the pen out of Tom's hand and add his thoughts to the journal too. Tom laughed whenever he read something Hogan wrote because his penmanship was awful, large block lettering, like a child's. *Be careful with Carol*, a boldly printed entry read at the bottom of one page, *she's no friend to Golf.*

In the back of the journal was a page labeled "Banking". Marty had strongly suggested that Tom put aside some cash for a golf fund that could be accumulated and spent without Carol's notice. Over the years, by slipping anywhere from twenty-five to fifty dollars a week past Carol's eagle eye, Tom was able to put aside a tidy sum. He'd opened first one, then a second checking account—Marty called them "wedge accounts"—even keeping his stash in separate banks for added security.

If Carol ever sees this she'll come at me with a meat cleaver.

One winter's night, when Tom wished he was anywhere but the frozen tundra of Connecticut, he and Hogan were working on a fantasy driver that Tom had designed. He had fastened aluminum wings to the sides of an old steel head driver to give it better aerodynamics. He then inserted a CO_2 cartridge into the rear of the club head, which was activated by a button on the grip. By pressing the button on the downswing, a blast of CO_2 would give the club a terrific burst of speed, like a booster rocket. It was certainly illegal for tournament play and most likely dangerous, but Tom loved the idea and couldn't stop tinkering with it. He called it his "Devil's Stick." Hogan, who loved anything to do with greater distance, was jazzed about it.

They had the club clamped in vices on the workbench and Tom was busy applying a chrome finish on the airfoil wings when Carol banged on the door. Tom was so startled that his hands jerked and he flipped the bottle of metal polish across the room, nicking his finger on the jagged edge of one of the wings.

"Tom?" Carol asked through the door, "What on earth are you doing in there?"

Tom shook the sting out of his bleeding finger and put his other hand to his chest to keep his heart from bursting through. He was glistening with sweat all of a sudden and had to concentrate to keep his tone neutral.

"Carol, I don't knock on your door when you're meditating, do I?"

There was a terrible moment's silence before Carol responded. Tom stood still, overcome with an overwhelming surge of guilt, a terrible mixture of dread and shame, like when he was a teenager and his mother had caught him lifting a dollar out of her purse, or worse, the unbearable moments when she'd suggested he was spending far too much time in the bathroom.

"I'm sorry, Tom, I just came down for some rolls of toilet paper."

Tom said nothing, hoping she would just go away.

"Who are you talking to? Is your friend Tank in there with you?"

"No, no." Tom said, somehow managing a laugh. "I'm just working on one of my clubs…talking to myself, I guess."

"Well, don't spend all night in there. Come up and be with your family."

Tom heard Carol's feet hit the stairs leading up to the kitchen; only when he'd heard the basement door close behind her did he allow himself to relax and take a normal breath. He braved a glance at Hogan for the first time since Carol had knocked. The old man was tapping a cigarette out of his pack of smokes.

"Look at you," Hogan smirked and stuck the butt in his mouth. "You look like you're ready to cry."

Carefully, Tom put the Devil's Stick back in the gun rack he had mounted on the wall where he kept his favorite creations. As the club found its resting place, a great pang of emotion moved through him. *Defend your family! Protect your wife!* He turned back, fists clenched, full of determination and fight, but his spirit guide was gone.

Carol left the following weekend with her "Psychic Junkies"—the name she had given her group of spiritual associates—for a two-day yoga retreat at Kripalu, a spiritual retreat in the Berkshires. While she was gone, Tom mounted a catch-plate on the outside of his bunker door and fastened a padlock to it.

Chapter Five
A Funeral

Small motors whirred under neat strips of AstroTurf as Carol watched Jerry Mahoney's casket slip from view and sink into the grave. She felt no visceral attachment to the lost soul disappearing before her; instead her brain was racing, trying to process the avalanche of emotions as she encountered this other world her husband inhabited. The people she had just met, the funeral mass, all the little details she had picked up on were feeding a growing sense of dread. She couldn't put her finger on it but something more than the husk that was once Jerry Mahoney was being buried today.

The morning of Jerry's funeral was a spectacular one, sunny and warm with an enticing breeze. Within minutes of arriving at the church, Carol could see that she was the only non-golfer in attendance. Everyone seemed to know everyone else, which made her feel invisible, like a ghost watching the proceedings from a separate dimension. She noticed right off that most of the mourners there, male and female alike, were milling about dressed in argyle sweater vests and brightly colored trousers. Some were even wearing shorts. The aroma of sunscreen was prevalent, and as mourners mingled around the entrance to the church, Carol noticed that they all seemed agitated; tense, constantly looking at their watches and texting on their cell phones. They reminded her of under-dressed commuters waiting for a late train.

They ran into Tank and his wife, Connie, on the front steps of the church. Because of the solemnity of the occasion introductions were brief, but if first impressions held any weight, Tank and Connie were not at all what Carol had been expecting.

Carol had met Tank briefly before, when he came to the house once or twice to help Tom build his hidey-hole in the basement; but she had never associated him with golf. Tank's real name was Jack, but it only took a glance to see how he had acquired the nickname. Looking at Tank, it appeared he did not possess a single athletic bone in his body. He was short, probably just over five feet, and what he lacked in height he made up for in girth. Tank was obese; in fact, he was almost perfectly round with a beefy red face and slicked back, jet black hair. Carol giggled inwardly when he shook her hand—he had a lit cigarette in the other—because with his tight fitting suit, open collared shirt and a rope of gold around his neck, he was right out of central casting for a mafia film. Until that moment, Carol had perceived golf as a sport generally played by people of a certain social elevation or distinction. Tank was neither.

When Carol turned to greet Tank's wife, Connie, she had to bite her tongue to hold back a gasp. Connie was taller than Tank by a good six inches and anorexic-skinny. The work she'd had done on her face was extensive, jarring in fact. The flesh was stretched so tight, so smooth around her skull, it seemed translucent. Connie's lips, Carol feared, were so packed with collagen that a full smile, a friendly grin even, would bring them to the bursting point. The extravagantly teased and frosted hair that exploded around her head completed the picture. Although Connie was not smoking, Carol guessed she was a pack-a-day girl by the raspy, lived-in quality of her voice. It was barely ten a.m. but if Carol's nose was working properly, Connie had already braced herself with a cocktail or two.

As the four of them walked down the center aisle and found an empty pew, Carol took in Jerry's coffin, draped with the flag of Ireland. His widow—Helen, Tom said her name was—sat in the first row with her two twenty-something daughters perched beside her. Behind them there were four or five rows filled with mourners, but beyond that the rest of the pews were empty. Tom had predicted the turnout might be large because Jerry had been president of the men's golf association on and off for many years, but that turned out not to be the case.

"What happened to all his friends?" Carol asked Tom under her breath.

Tom smiled and shrugged. "The weather's played against him I'm afraid."

Once seated, Tom pointed out Dr. Silverstein and his wife, Sue, already seated several pews ahead. Silverstein was tall and pale. Talking to his wife, he seemed all hands and elbows. He reminded Carol of Art Garfunkel, a folk singer from the seventies; he even sported the same explosion of curly hair. Sue was nice looking but small and plain, the kind of woman who, if not in possession of a vibrant personality, went through life unnoticed. Tom got Silverstein's attention and waved. Sue turned her head and gave a shy nod.

Tom and Silverstein proceeded to engage in a lengthy pantomime routine with their hands, Silverstein pointing to his watch to indicate that he was sitting up front because he got there on time and Tom indicating that they'd sat in the rear so he would be able to get out sooner to go hit balls. Silverstein answered by slapping his forehead as if to say, "How could I have been so stupid!" They kept up their childish behavior until Carol gave Tom a sharp elbow.

The service began with one after another of Jerry's pals getting up to speak at the lectern; not about what a good man Jerry had been or the kind of spiritual life he had lived, but instead going on endlessly about his golf game and his contributions to the men's golf association. Each speaker found a way to include the sentiment, "…wasn't it just wonderful that he died on the golf course, doing what he loved most." To them, it was as if Jerry had hit some celestial jackpot.

During each eulogy, Jerry's widow would let out a sound that was neither a sob nor a moan of grief, but something more akin to a low-toned animal growl.

Father Charlie's performance was disgraceful. For one thing, during each of the speeches he kept tapping his foot and checking his watch as if he had pressing business to attend to. If a speaker went on too long Charlie signaled the organ player in the balcony, who then vamped a few up-tempo bars of Amazing Grace until they wrapped it up. Charlie rushed the service to the extent that the congregation was standing and sitting and kneeling so fast, Carol was afraid some of the older mourners might injure themselves trying to keep up.

In their years of attending Sunday Mass, Carol could not remember a sermon Charlie had given where he had not jack-hammered a golf reference into it in some form or fashion. Today was no exception. He'd found a passage from the New Testament and twisted it to suit his purpose.

"And Jesus said, 'I am your shepherd.' What does Jesus mean by that? He means care- taker, doesn't he? I will watch over you. I am your caddy and will keep you in the fairway and out of the rough. As your caddy, if I see you driving toward a hazard, I will turn you gently until you are headed safely toward the green." Then he finished his clumsy metaphor with a line Carol thought was inappropriate for a funeral service.

"And once on the green, I will see you to the hole."

He ended his sermon by assuring the congregation that in heaven Jerry's swing flaws were forever corrected and that Jerry and Jesus were on some heavenly golf course "…teeing off and finding nothing but short grass!" Carol had been drifting off, but the term "short grass" caught her attention. Ever since Tom had become golf-crazed, sometimes during foreplay he would catch her off guard by using that phrase when he slipped his hand down her pajama bottoms. She'd suspected it had something to do with golf and now she knew.

Of the thirty or so mourners who attended the funeral mass, only five or six showed up at the graveside service to witness the internment. *What happened to this man's community?* The only touching gesture was the bag full of gleaming golf clubs standing guard next to the open grave. Father Charlie remained true to form, continuously checking his watch and directing the funeral home attendants with practiced precision. At one point when the breeze blew back his vestments Carol spotted two-tone golf shoes underneath.

As the coffin was lowered into the ground, Dr. Silverstein surprised Carol by making a joke. Silverstein snorted and turned to his golfing companions, saying loud enough for everyone to hear, "Poor Jerry. He has a terrible lie." As the coffin continued downward, Silverstein's mouth was quivering with so much suppressed mirth he could barely articulate the punch line. "I don't think he'll ever get out of it."

Tom and Tank started to sputter so loudly that even Father Charlie looked up from his prayer book and like a disapproving parent, shot a look of admonition at the two men.

As the graveside service wound down, everyone stood in line to toss a handful of dirt into the grave. When it came time for the widow Helen to do the same, she paused for a moment, peering down at the coffin below.

"Here, Jerry!" she suddenly shouted, then lashed out with a vicious swipe of her foot and kicked at the bag of clubs. A collective gasp went up as the whole set tipped and fell into the open grave, making a God-awful bang and clatter as they smashed onto the casket. Her head held high, Helen dusted her hands and said, "Don't forget your friends!"

The gathering at the Mahoney home afterward was a dismal affair. Jerry's daughters were huddled in the kitchen with their mother, who nursed an enormous Bloody Mary in a quart-sized cut-glass beer mug, while family friends and distant relatives milled about eating and chatting softly around the dining room table. The only golfer friends who had bothered to show up were Tank, Silverstein, Father Charlie, and Tom.

Tom and his pals had ensconced themselves in what had been Jerry's study. On the way into the room, probably the family den at one time, Carol noticed a large brass plaque on the door that read "PRIVATE". The room itself would have made a beautiful library with its wonderful dark mahogany shelves and paneling, but it had been turned into a shrine. The bookcases were crammed with books about golf: golf instruction manuals, golf history books, biographies of great golfers through the ages. The walls were festooned with photographs of golf courses and glossy pictures of Jerry posing with his pals in front of various clubhouses. There were framed posters of famous golf holes; *The Eighteenth Tee at Pebble Beach*, one title read. Carol was astonished to see golf paintings as well. One was a gilt-framed oil painting depicting a massive old clubhouse titled, *The Royal and Ancient*. An entire wall was taken up by a glass-enclosed case displaying hundreds of golf balls. Miniature shelving had been constructed to provide each ball its own cubby hole, labeled with the date and name of whatever course the ball had been played on. Finally, mounted above a fireplace, the centerpiece of the room was the largest flat screen television Carol had ever seen. Hanging under the set was a sign that read "Go Ahead. Change the Channel. I Dare You!"

Jerry had installed a wet bar in the far corner of the room and a green neon sign, *The 19th Hole,* flickered above. There were four stools in front of the bar where Tom and his pals had gathered in a hushed pow-wow. Connie and Sue were sitting on either end of a sofa stationed in front of the monolithic television with Carol sandwiched in-between them, when one of Helen's daughters stuck her head in the door to ask if anyone needed anything.

Connie shot her empty glass out in the general direction of the young woman. "How about another vodka tonic, honey, that'd be swell." No one else seemed to need anything and the girl hurried out.

Connie eyeballed Carol for a moment, then fished around in her purse, found a pack of cigarettes and took one out. Reaching to the coffee table in front of them, she grabbed a small decorative bowl full of multicolored golf tees and dumped them out. She lit her butt, inhaled deeply and tossed the spent match in the bowl.

"So," Connie said tilting her head in the direction of the men, "I see they wasted no time in finding new meat."

Carol nodded. "Tom is very excited about it."

Connie's lips twitched until she bared her teeth, an expression her plastic surgeon must have thought would pass for a smile. Sue, for her part, was sitting on the other side of Connie with her hands in her lap, silently staring off into space. Seeing her up close for the first time, Carol noticed a slight but persistent tremor over one of her eyes.

Connie leaned back in her seat and blew a cloud of smoke towards the ceiling, then nudging Sue she turned to Carol and asked in a hoarse whisper, "Tell us, Carol, how long has Tom been playing?"

"Tom picked up the game about ten years ago..." she said, trying to sound enthusiastic. "...and he's been hard at it ever since."

Connie and Sue shared a knowing glance then Connie pulled her bag off the floor from next to her feet and opened it. She rummaged around for a moment, came out with a pen and an empty book of matches, and scribbled on the inside cover of the matchbook. "Here's my number, honey," she said, handing the matchbook to Carol. "Call me sometime."

Seeing no alternative, Carol took the number and slipped it into her purse. "Why, thank you, Connie."

Connie leaned in closer still and probed more deeply. "What do you do, Carol? Do you work?"

"I used to be an elementary school teacher, but I've stayed home since the twins were born."

Connie struggled to orchestrate her lips into another grimace, but gave up halfway. "Oh, you have children, how wonderful for you." Connie took another drag on her cigarette. "Tank and I never had children." A cloud of mist passed over her eyes, and then, just as quickly, vanished. Sue came out of her trance, reached over, and patted Connie's arm in a sympathetic gesture just as Jerry's daughter returned with Connie's drink. Standing in the doorway behind her was Helen.

Helen came into the room and stood stock-still as she looked around, taking it all in as if seeing for the first time. "Well..." she cried out, exhaling a large boozy breath, then dramatically waving her arm at the mountain of golf paraphernalia that filled the room, "...first thing we're gonna do is...we're going to get rid of all this crap!"

The men, who had been talking and chuckling at the bar in subdued tones, became still. Helen let her eyes rest in the direction of the wives for a moment and when she saw what Connie was using for an ashtray, she chuckled. "Oh, Jerry would have loved that." She shook her head then swept her attention to the men.

"Make an old woman happy, would you, Tank?" she said. Tank stood up from his bar stool, threw a nervous glance at his companions, then looked back at Helen and waited. It reminded Carol of two outlaws squaring off just before a Western-style gunfight.

Finally, Helen sagged. Tears filled her eyes and she let out a long sigh. "On his last day on this earth, can you tell me Tank, was Jerry happy? Was he having a good time?"

Tank gave Helen a tender smile and then came at her with outstretched arms. Helen put her hands protectively out in front of her, a vain attempt to fend him off, but Tank was having none of that. He brushed Helen's arms aside, engulfing her with a consoling bear hug.

"Oh, Helen," Tank said warmly, stepping back and clutching the widow by her shoulders. "Jerry was having the time of his life!"

Carol felt everyone in the room let out a breath of relief. Connie raised her already half-empty glass, rattled the ice and said, "Here, here," then drained the dregs in a swallow. A glow of peace came over Helen's face, her eyes began to brighten and a faint smile crept into the corners of her mouth. She took Tank's hands from her shoulders and held them in hers.

"Was he...," Helen started, her expression filled with hope, "was he....winning?"

Tank held on to Helen's hands, tilted his head and frowned in deepest regret. "No, Helen, he wasn't." Tank said softly. "Unfortunately Jerry was down forty dollars at the end, but I want you to know, and this comes from all of us..." Tank jerked a thumb at his three friends standing at the bar, "...you take all the time you need getting that back to us."

As if someone had thrown a switch, Helen's face drooped into neutral. She pried her hands loose from Tank's grasp and crooked a finger at him.

"Come into the kitchen and I'll write you a check," she said, then as she was about to turn back out the door she stopped and added, "…you fat fuck."

Chapter Six
One of the Boys

After the funeral and reception at the widow Mahoney's house Tom changed into more casual attire—slacks and a short-sleeve shirt, then on the way downstairs he ran into Carol coming up with the vacuum cleaner in tow.

"Heading to the office?" she asked as she clumped past him on the stairs.

"Yeah, I might as well make an appearance and put in a few calls." He stopped and looked back at her. "And what do you have on for the afternoon?" Carol turned at the top of the stairs and looked down at him.

"I just put a load in the washer. While I'm waiting I thought I'd give the boys' room the once-over. At some point I'd like to meditate and send blessings to one of my friends who suffers from migraines."

"Good for you." Tom replied and was about to continue on his way, but then stopped and looked back to Carol.

"Thanks for coming today. I was glad to have you with me."

Carol smiled back at him. "It was interesting, that's for sure." Then Carol's expression darkened. There was something gnawing at her and he would have to address it.

"What?" he said, a splinter of fear fluttering in his gut. She had the look she got when she wanted to "have a talk." Now was not a good time.

"How much time are you planning on spending with these new friends of yours?"

Tom stood still on the stairs, making sure to maintain his smile. *Keep it light,* a voice whispered in his ear. *Be her friend.* For a moment he was tempted to fully explain what it was that drew him to this particular foursome, that excited him to his very core, but the voice in his head was trumpeting. *Tell her nothing,* it said. *She'll think it's wrong... all of it.*

Tom held up three fingers of his right hand, the only part he remembered of his Cub Scout pledge. "I'll keep it to a minimum. I promise."

Carol looked back down at Tom and he could see her relax a bit. "I know Father Charlie's a character, Tom, everyone knows that, but those other friends, Tank and Connie and Dr. Silverstein and his wife, Sue...?"

Tom continued to look up at Carol and gave her a slight nod of encouragement.

"They're a little...." Carol paused and a naughty grin crossed her face, and even though no one else was in the house, she half whispered, "f...ed up."

Tom laughed and nodded. "Yes, I guess they are. The thing is, they're better golfers than I am and believe it or not I learn something new every time I play with them."

After leaving Carol, Tom stopped by the office to give Larry a little face time. He poked some paper around on his desk for a few minutes, then announced to no one in particular that although the day was pretty well shot, he was going to hit the road and "rap on a few doors" anyway. He played a few hands of solitaire on his computer then made a show of picking up a variety of brochures and was half way out the door when Larry stuck his head out of his office and beckoned Tom to join him. Tom headed back towards his father-in-law, flashing his brightest smile. *Fuck me!*

Tom had been lucky with his father-in-law. Larry had started Kaymer Medical some thirty years ago and Tom was a good fit from the start. His off-beat humor made him a natural salesman and after a few years of learning the ins and outs of selling their high ticket items like electric transport chairs and stair elevators as well as run of the mill items like ambulance medical kits, crutches and urological supplies—you name it, they sold it —he started to earn his keep. He took over the grind of driving around the tri-state area making personal sales calls—Larry's ever increasing girth had made road trips exhausting for him—and because Tom loved any excuse to be out of the office anyway, he found this part of the job enjoyable.

Although Larry fought Tom every inch of the way, Tom was determined to bring the firm into the age of the internet. He built the firm's first web site and showed Larry you could move real volume without ever having to get out from behind your desk. Larry rewarded Tom with his daughter's hand in marriage as well as a substantial down payment for their house in Westwater; an upscale town Tom had never dreamed of living in. Later, after the zany cable television ads that Tom wrote and produced became a huge success—they starred a loud-talking, wire haired, screwball actor who kept shouting into the camera, "We're the doctor in your house!"—Larry changed the name of the company to Kaymer and Son and gave Tom his own office.

Larry pointed to the chair in front of his desk. It must be important, Tom thought, he's still eating his lunch. Normally Larry liked eating his lunch in private, but a half eaten Italian sausage grinder was on his desk, sitting in an explosion of red stained sandwich wrapping paper and napkins. Larry sat down and took a few savage bites of his meal. Tom swiveled towards the window that looked out on the parking lot of the two story building that housed their office rather than watch the gnashing of teeth and the gush of marinara sauce into Larry's beard.

"I got a call from Carol this weekend." Larry said between swallows.

"Oh?"

"You know, just to say hi. When I asked her how things were going between you two she let out a long sigh. 'Well Dad, its golf season again,' she said."

Tom swiveled back in time to catch Larry squeegee the droplets of red out of his beard with a napkin and suck a long series of gulps from a super-sized soft drink container. *Fat Jesus*, he thought and had to strain from letting a smirk creep into his expression. That's what Larry had come to look like in Tom's eyes. If Jesus had lived to be sixty-eight, put on an extra hundred pounds, preached in a leisure suit and liked gold chains, he would have looked just like Larry.

"She didn't say anything else about it but I gather she's unhappy. You're not making my daughter unhappy are you Tom?" There was a mischievous glint in the old man's eye but his tone was flat.

"I'll tell you what," Tom said, getting out of his seat, "I'll keep a lid on it."

"Good," Larry said. "I know you're having fun with this golf business, but you're not in college anymore. You're not in some Frat House having the time of your life with your pals. You may be tempted Tom, but remember this…" Larry was eyeballing Tom now, making sure he was getting every word. "…you can never go back."

"Got it,*"* Tom said. *Job, family, lifestyle, it's all in play.*

Larry nodded his shaggy head while another section of his meat tube disappeared into his mouth, then he held his hands to the sky indicating their surroundings. "What's not to like?"

Twenty minutes later, with his bag of clubs standing next to him like a sentry, Tom leaned against a giant oak adjacent to the tenth tee, waiting for his pals to come off the front nine. For Tom and his golfing companions, this was a time of celebration. Today his permanent status in the foursome would be cemented; a pact would be sealed, relationships forged. *By God I am a lucky man*, he thought, *I have it all; a beautiful wife, two wonderful sons and the perfect job for a golfer.*

Getting a quick nine in on a weekday was a simple matter for Tom. He had ample opportunity on most days to leave the office under the pretext of visiting any number of their retail clients in the tri-state area. Even though the internet was rapidly taking over the bulk of their sales, Larry remained a steadfast believer in pressing the flesh. He seemed pleased that Tom was agreeable to keeping Larry's hard won relationships with long time retailers personal and friendly. Of course, Tom was doing nothing of the kind. Most often he would slip out of the office, park himself at a nearby driving range, and in between practice buckets he'd network over the phone or on his laptop.

The only thing that tainted Tom's excitement while he waited in the shade for his friends to play up to him was that he'd lied through his teeth to Carol. These guys played three, sometimes four times a week. For Tom to get that much golf in on top of his daily buckets for practice and his weekly lessons with Marty while staying under Carol's radar was going to require stealth and a level of dishonesty that gave him a jolt of anxiety whenever he thought about it.

Tom took a 7-iron out of his bag and began taking some warm-up swings. As he swung and stretched he thought of something Dr. Silverstein once said to him. "It's a paradigm, Tom. We lie to our wives about how much time we spend on the golf course to spare them from worrying about how much time we're spending on the golf course, only to break their hearts when they discover how much time we're actually spending on the golf course."

If Carol knew how much golf Tom intended to play she would almost certainly see it as a threat to her concept of family, her sense of security. Four or five times a week would anger her, frighten her even, and she'd fight him every time he picked up a club. She was already sniffing him like a bloodhound every time he walked in the house. What next? Would she make him turn out his pockets looking for tees and ball markers? Cavity searches? Tom didn't always agree with the golf advice that came from the Hogan voice, the same voice that had recently suggested he uproot the whole family and move to South Carolina so he could golf year round, which was just insane, but when it came to the lies he was telling Carol, Tom was in full agreement. *The less she knows, the better,* the voice had hissed.

Looking back down the ninth fairway, Tom saw Tank, Father Charlie, and Silverstein mount the tee box. Father Charlie must have seen Tom also, because he started waving and when Tom waved back, the three of them threw their hands in the air and Tom heard a faint cheer coming at him from the distance. His heart leapt and any feelings of guilt he'd harbored a moment before melted into the ballooning joy inside him.

Several years back, Marty had taken Tom out on the course for a playing lesson. They drove out to the back-nine in Marty's metallic blue, jazzed-up golf cart that had been rebuilt to look like a miniature vintage convertible sports car. The cart had tail fins and working headlights; it was even fitted with a dashboard radio and cigarette lighter. Because Marty reserved this honor for only his most promising students, Tom felt privileged every time Marty took him out in it. While they were searching for an open hole to play, they'd run into Tank's foursome and Marty had stopped to introduce Tom. "You guys would be a good match," Marty had said. Looking back, Tom realized that Marty must have heard some scuttlebutt around the clubhouse that Tank, Silverstein, and Father Charlie had become disenchanted with Jerry. Even then, Marty was planting a seed for the future of the foursome. Marty was sensitive to things like that.

As they drove away from the group, Marty had explained that Tank and his crew were above average players and if Tom was lucky enough to get in a group like that it would undoubtedly elevate his game. Tom immediately signed on with Tank to be an alternate player for their group. When one of them couldn't break away from work or got ill, Tom filled in, so he ended up playing with them often. Now, to become a permanent member of this foursome thrilled him. What little he'd told Carol was true. He learned something new whenever he spent time with them, but it wasn't necessarily about golf.

Early on they'd discovered they were all huge fans of the movie, *The Godfather*. Tank was their Vito Corleone and he did a pretty good impression, too. If one of them hit a ball out of bounds, he'd wipe an imaginary tear from his eye and in his Don Corleone voice mumble, "I never wanted this for you." If someone landed behind a tree or had a difficult lie, he'd mumble in his best Marlon Brando, "I want you to use all of your powers, all of your skills and get the fuck back in the fairway!" It never failed to make them laugh like hell and it sure took the sting out of carding a snowman.

Coming off the ninth hole they approached Tom, all smiles. There were hugs and the shaking of hands; they greeted him like a new Mafia Don. "Couldn't wait, could you?" said Tank with a smile.

Silverstein gave Tom a big hug and kissed him on both cheeks, doing his best Santino. "Look at youse! Jerry's not even cold in his grave and here youse is."

Tom looked at Father Charlie and started laughing. "Do you think you could have performed the service any faster? I was kneeling and standing so fast, it felt like an aerobics class!" Charlie blushed and looked away, a perfect Fredo.

Tank was funny just to look at and hilarious to be with on the course. For all his physical shortcomings, he had a wonderful athletic rhythm that made him a damn fine golfer. On top of everything else, Tank had been a well-respected plumber in his day but was basically semi-retired now, so if you needed someone to stay on the phones and get a tee time, he was your go-to guy.

Sheldon (Sol) Silverstein was a gem. They all eagerly anticipated spending time with him because as one of the town's most prominent gynecologists he had seen, touched and thoroughly examined half the vaginas in town. Whether out on the course or having a beer in the clubhouse, Sol had the delightful habit of dispensing with the concept of doctor-patient confidentiality. He regularly entertained his friends with what he called "Tales from the Stirrups." When playing with Sol, all you had to do was point to a woman pushing a stroller down a sidewalk or a group of women jogging around the course, and nine times out of ten he would describe in minute detail any interesting characteristics of their private parts. The town's newest female librarian might be standing on the tenth tee, and while wolfing down hot dogs at the halfway house, Silverstein would point his chin in her direction. "She has a Brazilian, if memory serves." It was hilarious and they'd all giggle like twelve-year-olds, Father Charlie too, even when it was clear that he had no idea what they were talking about. Somehow that made it even funnier.

Growing up Catholic, Tom had run across his share of priests and for the most part they were all like Father Charlie; they never seemed to lose their baby fat. Charlie was forty-something but looked like a red-cheeked twenty-five-year-old, probably something to do with the low stress of rectory life and the lack of complications inherent in married life. Charlie had great form and his swing was the most graceful thing Tom had ever witnessed, almost too graceful. It looked like he was performing ballet. He could hit the ball straight, but never very far or with any great force. Charlie's stock line after he hit off the tee was always the same, "Short but safe." At first Tom felt inhibited playing with Charlie because he was under the assumption that he'd have to watch his language, but that wasn't the case. Charlie's own language was impeccable but when it came to his friends, he never judged. If one of them hit a terrible shot and let loose with a string of profanities, Charlie would make the sign of the cross in his direction; that was the extent of it.

There was something else that made playing with Charlie so damned irresistible. Charlie heard confessions. Tom was pretty sure that priests were required to take some kind of oath that made it a sin for them to reveal to anyone, even the law, what they heard in the sanctity of the confessional, but Charlie must have nodded off that day in the seminary or missed the class completely, because from the first tee to the last, Charlie was a spewing fountain of dark deeds he'd picked up while administering the sacrament of absolution.

As they climbed onto the tenth tee box someone called out from behind, "Father Charlie!" They turned to see Jaspar Vindu, the town's leading divorce attorney who, everyone knew, had political aspirations. An exceedingly tall and impeccably groomed man, Jaspar had been born in Calcutta, which they were all surprised to learn had a substantial Catholic population. He'd moved to the U.S. as a teenager and was a millionaire by the time he was thirty-five. He was known for being smart and genuinely warm, but Tom suspected that the root of his local popularity lay in the fact that everyone in town loved imitating his exotic Indian accent.

Jaspar came bounding up to the tee, shook everyone's hand and clapped his arm around Charlie. "I see that once again you are doing God's work by sneaking yourself out onto the golfing links, your holiness?"

"Stop calling me that," Charlie sputtered. "I take it you're doing important legal research out here as well." The two men grasped each other's hands.

"My good friend, may I have a moment of your time? I have something I must urgently discuss with you."

"Of course, Jaspar," Charlie turned to his partners and shrugged. "Even out on the course there are souls to be saved."

Everyone laughed, and as Jaspar was pulling Charlie off the tee he said to the others, "Please do not listen to Father Charlie, my friends. He has enough information on me to put me behind bars, I am not kidding you!"

The two men walked off a short distance and began a discreet, quick back and forth. By the time Charlie returned, the others had already hit.

"He's got quite a sense of humor." Silverstein said.

Charlie teed up and then looked over his shoulder to make sure Jaspar was well out of earshot. "He's going to need it. He tells me he's under investigation for sexual harassment."

Tank shot a quick glance in Jaspar's direction. "No kidding." he said with obvious relish. "He doesn't look the type."

Charlie hit a weak shot to the right hand rough and they marched off the tee.

"Oh, my God, you have no idea! There isn't a divorcée in town that's safe from Jaspar." Charlie assumed Jaspar's accent. "Oh, forgive me father, I am begging you. I only touched her buttocks that one time."

When the laughter died down, Tom spoke up as they wandered toward their second shots. "What did he want?"

"He wanted to make sure he's safe; that my lips are sealed when it comes to what he has shared with me in the confessional."

Silverstein threw in his two cents. "For what it's worth, I happen to know his most recent girlfriend has a urinary tract infection."

Tom waited until the group walked a bit further up the fairway, and then asked a question of his own. "Is he safe, Charlie?"

Charlie bit his lip and gave a half nod. "As long as the prosecutor isn't in my foursome, he is." That earned a chuckle from everyone as they separated to line up their next shots.

When they rejoined at the green, Tom, emboldened by his new status as a full-time member of the foursome, finally asked a question that had plagued him. "Are you guys allowed to be sharing all this shit?"

Charlie and Silverstein looked at each other for a moment and then glared at Tom.

"I mean, can't you get in trouble for talking out of school, so to speak?"

Silverstein marked his ball and then spoke for both of them. "Technically, yes, Tom, it's a little dangerous. I could lose my license just like that," he said, snapping his fingers for emphasis. Then he tilted his head in Charlie's direction. "And our Catholic brother here could be stripped of his priesthood."

Charlie nodded grimly, "Defrocked."

As they were lining up their putts, Silverstein tried to explain their actions. "Let me put it this way, Tom. Charlie and I deal with a mountain of secrets in our jobs and we've found over the years that it's therapeutic to share; unburden ourselves, if you will. If you're uncomfortable, we can always find a partner who can handle it."

Tom had put his foot in it and his face flushed bright red. Charlie put his hand on Tom's shoulder and lowered his tone.

"This is a sensitive subject for us, Tom. You see, our late friend Jerry threatened to betray us. For years he listened to our stories, even encouraged us along the way, and I daresay he enjoyed all of it. But then his game went south and he became miserable to play with. His swing was truly a wicked thing to watch, an abomination. When we couldn't take it anymore and finally approached him with the notion that he might want to find himself another threesome, he went berserk. He threatened to go public with our transgressions if we kicked him out."

A silence fell over the men and Tom, looking around to make sure they had the green to themselves, tried a little levity. "Did he fall over that cliff or was he helped?"

Tank barked a laugh and took out his flask of scotch; "swing grease," he called it, and handed it to Tom. "Oh, he fell, Tom, he fell. Did we dive headlong over the cliff to his rescue? We did not."

Charlie crossed himself. "It was a miracle the way it turned out. I felt the hand of God in it."

Tom pictured Jerry hanging over the side of the cliff, clinging to a root and crying out for help, while Tank and the boys calmly putted out. He gave his companions his warmest smile. "Your secrets are safe with me." From then on Tom came up with a stock phrase whenever Charlie spilled a confessional secret. "They'll be in our prayers, Charlie."

This seemed to make Charlie feel better about the unseemliness of it all. "Oh, that's good of you!" he'd say and then inevitably follow with, "Let me tell you who else needs your prayers…" And on it would go. It was great stuff.

Like most relationships, Tom's friendship with all three of them was tested periodically. Tank drank and smoked his way through every round and would let forth the most wrenching coughs on someone's backswing, which Tom sometimes suspected might be deliberate.

Silverstein, informative as he was about local genitalia, could drive you positively crazy during a round of golf. Sol never found a lost golf ball he didn't like. He had the longest ball retriever Tom had ever seen, and if he passed a water hazard of any kind on a hole, even if he didn't see a ball at the water's edge, he would stick in his ball retriever and blindly fish for balls. He loved wandering into the woods whenever play was slow, whacking the bushes with an iron, looking for wayward balls. He was in the woods so often he kept a snakebite kit and a pair of tweezers on him at all times for tick removal. As funny as it was, it was also a royal pain in the ass since he had to be called back to the fairway when it was his turn to hit. Only after one of them shouted his name two or three times, with an expletive or two thrown in for good measure, would he come out of the woods holding several balls in the air like he'd won the fucking lottery. At the end of every round, Silverstein's bag was bulging with treasure and in his garage at home he had the largest golf ball collection Tom had ever seen. Silverstein claimed he had millions of them and no one doubted him in the least.

On top of how much golf he was actually playing, these were the things Tom kept from Carol. She wouldn't approve of any of it; most likely she would find it all sophomoric, appalling even. So to protect her, to keep her happy—during golf season anyway—he lied to her at least once every single day and he honestly believed it was for her benefit more than anything else.

Journal Entry #216

What a day! I was out on the course with the boys shooting the lights out when I got a call from the assistant pro. "Your father-in-law's in the pro shop sniffing around. He sounds pissed off. Your cars in the lower lot so he probably won't see it, but you'd better high-tail it." God damn it. Larry'd asked me to sit in on a meeting with some website computer geeks and I forgot all about it. Stupid, stupid, stupid! Had a taxi pick me up off the fourteenth hole and take me to my dentist. He assured me he could save the tooth with a root canal but Larry's going to want some hard evidence. "Pull it!" I told him. "Just pull the fucker!"

Chapter Seven
Felony Golf

Any day Tom was on the road making sales calls was a good day. He wasn't expected back in the office on days like this, so a quick nine holes to end the afternoon on a crisp autumn day was a private affair between Tom and the golf gods. Playing a few holes without Carol's knowledge, without her permission if he was honest about it, was like free golf. Also, the idea of doing something sneaky, of getting away with something, somehow added an extra pinch of pleasure.

He'd just wrapped up a successful sales call in Madison, an hour east of Westwater, and was driving back toward home stroking his Fu Manchu while admiring his flamboyance in his Greg (The Shark) Norman cowboy hat in the rearview mirror. The look was over the top, no doubt about that, but when he was on the course and hitting sizzling iron shots, the mustache and hat made him feel like a gunslinger. Unfortunately Carol didn't care for it and adamantly refused to allow him to wear the hat in her presence.

"Oh my God, Tom," she'd said when he first walked in the house with it. "You look like you've been out trick-or-treating in that get-up."

As he approached the southbound entrance to the highway that would take him home, he passed a strip mall with a variety of stores, including a sporting goods store in the center. He only noticed it because of the enormous banner fluttering over the entrance of the parking lot announcing, "Season End Clearance Sale."

A puff of cigarette smoke drifted over from the passenger seat and Tom smiled. "Hello, Mr. Hogan." They were like old friends now and Tom's affection toward him was so strong that he was tempted to reach over and give Mr. Hogan a friendly pat on the knee, but he checked himself. Putting your hand on the knee of someone of Hogan's stature was inappropriate. Tom didn't need to be told that.

Not going to see what they have?" Hogan inquired as if it didn't matter one way or the other.

"You're awfully fast and loose with my money," Tom laughed.

Hogan flicked an ash in the direction of the passenger window, not quite making it.

"You're a little light on wedges, Tom."

This was true, Tom thought, but it was the rare moment on the course when his sand or pitching wedge wouldn't do. Still, a good gap wedge would round out his arsenal nicely. He turned the car around and headed back.

Now and then Tom worried that this whole relationship was in his head, that Hogan was in fact pure imagination. Tom hoped with all his heart that this manifestation sitting next to him was a true spirit guide that he had somehow tuned into because of his consuming desire to be a better golfer. In the end he decided it didn't make a difference anyway. Tom couldn't help himself; he simply loved having the Great Man around.

Before he had taken up golf, Tom used to conjure detailed and intricate sexual fantasies to occupy his mind during the long hours on the road, but these chats with Hogan were much more fulfilling than any pornographic escapades he could cook up, and they left him clear-headed and inspired, instead of just horny.

Tom pulled into the parking lot of the strip mall, found a space and turned to Hogan. "You coming in or do you want to wait in the car?"

Reaching for the door handle, Hogan looked up with genuine admiration. "I really like that hat by the way," he said and followed Tom into the store.

The shop was an immediate disappointment. It was a generic kind of sports store that catered more to the jogger and casual athlete than to a serious golfer. It was stocked mostly with running shoes and racks upon racks of sweatpants and sweatshirts in an assortment of professional team logos. The golf section was crap. All the clubs on sale were boxed sets, Chinese imports with brand names Tom had never heard of. The ones he did recognize were very low end. Tom surveyed the available stock, immediately realized there were no individual wedges for sale and was about to leave when he noticed Mr. Hogan standing next to a wooden barrel full of no-name drivers. The sign above the barrel read "Titanium Drivers, 50% off." Tom's own driver was of much higher quality, but Mr. Hogan wasn't budging. "We didn't have titanium in my day," Hogan lamented. "I used to be able to hit the skin off the ball, but with one of these babies..." he trailed off. Tom reached into the barrel and pulled out a driver.

The clerk behind the counter had been watching the lone customer out of the corner of his eye from the moment he'd entered the shop, and the way this guy was mumbling to himself was disturbing. It was weird but the clerk couldn't shake the feeling that this man with the cowboy hat and the flaming red facial hair was behaving as if he was with someone else. *Was it my imagination,* the clerk thought, *or did this guy pretend to hold the door for someone on the way in? Oh shit, this guy could be real trouble and now he's got a driver in his hands.*

"May I help you with something?"

Tom turned, holding the enormous metal club head up close to his face and inhaled. "There's nothing like the smell of titanium in the morning." The clerk gave no indication of grasping the film reference but simply continued his blank stare. Tom suppressed the urge to tell the clerk to fuck off and leave him alone. The slouching, pimple faced guy was wearing a nametag, "Store Manager." which gave Tom a feeling of cold indifference. This guy wasn't even a real salesman, just some slug doing a job, waiting to figure out what came next in life. *To you*, Tom thought, *I'm not even a customer, I'm an irritant.*

"Nah," Tom said, not bothering to make eye contact. "I'm just looking."

"That's fine," the clerk replied before heading back toward the cash register, "look all you like, but no swinging the clubs." With that the clerk pointed to a large sign on the wall behind the club display area. It read in bold letters, "Swinging Golf Clubs in Store Is Forbidden. This Rule Is Strictly Enforced." Tom read the sign and then held up his hand to the clerk indicating that he understood.

"He's a little man in his little kingdom and he has his little rules," Hogan snickered as the clerk walked away. Tom chuckled along with his friend, and then turned his attention back to the driver.

"You know," he said to Hogan, who was slipping a cigarette between his lips, "this club doesn't feel half bad." Tom threw a glance at the clerk and then in a quiet aside to Hogan he whispered, "You can't smoke in the store." Hogan pulled a face but put the cigarette away.

Tom was waggling the club back and forth. "What's interesting about it is that it's got a stiff shaft, which is unusual for a generic brand like this, and the club face looks very forgiving." He sensed Hogan was losing his patience, probably because of the tobacco thing, and he started to put the club back in the barrel.

"It's pretty cheap," Hogan said. "You should buy it."

Tom shook his head in amazement, not believing for a second that Hogan would throw his money around like that.

"I'm not buying it without swinging it, that's for damn sure."

"Then swing it." Hogan insisted, a flash of ruby sparkled in his eyes. Tom glanced in the direction of the clerk, whose attention seemed to be focused on a rack of sunglasses next to the counter. Tom was tempted. With one or two aggressive swings he could get a pretty good idea how the shaft would respond out on the course.

"Oh, that's right. You don't want to get yelled at by the store manager!" Hogan threw his head back and let out a howl.

Tom knew it was a mistake, even while he was doing it, but refused to look weak in front of his hero. He glanced in the direction of the counter and saw the clerk with his back momentarily turned. *He has his eye on me,* Tom thought, *but the hell with it, one swing and I'm out the door.* Stepping back from the barrel he took the club in both hands, waggled it a few times to get a feel of the heft of the club head, the flex of the shaft.

"Excuse me sir…" he heard over his shoulder, a sudden pad of footsteps rushing towards him.

Mischief was in the air and Hogan's eyes were slanted almost shut with glee.

Fuck it. Tom rushed into a solid stance, fixed his eyes on where the ball would be teed up, and swung the club back with all he had.

The next few minutes were fuzzy in Tom's memory. He heard, more than felt, a dull but solid thud as he whipped the club back, and an instant later saw a glob of blood and hair spray onto the wall, immediately followed by a second thud as the clerk's crumpled body hit the floor. The bottom fell out of Tom's stomach as he threw the club back into the bin and turned to see Hogan already by the front door, waving at Tom to follow him out. He glanced down at the clerk who was holding his hands to his head and rolling around on the floor in agony. Tom was pulling out his cell phone to dial 911 when he realized the implications of what he'd just done. "Oh, dear Jesus," he said. Panic took hold and he bolted for the door.

Tom carefully watched his speed as he turned onto the highway and headed home. The last thing he needed was to get pulled over. He was hyperventilating and sweat was pouring off him. In a moment he'd throw up, he was sure of it.

"Look what you made me do!" he shouted at Hogan, who sat perfectly calm while lighting up a smoke.

"Relax." Hogan's head was in a cloud of smoke. "I didn't make you do it, that's number one. Number two, you were alone in the store, no one saw you."

"Oh, yeah?" Tom said wiping sweat from his eyes, "What about the clerk? He saw me all right."

Hogan chuckled. "Calm down. All you have to do is throw out that hat and shave. And number three, listen to me, Tom, here's some really good news." Hogan lipped a dense blue smoke ring into the windshield. "Your backswing looks fantastic!"

Chapter Eight
Winter

Something was wrong with Tom. Carol sat under a healing pyramid she'd set up in her meditation room sipping a cup of chamomile and prayed for a blizzard. Tom had already played 18 holes of December golf that morning with his pals but apparently that wasn't enough. After getting himself all revved up watching a re-broadcast of one of the major summer tournaments on television he ran out to the car, grabbed an iron out of the trunk and started hitting balls into the practice net that he'd set up in the garage. Originally Tom had the net set up in the side yard but the neighbor in the house behind them threatened to call the police if Tom put one more ball through the net and dented his aluminum siding. Instead of being remotely contrite Tom went into action mode. He jumped on his computer, consulted several of his golf blogger friends he'd been following then flew from the house. Exiling both cars from the garage he set the practice net up inside. Unfortunately the garage was attached to the house and directly adjacent to the kitchen, so while it may have prevented a law suit of some kind, the cannon blast and reverberation of each shot was like a hammer blow to Carol's brain.

This was after a week of behavior that bordered on the bizarre. For the first time in memory Tom had arrived home early from work in nothing short of a state of panic. Without so much as a kiss hello he ran upstairs and locked himself in the bathroom. A half hour later he waltzed downstairs a different man; he'd shaved his sideburns and mustache.

"Oh my God," Carol gasped, "What happened?"

"What do you mean?" Tom strolled past her and into the den like nothing had happened.

"Your face," Carol said. "I mean I love it, you look ten years younger...but why?"

"Oh," he replied as if she'd asked him about the weather, "I felt like it, that's all."

But there was more to it than that, Carol was certain. For the next week he kept looking out the window every time a car went by the house and when the phone rang he damn near jumped out of his chair. *What in God's name have you done, Tom? What have you done?*

Instead of trying to meditate her way past the pounding explosions coming from the garage Carol embraced them. Each tremendous whack was like a physical blow driving her closer and closer to taking some kind of action. *What can I do, I can't be the only one. What do the other wives do?*

The healing energy under her pyramid provided some clarity. Scattered thoughts came into focus. It was a giant game of connect the dots. Years ago, Carol had seen no connection between everyday life and golf; now she saw it everywhere. It came at you on television and radio. A huge variety of products devoted their entire advertising campaigns to the idea that if you lost twenty pounds, you could play golf again. If you took such and such vitamin your game would improve. Why, if you take this sleep aid your putts will go in. There were golf movies and even theatrical productions about golf. And Tiger Woods! Oh my God, his picture was everywhere. Her physician had golf magazines galore in the waiting room, her dentist too. Once, during a gynecological visit, the doctor examining Carol used a similar string of words that she'd heard golf announcers use on television. "Okay," the doctor said in a hushed tone, extending his fingers toward her cervix, "we're in the fairway and approaching the green."

On the rare occasion she was shopping with Tom, Carol would notice out of the corner of her eye a stranger giving Tom a small wave, wink or nod. They were all signaling to each other as if everyone in town were in on some common secret, everyone but her. It was beginning to feel like *The Invasion of the Body Snatchers*, but in Carol's version people weren't turned into aliens, they were normal people who, if they fell asleep, woke to find themselves slaves to an eighteen-handicap, and it didn't matter if you asked them how they were or how their day had been, the answer was always the same, "Oh, par for the course." And these friends of his were just awful. They never talked about anything but golf. She hated herself for thinking it but they were not her kind of people at all. They seemed…inferior…their obsession had stunted their souls somehow. "Low companions," that's what her mother called them.

Whack! Carol's heart skipped a beat with each ball Tom hit in the garage. Could it be, she thought to herself, that she was the one with the problem? Was she the one who was missing the connection? *Whack!* Was she the only one in town who thought that golf might not be a good thing? That it might be, if not an addiction, at least a compulsion of such magnitude that it was capable of having negative effects on society at large, just like video games or fast food or rap music? Something has to be done. *Whack! Whack! Whack!*

***

Journal Entry #298
Winter sucks. I wish I had the balls to move the family to South Carolina so I could play year round. I floated that idea to Carol once. She laughed in my face and called me an

idiot. If I had the nerve I'd put my foot down and demand it.

I love my boys with all my heart but when it comes to their feelings toward golf, they seem to have sided with Carol. They've been old enough to play on the course a couple years now but show no interest whatsoever. I'll probably lose them to tennis. What a shame!

***

"Could we possibly talk about something other than golf?" Carol had to shout to be heard above the din but she'd held her tongue long enough. Dinner guests or not, the conversation had stayed on golf from the moment Tom's friends had tracked muddy snow into the house, smashing the magic of winter's reprieve from the topic. She had allowed Tom to sweet talk her into letting him have his friends over on the condition that golf didn't dominate the evening. So much for good intentions.

The silence at the table was jarring and all eyes were on her. "Honestly, we girls don't have the slightest interest." Connie and Sue didn't bother to nod their approval, as if they didn't possess thoughts of their own. Tom just stared at her with wine-moist eyes and flushed cheeks. Father Charlie took his napkin from his lap and dabbed at his fleshy lips.

"You're one hundred percent correct, Carol. Let's change the subject. Tom tells us your interests lie in Eastern religions and the paranormal; anything new on that front?"

"Oh boy," Tom sighed, "here we go."

"Well..." Carol stammered, "I'm reading a fascinating book about the spiritual nature of water. It claims they're beginning to believe that even water has intellect, that it has a soul."

The room came to a standstill—forks and glasses suspended in midair—Sue and Connie's faces went blank as slate.

"Goodness," Father Charlie said. "How have they determined that?"

"Well, for example," Carol continued, excited all of a sudden, "they've subjected spring water to punk music, you know, heavy metal? When they freeze the water and make snow crystals out of it, the snowflakes are all deformed."

Tank rattled the ice in his glass and chuckled. "What the hell's that supposed to mean?"

"It means that we are all a part of everything and everything is a part of us."

Father Charlie clasped his hands in front of him as if he were about to pray. "Are you saying that water has..." he paused for a moment fighting back a laugh, "feelings?"

Carol looked to Tom for help but found none. He was starting to laugh like the rest. It was the most awkward moment in Carol's memory. Instead of coming to her rescue and at least claiming to respect her spiritual research he threw her under the bus.

"I have always felt a pang of sorrow when I flush the toilet...now I know why."

Silverstein held up his water glass and declared, "Damn, I don't know whether to drink this or ask it out on a date."

Connie reached over and patted Carol's hand while tears of laughter were spoiling her makeup. "Oh now Carol," she said like a parent talking to a wayward child, "when you're alone...you don't talk to the water, do you?"

For the rest of the evening, whenever there was a lull in the conversation someone made a snarky 'water' comment like, "Oh dear, I've spilled my water! Should I get a sponge or call 911?" and everyone just laughed and laughed. Things went downhill from there.

Within minutes the men were back at it: the coming season, the questionable quality of the greens at the course and then settled on the topic of golf gadgetry and the wonderful array of items available on the internet. That's when Tank, red faced and high as a kite from the four scotches he'd slurped down during dinner, reached into his shirt pocket and tossed a small foil packet down on the dinner table. The sight of a condom sitting on her dinner table made Carol wince. It was something he'd found on the internet and *"...couldn't stop myself from ordering a box."* Colorfully packaged as a golf novelty item, the silver foil wrapping was covered with hot pink lettering, "Stop spraying your shots!" on one side and, "Guaranteed to go in the hole!" on the other. Carol had watched in dismay as the gaudy prophylactic was handed from person to person, a perverted show-and-tell. Given the green light to take the conversation into 'adult' territory, Dr. Silverstein had proceeded to regale the table with his "Tales From the Stirrups" as he called them, an unrelenting cascade of stories, all describing the fascinating nuances of the female genitalia he'd come across in his scintillating career. Now that the conversation was in the gutter, Carol excused herself from the table and took sanctuary in the kitchen.

***

In the middle of the coldest January in a decade, Tom sat golf-starved and lonely at his basement workbench under a single hanging lamp, tapping his fountain pen on the smooth leather cover of his golf journal. Having just made an ass of himself in front of his wife and twin sons, he skulked down to the solitude of his bunker like a whipped dog to escape Carol's frosty glare. From the bunker he could hear the stomp of her heavy march overhead and the clatter of dinner pans hitting the stove. At some point he'd have to crawl back upstairs and apologize for his madness, but he'd have to wait until she simmered down.

Tom flipped through the pages of his swing notes, occasionally smiling at some of his sillier entries. When he read, *Marty videotaped my golf swing and showed it to me. My God, I look so spastic. I swing like someone's juicing me with a cattle-prod*, he laughed out loud. As he continued to turn the pages, it dawned on him that he'd have to get a new journal soon. He must have written over two hundred pages and only had a few blank sheets left. Flipping towards the back, he found an empty page. Then he sighed and picked up his pen.

Journal Entry # 300
Another row with Carol: I told her I was going out for a walk this afternoon and she caught me putting my clubs into the car. "You can't play golf today, Tom, it's twenty degrees outside. The ground's frozen solid." God, what a negative Nelly!

"Yeah," I said right back, "but there's no wind!" She went ballistic calling me obsessed and I shouted right back, "You're the one who made me take the net down, what am I supposed to do?" I told her winter golf was no different than ice fishing. That was a mistake. She called me insane, right in front of Max and Zachery.

Then the boys were standing behind her yelling at me for yelling at her...what a shit storm.

All this because I was foolish enough to invite the gang over for dinner last week. What a cluster f--k.

We're all talking about the coming season and the first quiet moment Carol starts yapping about her "water has a brain" theory. Talk about awkward. You could have sailed a ship through that silence. Later I took Tank, Silverstein and Father Charlie into the garage to show them my set up, stereo, space heaters, golf net and five minutes later Carol barges in and says we're all being rude and tries to guilt us back to the table. I'm the rude one, right? It's all my fault, right? How would she like it if I guzzled beer as a hobby like half the salesmen I know. There's an obsession she could sink her teeth into. Watching her husband get a nice beer gut and me sliding into bed each night smelling like a brewery. Yeah, that'd serve her right. I just play golf and that makes me the bad man.

All right, all right, calm down. Be careful or you'll get nutty as her.

She's acting like my behavior is depraved. Is she comparing golf to child pornography? Is that where she's at? She's constantly checking my credit card receipts looking for golf expenditures. She waves them in front of my face like some deranged prosecutor with a piece of damning criminal evidence. "What about this charge, Tom," she screeches, "What about this!" If she sits on a golf tee that fell out of my pocket she reacts like I planted it there on purpose. God Almighty, it's maddening.

I know I do some stupid things Carol, I admit it, okay? I took a full swing in the den last summer and smashed a glass lamp shade. You'd think I had fired a machine gun in the house they way she reacted. Sometimes I just want to drop to my knees in front of her and scream, "It's just golf, Carol, it's just golf. I don't smoke, I don't drink to excess. I go to work almost every day and I come home sober at night. And hey Carol, I only ask for sex on our 'fun' nights like a good boy. What more do you want? Well, there's nothing for it now. Just have to go upstairs and face the music. Keep smiling 'til she smiles back I guess.

Chin up, spring's right around the corner.

Journal Entry #316

Found it! Found it! Today, during my weekly lesson with Marty I found the secret to the golf swing. How could I have been so stupid not to see it before now? Okay moron, here it is. On your takeaway, turn your back to the target, making sure that you have planted your weight on the inside of your right leg. At the same time make sure you've hinged your wrists at the top of your swing when you have achieved what Marty calls 'the tray position.' Once you set the angle at the top of the swing, drop your hands straight down making sure the back of the left hand doesn't cave and force you to come over the top but instead stays flat so you can roll your forearms over and release the club as you step into the ball. The key to all of this is keeping your hands and wrists loose at the top so you have a timed flex in your wrists when you let go and fire. It's your tight grip that's killing you! It is shrinking your swing and making you release too early. That's why you keep hooking. Relax, damn you, relax.

It's a shame I made Carol cry by being so late to the boys' birthday party. Now Larry's pissed at me too. Well, too bad, it was worth it. I was crushing the ball. I hit every iron in my bag and the ball was jumping off the clubface on a perfect trajectory, then ballooning into the sky at heights I didn't think possible. Oh my God, what a great day. No more hooks. Yea!

Chapter Nine
Augusta Green

Carol caught herself looking in the rear view mirror as she drove and shook her head. *What am I checking my make-up for?* She was not paying Connie a social call; she needed help and Connie was the person of last resort before she allowed her mind to venture over the horizon; marriage counseling, separation ...divorce. But, before she delivered Tom with the ultimatum, *"it's either golf or your family,"* there were things she needed to know, nagging suspicions that needed confirmation.

Tank and Connie's home was located in a part of town that Carol was unfamiliar with; some nicely cared for cottages mixed in with small tract houses in various states of repair. Some had been kept up nicely while others looked uncared for. In Carol's neighborhood they were restricted from storing recreational vehicles openly on their property, but here many of the properties were littered with tarp covered motor boats, ski-dos and such, even the occasional Winnebago. Several homes were boarded up, but Carol, who enjoyed flipping through the real estate section of the local paper every week, knew this was more a product of the times than a statement about the kind of people living there. Carol had never been to Connie's home before and was a little anxious about what she might find, but when she pulled in the driveway she was pleasantly surprised. Emerging from the car she noticed that the house looked freshly painted and what little property they had was tidy and well tended.

It had only been a month since Carol had seen Connie face to face — in an unwelcome coincidence Tank and Connie had shown up at the same restaurant where Carol and her parents were celebrating the twin's birthday with a festive family brunch — but when Connie greeted her at the door today, Carol was still jolted by her appearance. Connie's bleach-blond hair now had a slight orange tint; it was curled and teased away from her shrunken skull to such an extent that she looked like an ancient, windswept Little Orphan Annie. She wore a tight mock turtleneck and an even tighter pair of Capri pants that only accented her already skeletal appearance. On the front steps Carol was forced to endure a tepid embrace, careful not to smudge Connie's extravagant make-up or get any on her blouse. During their little hug Carol made a point of taking a sniff and though it smelled like Connie had just finished a cigarette, she could detect no alcohol. It was only eleven in the morning, but still…

Connie escorted Carol down the hall toward the rear of the house and into the kitchen. "I'm having a screwdriver," Connie announced, "Can I make you one?"

Carol resisted the impulse to lecture Connie on her alcohol consumption and instead tried to lead by example. "A cup of tea would be nice."

"Suit yourself." Connie said and put the kettle on the stove.

The kitchen was small with a tidy breakfast nook that looked out on a small patch of fenced-in backyard. The shelves on the walls displayed a collection of hundreds of tiny, fragile porcelain figurines. There was a framed *home sweet home* needle point hanging on one wall and a triangle of dried flower wreaths on another. A mobile phone sat on the kitchen counter and pinned to the wall next to it, a large calendar. She was sitting close enough to the calendar to see that almost every day of the month had a time entry scrawled in red pencil. *Tee times, no doubt.*

What struck her the most was how immaculately clean the room was. The counter and tabletops positively sparkled and the stovetop looked as if it had never been used. *This is what a house with no children looks like,* Carol thought.

After Connie fixed her drink they sat at the kitchen table while the water heated. Connie took out a cigarette and tapped the tobacco end on the table a few times while holding Carol in a vacant stare. Other than the ticking of the clock over the stove and the tinny drumbeat of the water beginning to simmer, the two women faced each other in silence. Carol's discomfort grew until she felt compelled to speak.

"How long have you lived here?"

Connie lit the cigarette, took a big drag and blew out a cloud of smoke. "Since Lincoln was president." Then she cackled and took a large mouthful of her drink. Connie sat still with her eyes closed for a second, embracing the moment as the alcohol hit her stomach. When she opened her eyes they were bright and sparkling, as if she were seeing Carol clearly for the first time since she'd entered the house.

"You'll have to forgive me," Connie said holding up her drink. "Since I retired I have the days to myself and besides puttering around the yard and doing a little upkeep on the house, I have an awful lot of time on my hands." She rattled the cubes in her drink and said, "This makes the time just fly by."

Carol waved, her hand dismissing Connie's apology as if pre-noontime cocktails were the most normal thing in the world. "Tank's work keeps him busy all day?"

Connie grunted and strained the corners of her mouth into a frown, but the tightly tucked flesh of her face resisted and her expression snapped back to neutral. "Very funny," she said. The kettle began to whistle and she brought down a mug and teabag from the cupboard. She poured the water, all the while shaking her head, the sound of her breath coming in a series of short moans. She handed Carol the tea and settled back into her seat with a great sigh. A gulp of drink, a cloud of smoke and then, "I have to say, you calling me came as quite a surprise, Carol."

Carol raised a hand, trying to think of a gentle way to apologize for not making an effort to befriend Connie over the years, but she floundered searching for the right words and Connie took the lead.

"The boys have been playing together for how many years now... and this is the first time."

Again Carol opened her mouth, feeling the need to explain the situation as best she could, but Connie waved her off.

"You don't have to apologize, honey, I understand. For one thing, you have children. I can only imagine how busy that keeps you." Connie took another drag and blew some smoke over her shoulder. "And let's face it; we're not your kind of people. We're never going to become best friends. I know that as well as you."

Connie took a sip of her drink seeming to offer Carol another chance to protest. She opened her mouth but Connie shook her head. This was a speech, Carol realized, that Connie had long practiced in her head.

"It was sweet of you to have Tank and I over for dinner last winter," Connie continued, "but let's be honest, that was Tom's idea, wasn't it? And the twins' birthday party, you didn't even know we'd been invited did you?"

Oh my God, the dinner, Carol thought. She'd almost been able to wipe the stain of it from her mind.

Between her eyes she noticed her nostrils were flaring open and closed with each rapid intake of breath. She couldn't dwell on that terrible evening now; above all she needed to be focused and centered, in the present, if she had any hope of controlling the future.

"You're right, Connie, I didn't come here on a mission of friendship," Carol managed to say, "I came because I need to know the truth about how much golf Tom is actually playing."

"Well, I can tell you that…" Connie started, but Carol cut her off. She also had a speech.

"I got a Facebook message a few weeks ago from an old friend, a sorority sister from college, who tells me her husband played in some charity golf tournament with Tom and Tank all the way up in Hartford for God's sake. This was on a Wednesday, Connie, a Wednesday!"

"Oh yeah," Connie started, "Most of those charity events are played during the…"

A dam of some kind had broken in Carol. Incapable of listening, she could only spew.

"I'm at the end of my rope, Connie. I'm not one for sports analogies, but I remember my father used one whenever he had red flagged an employee's misbehavior and was on the verge of letting them go. 'Strike one,' he'd say, and then, raising an index finger, he'd list off the offending employee's crimes. 'Strike two, strike three,' Carol shot three fingers up, jutting skywards, 'he's outta here' he'd say! Now my Tom has put himself in the same position; three strikes have been called, and I, Carol the umpire, have to make a decision."

"My, my," Connie smiled. She got up and opened the freezer and tossed a few more cubes into her glass, then pulled out a frost covered half gallon bottle of vodka and topped off her drink with a healthy splash. "Somebody's got a bee in her bonnet." She took a mouthful of her drink and then turned back to Carol. "Why don't we go into the living room? It's not much, but it's more comfortable than this."

Connie sashayed into the living room adjacent to the kitchen, scooping up her cigarettes and ashtray as she went.

It was a small room, not nearly large enough to accommodate the enormous sofa with matching love seats on either side that dominated the cramped space along with the glass-top coffee table that sat in front. Mounted over a dormant fireplace was a large flat-screen TV.

"That's an interesting fabric on the sofa, Connie." The sofa was the centerpiece of the room and in immaculate condition; in fact the upholstery looked brand new. It was the color that caught Carol's eye, an intense emerald green that clearly clashed with the gray carpeting and turquoise blue of the walls. "What color green is that?" she asked with bewildered interest.

Connie turned her attention to the sofa and her expression went slack. "Tank picked it out." Connie took several gulps of drink followed by a long, pensive drag on her cigarette, then nodded toward Carol as if sharing a common secret. "It's Augusta Green." She waved a hand over the sofa while naming the color, as if she were intoning something mystical. Whatever Connie was trying to suggest was not registering with Carol.

Connie noticed Carol's confusion and repeated the phrase, this time making quotation marks in the air with both hands, putting an exaggerated emphasis on the word "Augusta."

"Oh, *that* Augusta, from the Masters," Carol held up her hands in apology. "Got it, got it." An ash from Connie's cigarette fell on the arm of the sofa and she laughed—it was a short, breathy laugh that sounded very much like the quack of a duck—then she quickly brushed the ash off with a few flicks of her hand.

"If Tank saw that, he'd have a fucking heart attack, pardon my French," Connie said and then kicked the sofa hard. "Look at the stupid thing! It looks ridiculous in here, but Tank, he just had to have it." Connie plopped herself down on the green monster, threw her feet up on the coffee table and sipped at her drink. "So," she said after a heavy sigh, "you know about the Masters, huh?"

Carol nodded. She knew all about Masters Weekend, a four-day span when golfers all over the world kneeled and prayed at the altar of the Augusta National golf course. If there was a high holy week in golf, this was it. Weeks before the tournament Tom started ranting about the slope of the greens and something called Amen Corner as if it had meaning to her. Tom's shouts of ecstasy and moans of despair while he watched from the den were so disturbing that every year Carol took the kids to her parent's house for the weekend.

A cloud of cigarette smoke drifted Carol's way and broke her reverie. "So what's our little Tommy been up to?" Connie cackled, "Something naughty?"

Just thinking of the Masters filled Carol with a sudden panic, and teary eyed, she swept back into her desperate sense of urgency.

"Strike one," Carol said, holding up one finger, picking up where she'd left off. "He's sneaking more and more cash every week out of our accounts to spend on his golf, much more than we agreed to. Last week he bought a three dollar carton of milk with his debit card and took back fifty dollars change. Like I wouldn't notice? When I dared mention it to him he went through the roof like I'm accusing him of stealing!"

Connie's head bobbed slowly up and down. She took a sip. "Tank tells me Tom takes a lot of lessons. Marty doesn't come cheap, I can tell you that."

"Strike two." Carol said, veins now bulging on the surface of her forehead. "He's always lied to me about the amount of golf he's playing, but now it's getting out of hand. He sneaks in a few holes in the evening almost every night before coming home from work. I can tell from the bits of grass on his socks – and on the weekends, well, he's barely home. He takes phone calls at all hours of the night from total strangers. He says they're business calls but then he picks up the phone and runs down to his bunker in the basement. Does he think I'm stupid? I look at the caller I.D. and other than Tank or Dr. Silverstein and Father Charlie; I don't know any of these people."

Connie was alternating between her drink and her smoke, her head continuing its sympathetic bob. "Well, Carol, that's golf. It's a very social game."

"Strike three…" Carol cried out. The physical release of verbalizing her fears about Tom's obsession was making her hands shake and voice quiver. "…my God, you saw what happened at the boys' birthday party last week. He said he was just going to hit a small bucket before the brunch *'to get the kinks out'* he said, *'he'd meet us there'* he said, and then shows up an hour late, drunk with the idea of supposedly finding the secret of the golf swing. I mean heaven help me, Connie, what am I going to do?"

Carol pulled a tissue out of her purse and wiped her eyes while Connie snubbed out her butt.

"I'll tell you what, honey, why don't you take a load off," Connie said, pointing to the love seat next to her. "Go ahead," she urged, then held up her drink and rattled the ice. "Are you sure you wouldn't care for something with a little kick? We might as well relax. The boys won't be off the course until two, at the earliest."

Carol sat down and looked at Connie. "No, no, I could never drink in the morning." She regretted the words as soon as they'd passed her lips and tried to cover her rudeness by pressing on. "Oh, is Tank playing today?" She blew her nose and stuffed her tissue back in her bag. Connie tilted her head, squinting her eyes at Carol as if someone were pulling her leg.

"Yes, and so is Silverstein and Father Charlie and your darling Tom."

Carol thought for a long moment, getting her facts straight before saying something stupid. "Oh, no, Connie, not Tom, he has a sales meeting up in Monroe today. He won't be back until late this afternoon. I heard him talking to my Dad about it last night."

Connie blinked at Carol for a moment and then started to laugh, softly at first but then louder and louder. The sound of Connie's phlegmy laugh made Carol grimace. It was a mirthless, world weary sound, full of rancor and bitterness. Whatever it was that was leaking from Connie's soul was so rank, so full of bile, that Carol braced herself in case she'd have to endure the smell of it. She began to rise from her seat in an unconscious effort to flee, when Connie lurched forward in her seat and her bony claw shot out in a blur, snatching Carol's elbow tight.

"Now you listen to me, little lady, and you listen good." Only inches away, Connie's face trembled and twitched, cracking open layers of foundation, exposing a milky gray pallor below. "Your husband is out on the golf course right now with my Tank and those two other fools. Golf has your man by his private parts, missy, and won't let go. Get that through your pretty little head. It won't ever let go."

Carol yelped and yanked her arm out of Connie's clutch, then jumped out of her seat like she'd been bitten by a rat. She hugged her purse to her chest and looked to see if she could make it to the door before Connie could cut her off, but Connie had already blown past her on the way to the kitchen.

Over the rattle of ice cubes Carol heard Connie's rasp from the other room, "They didn't tee off 'til ten so they should still be on the front nine. We'll be able to spot them from the road."

There was the sound of fluid being poured and after a moment of muted suckling sounds, Connie spoke again. "Can you drive, Sweety? I'm going to be a little tipsy after this one."

Chapter Ten
"It's like heroin."

Carol had been to the town park many times. During the summer the twins took swimming, golf, tennis and sailing lessons, all in the same facility. It was the "jewel in the crown of the town," as local politicians and realtors were often quoted, but the real gem of the entire park was the golf course. Entering the park, one drove down a long tree-lined avenue with wide open fairways on either side. Most residential real estate deals in town were clinched while driving potential buyers down this very road; it was that impressive. The course itself, according to Tom anyway, was not as impressive as all that. On the one hand it was rather short, he said, and not as challenging as some might like, but on the other hand it was close and he claimed it suited his game perfectly.

Connie's head was swiveling rapidly left and right, trying to spot the men. "This is the sixth fairway on my right and the seventh on my left. They must be moving right along. Take this left turn right here. It comes out at a parking lot right in back of the tenth green. If they're not there yet, they will be shortly." Carol made the turn and found the parking lot without trouble.

They got out of the car and walked to the edge of the parking lot where the outer reaches of the course began. Sure enough, some forty yards from the edge of the parking lot, masked by a string of maple and beech trees, there was a green impaled with a red flag flapping in the breeze. There were a group of golfers just finishing up on the green but it wasn't Tom and the others. Connie pulled a compact out of her purse and knitted together the crackled façade plastered on her face. When she was done, she pulled out a cigarette and lit it.

It was a moment of compounded sadness for Carol. She was there to catch Tom in a lie and standing next to Connie who was trying to make herself pretty.

Suddenly, Carol decided she was getting cold feet. Even if Tom had lied to her, she wasn't so sure she wanted to confront him in the presence of his friends. They were husband and wife after all, not combatants. It wasn't worth it. "You know what, Connie…" Carol started, "…let's forget the whole…" but she never got the chance to finish. Connie threw her hands dramatically out in front of her in the direction of the green.

"Here they come. Just look at them!" Sure enough, about two hundred yards away, Carol saw a foursome marching up the fairway, their handcarts in tow. She wasn't sure about the others but Tank's outline was unmistakable. They stopped now and again as one or another of the group set himself and took a shot, trying to land his ball on the green. As they got closer, Carol was able to recognize everyone. The last among them to hit his second shot was Tom. Connie knew more about what was happening than Carol and she narrated in a hushed voice, not unlike a TV golf announcer.

"I see your Tom outdrove the veterans, Carol. Did you know he could hit the long ball?"

Carol held up her hand to shush Connie because with the breeze blowing in their direction, they could occasionally hear a word or two of conversation or a hoot of laughter from down the fairway. Carol's eyes never left Tom. He had taken a few practice swings, a swing Carol recognized, would recognize anywhere, because she had seen it a million times in the bedroom, in the kitchen, in the den, in the garage and in the yard. She felt herself tense up as he set himself for the shot. *What do I care?*, she thought to herself, but for some irrational sense of pride, she did care. Tom hit the ball crisply, high up into the air and on a direct line with the flag. It came down with a muted thump, landing on the front of the green and then rolling toward the center, not far from the hole. A war whoop came to them on the breeze and Carol watched as Tom did some kind of fist pumping action, then moon-walked a quick back and forth, receiving high fives from his friends as he went.

"Oh," Connie rasped, "he's getting good." Father Charlie had split from the group and disappeared into a deep bunker, but the other three came straight at them. "Come on," said Connie, "let's walk around to the side so we can catch them after they putt out."

They walked to the right around a clump of trees that guarded the back of the green, to a clearing just to their left where a blacktop path wrapped around the green and led to the next hole. When the men finished up on the green and placed the flag back in the hole with more hand-slapping high fives, they started toward the women. It was Silverstein who noticed them first. He nudged Tank hard in the ribs and pointed in their direction. "We have company."

When Tom turned and noticed Carol and Connie for the first time, his face went through a familiar dance of emotions. It was the same performance Carol had seen a thousand times since he'd started lying about golf. First the color went out of his face and he looked stricken. This was followed by a blank look and blinking eyes. Carol watched the life snap back into Tom's expression and braced herself for the onslaught of lies.

He walked toward Carol with a grimace of a smile that had all the warmth of a death-house warden. "What the heck are you two doing here?" he asked and gave Carol a hug.

"Connie and I are having a lunch date." Carol was smiling, offering a light touch. "And on our way to lunch, Connie mentioned that you guys were out on the course. I told her, no way, Tom has a very important sales meeting in Monroe." Tom tried to jump in right away with one of his lies, but Carol held up a hand. Any trace of a smile on her face vanished. "At least that's what you told me this morning." The cold intensity of Carol's voice sucked any joyful pretense out of the moment. Tank and Silverstein looked to Tom to see how he would handle the situation, while Father Charlie stood off to the side kicking sand off his shoes and smiling warmly at everyone.

Tom didn't miss a beat. He used his patient tone, one that he acquired over the years explaining life's basics to their sons, like how to start the lawn mower or plunge a toilet. "Yes, Carol, I know that's what I told you, but when I went to the office to grab some new brochures to take with me, I got a call from the guy who was hosting the meeting. He had to cancel due to a family emergency, so we rescheduled for next week, and wouldn't you know it, as soon as I hung up Tank called and said they had this tee time. Since the bottom had fallen out of my morning, I decided to play." Then Tom tossed in a line that infuriated Carol because it was such a cheesy attempt to play to her spiritual side. "It was kismet, Carol, like it was meant to be." There was a momentary silence while Carol and Tom locked eyes.

Everyone could see that the two were in the middle of a marital row, kept in check only by the public circumstances. Tank jumped in with what he thought was great news.

"Tom is playing really well today, Carol." Silverstein and Father Charlie both nodded vigorously and threw in their two cents.

"Oh my God," Silverstein said, "He's knocking the cover off the ball."

"All those lessons with Marty are really paying off." Father Charlie added.

Carol flicked her head in Charlie's direction to let Tom know that she'd heard the priest's remark and looked back at Tom just in time to see him wince. Charlie, realizing his mistake, turned pale and started walking toward the next tee box, whistling Danny Boy. Carol was able to piece together a smile on her face but inside she was seething. Her birthday had come and gone a few weeks ago and they'd both agreed to no presents so they could economize a little and put some extra cash toward the twins' college fund. Tom didn't even bother with a little bouquet or a card, but on golf he spent all he had. However, now was not the time to let him have it. She'd save that body blow for later.

"Well," Carol said through a clenched grin, "it seems today's your lucky day." She gave Tom a little hug and a playful rap on the forehead with the knuckle of her hand. "You boys go have fun. Connie and I have a million things to talk about, don't we Connie?"

Connie flicked her butt into a greenside bunker and surveyed each of the men with a cold stare, then settled her eyes on Tom. "I'll fill Carol in on everything, Tom, don't you worry." With that Carol and Connie locked arms and started back toward the car.

"Hey! You two enjoy yourselves," Tom shouted after them. "I'm so glad you're getting together." Neither woman bothered to look back.

After they'd buckled themselves into the car, Connie announced that she needed some food in her stomach. "Let's eat out," she announced. Carol felt tired and wanted nothing more than to go home, crawl into her meditation room, light a candle and see if a prolonged yoga session—maybe an hour standing in Vriksha, the tree position—could take her to a peaceful place, but

Connie was already on her cell phone. "Let's see if Sue can join us. It's time we brought you up to speed."

Sue Silverstein was waiting for them in a booth at the restaurant. Sue was so diminutive and sat so still, she looked to Carol like a little girl waiting for her parents while they parked the car. When they reached the booth Sue slid out and gave Connie a hug. The two women locked eyes and held each other as if commiserating over some shared loss. Connie reached out and tucked a runaway lock of Sue's hair behind an ear." Carol's just found out how much golf Tom has been playing."

Sue bit her lip in sympathy and moaned in her prepubescent voice, "Oh, dear." When they all were seated Sue reached over the table and patted Carol's hand. "Well, you were bound to find out sooner or later."

Carol felt like she was in the middle of a wake, and only now discovering that she was the grieving widow. "Girls, girls," she laughed. "I'm not saying that Tom doesn't deserve a good dressing down, but you're making way too much of this. All men drift away in one fashion or another. Some find other women, usually much younger women, some do other bad things like gamble or drink." Carol knew that might be insensitive given Connie's devotion to alcohol, but Connie seemed not to notice. "In the long run I feel lucky that it's only golf that's caught Tom's eye and not some…twenty year old sexpot in a thong."

Their drinks had arrived and Connie took a swallow of her vodka tonic that would have impressed a sailor on shore leave. "Carol, honey," Connie said as she dabbed her ballooned lips with a napkin, "you're just not getting it. You're in denial. Tom has been swept away. Can't you feel it? The nice, happy-go-lucky man you married, he's long gone."

What Connie said was mostly true. The man she had married was lost to her. She couldn't remember the last time they had gone for a walk or a bike ride together. She flashed on a vision of the two of them just lying in bed snuggled up under the blankets, sharing a good book and laughing like they had when they were first married. She felt a sob rise in her throat. Even so, the real Tom was still in there, she was sure of it.

"Don't they ever get bored with it?" Carol asked. "I mean, it's just a game."

Simultaneously, both Sue and Connie burst out in laughter; Sue in her high-pitched titter supported by Connie's brassy rasp. They weren't laughing with Carol, but at her, at her naiveté. They were pulling away a child's veil of ignorance, like telling a child there's no such thing as Santa Claus, and they were enjoying it. Connie took hold of Carol's chin and turned her face toward her own.

"Look at me, honey." Connie tilted her head to the side and forward, a mother giving bad news to a child. "That's the insidious part of the whole thing. It's just golf. It's just an innocent hobby, that's all. That's why nobody pays attention until it's too late."

Their food arrived and there was a brief flurry of noise and action as they snapped their napkins, rearranged their cutlery and compared each other's choices from the menu. When they resettled it was Sue who picked up the thread, and she dropped a bombshell.

"When was the last time you had sex with Tom?"

Carol's fork stopped in mid-air; she was taken aback that Sue of all people would come out of the gate, over salad no less, with such an intimate question. At the same time she felt a pang of panic because she instinctively knew where the conversation was heading. Carol and Tom had not been intimate in a long while. In fact, she couldn't remember the last time. Certainly it had tapered off after the twins were born and it was increasingly difficult to find time alone in the house, but…. "It's been a while, I guess," she finally said.

Sue's face remained impassive. "So who is Tom having sex with?"

"No one, Sue," Carol laughed, almost choking on a mouth full of salad. "Oh my God, you think he's having an affair? Is that what you're saying?"

Now it was Sue's turn to laugh. "Oh, Carol," she chirped while carving a portion of the chicken parmesan she'd ordered from the children's menu. "When a man gets an itch, he *will* satisfy it, he just will. Of course he's having an affair. He's doing it with golf."

Carol looked to Connie to see if she was buying any of this, but Connie was looking across the room, rattling the ice in her empty glass in the direction of the waiter.

"My husband hasn't had any interest in me sexually for years," Sue said, tapping Carol's hand to regain her attention. "I understand, of course, that because he's a gynecologist his sexual curiosity in female anatomy is naturally dampened, but I can tell you that as his compulsion for golf increased over the years, his interest in all matters sexual became non-existent. Desperate, I finally tried a little experiment I'd been thinking about for a long time. I snuggled up to him one night, slipped my hand into his shorts and began to…you know…"

Carol sat perfectly still, aghast at where Sue was taking this.

"Of course he immediately rebuffed me, claiming he was totally drained from a long day at the office, so I backed off and began to ease him into a conversation about golf."

Carol shot another glance at Connie, who had received her second drink and was looking back at her with glassy eyes.

"Hear her out, Carol," Connie croaked, "this is rich."

Carol looked back at Sue, whose expression was anything but comical.

"I asked him how he was hitting the ball and did he like the new driver he'd recently bought. Did it have a regular shaft or was it a long, stiff one? Does it have a really big head? He lay quite still while he answered my questions but when I reached inside his shorts again he was fully aroused and this time he didn't resist."

Connie was nodding vigorously and after swallowing a mouthful of penne, she said, "It's true, Carol. I used to do it with Tank. It works every time."

Carol fought the urge to gag and closed her eyes. She created the image of a brilliant, white-hot healing crystal and blasted the image of Connie and Tank frolicking naked in bed from her mind.

"Finally I asked Sol to describe the best round of golf he'd ever had. Tell me about it, I moaned in his ear. Tell me everything. He started by describing a course he'd played once on some pharmaceutical junket in California. 'It was soft and wet,' he said, 'like after an early morning shower with mist floating above damp and vulnerable greens. The course would lie down for an experienced golfer, he added, like a naughty girl.'"

Connie was cackling away now and tapping her hand on the tabletop to the rhythm of some inner thrill.

"What happened?" Carol finally asked.

"That's as far as I got. He ripped off my nightie and took me like an animal."

Connie burst into hysterics. "Can you imagine?" she shrieked, then cringed and coughed out an extended bout of smoker's hack.

"So why has it been so long between sexual encounters if all you have to do is talk about golf to get a little romance going?"

Sue sat up straight and looked at both women directly. "I don't judge other people's sexual habits, Carol, I'm not like that; but the truth is I don't like dirty talk in the bedroom. I never have."

Connie, who had almost recovered herself, pounded the table and set back into coughing. In between the yelping, wet wheeze of each cough, she choked out, "Stop it, Sue—you're—killing me."

By the time dessert came out they'd each shared their hatred of the game of golf, ruing the day their husbands had picked up the sport.

"I just don't get it," Carol tossed her hands into the air. "I never have. What's the attraction, chasing a stupid little ball into a hole all day?"

"Who the fuck knows, Carol," Connie said loud enough to make heads turn at nearby tables, "I think it has something to do with the swing. They think there's magic in it. At least that's what Tank is always saying. 'I had the magic today, Connie,' he says to me, 'I had the magic.'"

"Magic-shmagic," Sue sneered. "They're addicted to it, that's the long and short of it. I'm certain that if someone told Sol that he'd never be able to play again, he'd throw himself off a bridge."

"You say addicted," Carol said, "You mean like drugs?"

Sue leaned across the table and lowered her voice. "It's like heroin to them, Carol."

Connie pulled a swizzle stick out of her mouth. "Marty's their dealer, don't you see? Playing the big man, doling out free range tokens now and then, knowing full well they'll come crawling back for new clubs, shoes, cart rentals, lessons. The pro-shop is the crack-house of sports."

While the girls sipped their coffee and pecked at their desserts, Carol had time to catch her breath. Certainly Tom's behavior when it came to golf was obsessive and compulsive, but to hear other women use the 'A' word was terrifying.

"Have you ever done the math on how many practice balls they hit? It's ridiculous," Sue continued. "I calculate that over the past twenty years Sal has hit over two hundred and forty thousand balls."

Connie laughed. "That's five dollars a bucket you know. I wonder what that comes out to."

There was a pause at the table then Sue finished the thought. "That's a five star week in Paris, girls."

As this was sinking in the check came and the three women pulled out their credit cards. When the waiter had run off they sat in stunned silence.

The thought of missing out on something like Paris made Carol so sad she had to swallow a sob. She wanted desperately to leave but something was nagging her. She hated to rouse Connie who seemed to be using all her concentration to remain upright but she couldn't resist.

"You said you tried the bedroom golf talk with Tank and got the same response that Sue did," Carol said. "Why didn't you use that method and trick Tank into getting you pregnant?" It was well past nap time for Connie, but she managed to lift her head high for one last outburst.

"Oh, Jesus," she said, "that was years and years ago. By the time I thought of it my chance for kiddies had come and gone. Tank wouldn't have sex with me now if I painted myself green and stuck a flag between my legs." Connie croaked a feeble laugh, then she closed her eyes and her chin hit her chest with a thud.

On her way home, Carol tried to sort things out. For all the distance that had developed between Tom and her since he'd begun to drift farther and farther away into the world of golf, Carol believed that there was still a strong love connection between them. Tom was still handsome to her. He stayed in shape and although he was a stickler with sunscreen, he had developed a very attractive tan. He was losing his hair, and that was a shame, but with a golf cap on his head, his toupee, he called it, he still looked youthful. Tom maintained his wonderful sense of humor and managed to make Carol and the boys laugh with the hundreds of jokes he picked up on the road—the impressions he did of his customers were priceless. Finally, there was the sex. She really couldn't remember when they'd been intimate together, but she was pretty sure they had enjoyed it, and if she desired it in the future, she had just learned from Connie and Sue how to get it. *No, Carol thought to herself, I'm not going to turn into a bitter, drunken soul like poor Connie or simply surrender my husband to golf like Sue.*

It wasn't going to be easy though, she knew that much. Carol remembered the night of the dinner party and shuddered; the night Tank had tossed that disgusting condom around like it was a prized gold coin, and Silverstein had almost made her gag at her own dinner table with a grotesque story about some exotic patient's navel-to-knees pelt of pubic hair - but what happened after dinner haunted her most of all.

Carol had waited to bring the pie to the table until after Silverstein had finished his raunchy tale, and then gone back to the kitchen for the coffee. She returned to the dining room with a tray of mugs and found only Connie and Sue sitting at the table. When Carol asked where the men had disappeared to, Connie snorted then jerked her thumb in the direction of the garage.

"Well," Carol said to her guests, "they need to come right back in while the coffee is still hot."

Connie and Sue had shared a look. "Good luck with that," Connie said.

Carol left the two women at the dinner table, walked down the hallway to the garage door and opened it. The men were in there, all right, examining a set of Tom's handmade clubs from tip to toe. Tom had his space heaters going full tilt and a boom box in the corner was blasting a Jerry Lee Lewis tune from some classic rocker station. Each one of them had a fresh drink and Tom and Tank held lit cigars. Tom dumped a few balls onto the green Astro-turf mat in front of the net and started taking practice swings.

"Tom," Carol folded her arms across her chest, "how can you be so rude leaving Connie and Sue all alone at the table?" Tom looked up at Carol from inside the golf net with eyes she had never seen before. They were blank eyes. A cold detachment emanated from his face that sent a chill up her spine. He looked right through her as if she were a total stranger, a different species.

She was about to step down into the garage and give them all a piece of her mind when Tank, who was standing closest to her, reached over and started to deliberately close the door on her. Carol was so stunned by what Tank was doing that she'd thought it was a joke.

"We'll be in when we're done," Tank said as he closed the door and shut her out. It reminded Carol so much of the last scene of *The Godfather*, a film that Tom had made her watch a hundred times, that it would have been funny if it weren't actually happening to her.

When she returned to the dining room no one was there. Carol followed the sound of voices and found Connie and Sue shivering out on the patio in the back yard. Connie was having a smoke and Sue stood by her side in silence. When Carol came up beside them, Connie half turned. "How'd that work out for you?" When Carol said nothing, Connie tilted her head back and let out that horrible, twisted, screech—Connie's version of delight.

"Well," Carol thought to herself as she pulled into her driveway, *that may have been all right for Connie and Sue, but I'm not going to lose my Tom to golf. Not without a fight!*

Carol turned off her car and sat in front of her house for ten minutes thinking things through, then took out her cell and dialed Larry's office number. When she punched in his extension she got his voicemail. "It's me, Dad. I'm sorry to burden you with this, but I don't know where else to turn. I know Tom didn't go to that meeting in Monroe today; I assume you know it too. We need to talk."

Chapter Eleven
Larry Steps Out

It was the responsibility of the last employee leaving the office at night to perform a walk-through, ensuring that the lights and computers were all turned off. Larry trained everyone to do it, especially on a Friday night, when the very thought of needlessly wasting electricity over the weekend made him grind his teeth. Usually Larry was not the last to leave, but it was a beautiful Friday afternoon and very often if things were slow on a day like this, he let everyone go a little early. The truth was that Larry didn't mind being the last man out; in fact he enjoyed it. Walking from room to room with no one there gave him a chance to privately survey his kingdom. Counting the number of workstations warmed him and he smiled, remembering that when he'd started the business forty years before, there had just been one desk, a telephone and him. As he passed from one workstation to another he looked at the pictures on the walls; pictures of past Christmas parties with him dressed as Santa in several of them. There were pictures of him taken with various local politicians over the years as well as several plaques commemorating him for a lifetime of civic achievements, lauding him for his sponsorship of a variety of charitable causes.

Tonight though, he was furious as he thumped through the office-closing routine. He had specifically waited to see if Tom would return to the office after his morning meeting. Now, here it was almost six p.m. and no sign of him. If it were anyone else, he would have been worried and made some calls to be sure there hadn't been an accident, but after hearing Carol's message, that wasn't necessary. He knew exactly where Tom was and what he was doing.

In retrospect, Larry did not regret his only daughter marrying Tom. His son-in-law seemed to make her happy, or used to anyway, and Larry had two magnificent grandsons out of the bargain. What he did regret, and he regretted it more with each passing day, was that he had ever suggested that his son-in-law take up golf. God Almighty, what a mistake that was. Tom had become impossible when it came to his compulsion for hitting golf balls and if he weren't his son-in-law, Larry would most certainly have fired him long ago.

As soon as Tom started taking lessons he would burst into Larry's office every morning, where Larry was forced to endure a fifteen minute monologue as Tom described the latest epiphany he'd had about his golf swing. It got to the point where Larry was deliberately sending Tom out of town on overnight sales junkets just so he wouldn't have to listen to that bullshit first thing every day. When Tom was in the office, Larry had to watch him like a hawk. His most annoying habit was getting up from his desk every half-hour to practice putting. He'd hit balls into a little automatic ball-return device, which made a loud clicking noise every time it shot the ball back towards Tom and his putter. When he hit a poor shot he scolded himself out loud, as if there was someone with him, which was weird as hell. It set a terrible example for the rest of the staff and on top of that he would leave the damn golf balls all over his office floor. Sooner or later some poor bastard was going to trip over one of them and then there'd be a lawsuit.

Larry realized the extent of his daughter's dismay over Tom's compulsion for golf on the day Tom arrived an hour late to his grandsons' sixteenth birthday party. Brunch had been ordered and eaten and the birthday cake was coming to the table when they saw

Tom pull into the parking lot of the restaurant. He jumped out of his car—he'd managed to put on a shirt and tie, but hadn't seen fit to change out of his lime-green golf shorts—took two steps, then ran back and popped his trunk. He reached in, pulled out a golf club, and right there behind his car took a stance and began swinging the club again and again, each time studying the placement of his hands at the top of his swing. Then he tossed the club back in the trunk and made for the front door of the restaurant like a man on fire. Larry seethed as he watched his daughter physically cringe as Tom neared the table, dodging waiters as he came, beet-red and panting. When he finally collapsed into his seat it was clear he was in a highly agitated state. It was hard to tell whether it was panic or excitement but his breath came in short gasps and his movements were manic, beads of sweat dotting his flushed face.

When things settled down, Larry looked over at Tom. He was jittery and his eyes were dancing around in their sockets. He was snapping his fingers in a desperate attempt to connect with his golfing friend—who'd crashed the party with his "Bride of Frankenstein" wife—as if he had a secret he was dying to share. Larry felt a distinct pressure building behind his eyes, pulsing with each beat of his heart, and he feared for a moment he was going to have a stroke. He watched Tom, unable to control himself, lean over the table to his friend and say, loud enough for everyone in a fifteen-foot radius to hear, "I found it, Tank. I've found the secret of the swing." That's when Larry saw his daughter drop her head and choke back a sob. A primal rage swelled up in Larry that caught him by surprise, and in that instant he was tempted to grab a baseball bat, one of the Louisville Sluggers he'd brought the boys for their birthday, and smash Tom across the head with it.

Larry had been scrutinizing Tom's behavior around the office with hawk-eyed intensity for a long time, but since the restaurant scene he'd redoubled his efforts. He noticed that Tom had his golf magazine subscriptions delivered to the office and when one arrived Tom would take it straight into the bathroom, barricade himself in a toilet stall, and ogle the damn thing like pornography. Larry had lost count of the number of times he'd had to use his master key, barge into the bathroom and pound on the stall door shouting, "Not on my dime, damn it! Consider yourself red-flagged."

Now, as Larry lumbered around the office turning off a lamp here and there, the room darkened and from across the floor space he could see Tom's light burning in his office. No doubt his computer was on as well. Larry felt a pounding in his ears as his anger swelled, his breathing labored. As he weaved his way through the bullpen of workstations and cubicles, continuing to flick off any power buttons that had been left on, Larry came to a momentous decision. Years earlier he had envisioned the moment when he could hand the reins of his business over to Tom, sit back while collecting a healthy return to cushion his retirement. That wasn't going to happen now. Tom's insane compulsion to golf would lead to the downfall of the business; there could be no doubt about it. *No*, Larry decided as he neared the door to Tom's office, *now I'll have to sell the business outright*. He already had an offer for the company and if the sale went through, Larry would not only get the financial security he needed, but would also have the delightful satisfaction of seeing Tom get thrown out on his ass. "Christ," he clapped his hands and laughed out loud, happy with his decision. "With a new owner, the fool won't last a week." For the first time all day a beaming smile broke across Larry's face as he stepped into Tom's office and reached for the glowing lamp on the desk.

*   *   *

"Nailed it," Tom said. His shot, a hundred-and-eighty-uphill-yards to the sixteenth hole, was a thing of beauty. It was a 4-iron that stayed in the air a long time, had just a slight fade as it hit the front of the green, bounced once to the right and stopped a foot from the hole.

"Holy shit," Tank cried out, staring at the flag fluttering in the distance. "You can double bogie the next two holes and still do it."

After putting out on the eighteenth and a vigorous round of hand shaking with his companions, Tom walked off the green and directly into the corner room of the clubhouse to post his score. On his way to the clubhouse bar he stuck his head in the pro shop. Marty was seated behind the counter tapping something out on his laptop. He looked up from behind the computer screen and gave Tom a warm smile and a wave hello. Tom responded by lifting his eyebrows up and down a couple of times and biting his lip. Marty closed the laptop and tilted his head. "Okay, what'd you shoot?"

"My friend," Tom said, trying to sound nonchalant, "I just shot a 76!"

A grin erupted across Marty's face and he beat a flashy drum roll on the countertop in front of him; a triumph for the teacher as well as the student.

"Congratulations," he said as he hopped off his stool and came around from behind the counter to shake Tom's hand. Several strangers in the shop came over and slapped Tom on the back, congratulating him. It was an intoxicating moment. The celebration was interrupted by a disgruntled group of golfers who stormed into the shop in desperate need of an on-course ruling from the Pro, so Tom excused himself and drifted into the lounge, hoping for a congratulatory drink with his friends. In a corner booth he spied Tank, Father Charlie, and Silverstein hoisting drinks in his direction.

A tall frosted beer was waiting for him as he sat down and his friends raised their glasses in his honor. Tom felt the dual flush of pride and self-satisfaction fill him to bursting as they began to go over the highlights of his play. Another round was ordered and they began to plan their next outing, even though his partners teased Tom that he might have become too good for them. Glasses touched, laughter soared, and on it went.

It was getting late and Tom knew he had to go home and man-up to the wrath of Carol when Marty stepped into the lounge and started scanning the crowd. Spying Tom's group he made a beeline for their booth. Tom raised his hand to get the attention of the waitress, but Marty waved him off. "I can't stay, I have to get back to the shop," he said addressing the group. Then he turned his attention to Tom. "I just wanted to say congrats again. And do me a favor, would you, Tom?"

"Sure thing," Tom said, more than happy to accommodate his mentor and friend.

"Stop in the shop before you take off. I have something for you." With that, Marty tipped his cap and hurried out.

"What was that all about?" Father Charlie wondered aloud.

Tank, the only other member of the foursome who had ever broken 80, smiled and touched Tom's glass with his own. As they were finishing their drinks, Tank leaned back in his seat and regarded Tom. "What are you facing when you get home?"

Tom thought about it for a minute, then laughed softly and shook his head before replying. "Carol caught me with my pants down today. If I had to bet on it, I'd guess I'm walking into a full blown shit storm.

Carol's already been giving me the cold shoulder since I showed up late for the boys' birthday bash.

Father Charlie shook his head, "Of all the days to take a lesson from Marty, that was foolish, Tom."

A frown crossed Tom's face as he remembered the day. "Well, Charlie, it wasn't so much the lesson as it was the four buckets afterward. You're right though, I wish I could take that one back. Carol didn't speak to me for two solid days and I'm pretty sure Larry wanted to slug me." Tom shrugged. "But it's also the lesson where I broke the code. I found my swing that day," and lifting his glass he added, "and look where I am now."

Father Charlie made a sign of the cross over Tom's head. "All is forgiven, my friend. I absolve you in the name of the Father…"

The boys raised their glasses in Tom's direction one last time and got up to go.

"Let me give you some advice about Carol, Tommy," Tank said as they walked arm-in- arm toward the exit. "Do the 'rope-a-dope,' like Muhammad Ali. Just stand there and let her punch herself out. She'll get tired and start to cry and then you can say you're sorry and have make-up sex. It'll all work out." As they stepped out of the lounge onto the porch, squinting into the blood red smear of an early autumn sunset, Tank tapped Tom on the elbow. "Don't forget to see Marty before you go."

The high school kids who Marty had hired to run the counter in the afternoons were long gone, and Marty was alone in the shop. "Well, well, well," Marty chuckled, closing out his register and going through his lock-up procedure. "Look who it is, my prize student. You must be feeling rather full of yourself." Tom shrugged and gave Marty a sheepish grin.

"It was a great round, Marty, but it's going to cost me." He told Marty about Carol's surprise appearance at the tenth green.

Marty, who had been married and divorced three times, and was now engaged for the fourth time, was unsympathetic. "Wives are like volcanoes," he said. "They erupt every now and again. Lots of smoke and sparks and shit; you just learn to live with it. I take it your swing remained unaffected. That's a good sign." Then he slipped into the club's back storage room that also held his office, and returned holding an envelope.

"This is for you," he beamed, and handing the envelope to Tom, gave his shoulder a firm squeeze, the Marty version of a hug. "Think of it as a sort of graduation present. Today you went from being just an average, mediocre, golfer to an above average golfer - and make no mistake, Tom, there is a world of difference between the two. Only the top ten percent of golfers the world over ever break 80. The rest, the other ninety percent, are just hackers. But not you, my friend; you have sacrificed, you have put in the time and effort. Congratulations." Marty pointed to the envelope Tom clutched in his hand. "Go on. Open it."

Tom drove home from the golf course that afternoon with a level of rapture that compared only with the glory he'd felt when he witnessed the birth of his twin boys. Yes, Carol had caught him out on the course, caught him in a lie, and he knew there would be an explosion of some kind when he got home. This realization tainted his rush of elation, to be sure, but whenever his mind wandered to the impending fireworks with Carol, the leaden mixture of guilt and anxiety that tried to surface was immediately driven back by the purifying light of his monumental accomplishment.

* * *

By the time Carol got home from her lunch with Connie and Sue, she was cementing plans in her head. First thing the following week, she was going to start looking for a job. Although she preached against projecting into the future, always a negative energy drain, she could see far enough down the road that once the boys left the house for college she'd become an empty nester, leaving herself open to a life revolving around nothing but Tom's golf schedule. The next step would be a half gallon of vodka in the freezer. She would not let that happen. Then she smiled, because the very idea of finding a career and starting a new phase of her life excited her, and she felt uplifted. If Tom was determined to drown himself in golf, so be it. He'd have to do it alone.

She spent the rest of the afternoon in the kitchen, getting the boys a snack when they got off the school bus, and preparing steak and vegetables just the way she liked them for dinner. Tom walked in the door at dusk, carrying the odor of all things golf: sweat, cut grass, sunscreen and a few clubhouse beers. He was weirdly elated when he waltzed in and started playing it all warm and fuzzy. He kept trying to cozy up, trying to get Carol to give him a hug, but each time he came in close, Carol rebuffed him with a swipe of her hip.

"Did you have fun with the girls?" he asked.

As if fun was something you did with Connie and Sue.

"I learned how much golf you guys are playing, if that's what you call fun." They both knew a fight was brewing and she could tell that Tom was doing his best to stave it off.

"I don't play nearly as much as those guys, Carol, you know that."

He tried to help her set the table but she elbowed him away. If he thought he was going to get in her good graces by pretending to be helpful, he was mistaken. Not after the incredible lie he'd told her today, not after the years of lies and sneaking around. There was too much dirty laundry hanging between them and tonight they were going to air it out.

"No, Tom, I don't know that. That's just the point. You said you were going to some soul-crushing meeting and when I told that to Connie, she laughed in my face."

Tom nodded as if he understood the embarrassing situation he'd put her in but Carol knew that was not true. Tom didn't get it at all. Every defensive word that fell out of his mouth confirmed her suspicions.

"So every time a round of golf comes my way I need to call home and run it by you first, is that it?"

Carol was at the sink rinsing some utensils when she stopped and turned the water off. She paused to dry her hands, at the same time taking a few deep, cleansing breaths, determined to speak from a platform of calm and clarity.

"I guess that depends on how much golf you're actually playing. Connie says those guys play almost every day."

Tom was leaning back in his chair with his head tilted to the side. His placid expression made Carol's fury jump a notch because he was playing it as if *she* were the aggressor and he the patient and reasonable one.

"You're projecting, Honey. I told you I don't play as much as those guys," his tone a soft caress.

Was he mocking her?

"They're not like me," he continued. "None of them work full time. Tank is a semi-retired plumber; he fixes maybe one clogged sink a week. Silverstein has two other doctors in his office who cover for him whenever he wants, and Father Charlie, well, God only knows what a priest has to do during the week. He plays more than all of us, I think."

"Well," Carol said, switching to an upbeat tempo, a sarcastic gush, all wide-eyed and smiles, as if she were talking about something exciting and pleasant, "let's talk about your marvelous golf lessons."

Tom nodded and shrugged.

Now she lashed out, her tone pure venom. "How many are you really taking and how much are they setting us back?"

Carol was still at the sink when Tom stood up and leaned against the counter next to her. He lifted a few errant strands of hair off her forehead and looked deeply into her eyes, as if trying to connect with her soul. "Sometimes life isn't about the money, Carol."

God Damn it! He poked fun at her spiritual explorations, her desire to find a deeper sense of herself, her dharma, at every chance, and now here he was throwing her spirituality back in her face as if, somehow, he was living on a higher spiritual plane than she. All of Carol's Buddhist convictions, her passion for serenity and inner peace, abandoned her as she felt an overwhelming urge to slap Tom. She visualized her hand meeting flesh and pressing through to the meat of his skull, and it felt fantastic.

Tom began to slip his arms around her, incredibly reaching for an embrace. Did he think they were finished? That Carol was ready to make up? Was he that dense? She stiff-armed him and walked to the other side of the kitchen, putting the table between them.

"My checks from work," Tom said, his tone darkening, "they're still clearing the bank, aren't they?"

The desire to slap Tom disappeared, instantly replaced by something more deeply gratifying. Shoving one of his hands into the garbage disposal felt about right.

Ever since Carol had quit teaching to stay home with the boys, Tom had used the fact that he was the earner of the family as a way of getting out of prickly situations. She was getting sick and tired of that line, but that was a secondary grievance and she would not be sidetracked. This was about the golf, nothing else. The two of them squared off on either side of the kitchen table, steeling themselves for the eruption they both knew was rushing to the surface. Their faces hardened, their mouths opened simultaneously to shout something hurtful at the other, when the phone rang and shattered the tension like a blast.

Ashen-faced, Carol hung up from her mother's call. "Dad hasn't shown up at home and isn't answering his cell." Carol began to sway and Tom threw an arm around her waist and guided her to a seat at the table. "I'll call you as soon as I get to the office." He gave Carol a parting kiss on the top of her head, grabbed the car keys from his jacket pocket and raced out the door.

Driving over to the office, a nervous flutter in Tom's gut was telling him something was dreadfully wrong. Unless the business was in crisis mode, Larry was normally out of the building and home well before six. He trusted his staff enough to leave any unfinished work in their hands and Tom understood that after all the years Larry had put in, he had earned that right. In addition, Larry was getting up there, seventy-two, if Tom remembered correctly, and over the past few years he'd gotten as rotund as the Tankster, so there was persistent concern from Carol and her mother that Larry not tax himself. Tom had promised to keep an eye out and make sure the old man didn't push too hard, but the truth was he hadn't given it much thought.

The building was dead quiet when Tom punched in the numbers on the security pad in the lobby. The office was dark and perfectly still inside. As he went through the facility checking each room, he began to think it was all a false alarm and was about to call Carol's mother to see if Larry had gotten home yet, when he poked his head into his own office. Larry lay on the floor directly in front of Tom's desk. He was lying on his side and even though Tom had no experience in these matters, Larry sure looked dead to him. Tom knelt down and when he rolled Larry over onto his back, he gasped. His father-in-law's face was as gray as the carpet. Tom checked for a pulse and then stopped, realizing it was pointless since he didn't know how. He lowered his ear to Larry's chest and tried to listen for a heartbeat. With his ear pressed on Larry's torso, he could see under his desk. That's when Tom's own heart skipped a beat. There, nestled up against one of the legs of the desk, was a golf ball.

Tom didn't spend much time in the office, partly because he was out most days playing golf or even meeting clients now and then, but mostly because his relationship with Larry had become strained. Ever since Tom had made Carol cry at the twins' birthday brunch Larry had become cold towards Tom, brusque, strictly business. Since then Larry had kept such a close eye on Tom that it had become uncomfortable for him to be in the office for any length of time. If Tom so much as went on the internet to check on important PGA tournament scores or stepped into the men's room with a golf magazine to pass an eye over the latest swing tips, within an hour he found himself in Larry's office getting an earful. Everyone could hear Tom getting chewed out and he'd have to endure childish sneers and snide comments from the staff about being red-flagged for the rest of the day.

There were no windows looking into Tom's office, yet Larry had developed a kind of sixth sense. Every time Tom took a break from sales calls or paperwork and got up from his desk to stretch and get in a few minutes of putting practice, Larry knew. It seemed like all he had to do was hit two or three balls and suddenly Larry was standing in the doorway glaring at him.

Hearing no heartbeat, Tom snatched the golf ball from under the desk, stood up, and put it in his pocket. He sat on the corner of his desk, eyes closed, trying to get his heart to slow down while retracing his steps from that morning. He had stopped off at the office early, making a show of retrieving any messages and restocking his supply of company brochures before leaving to meet his buddies and…yes, he had taken a few practice putts, he was sure of it. Had he put the balls away before he left? Probably not, and most certainly he hadn't turned his light out either.

Tom got up and walked around to the back of his desk and dialed 911. After hanging up with EMS he steeled himself, picked up the phone again and called home.

The exchange between him and Carol was heartbreaking and when Carol was finally able to bring herself to hang up the phone he had to pull a hankie out of his pocket and wipe his own tear swollen eyes. He heard a delicate cough, looked up with a start and spied Mr. Hogan holding his putter, leaning against the wall next to the putting machine. "Don't touch anything!" Tom told him. "And don't even think about smoking. This is a crime scene." Tom surveyed the perimeter of the room, making sure there were no more golf balls for the authorities to find, then unplugged the putting machine and brought it back to his desk.

"Congratulations on breaking 80. I knew you could do it." Hogan said.

Tom's grief and anxiety diminished some, replaced by a nudge of pride. The warm tug of camaraderie from a fellow golfer could do that.

"Thanks," Tom said, then opened his bottom desk drawer and dropped the putting machine inside. Hogan frowned and glanced up at the clock on the wall.

"You've got a few minutes before they get here." Hogan said, holding out Tom's putter. "Let's see your stroke."

He was a cold customer this one, Tom thought, *but there was no questioning his work ethic.* Together the two of them focused their attention on keeping Tom's hands quiet through impact until he heard the buzzer in the lobby.

Chapter Twelve
The Slap

If it hadn't been for Carol's granite faith in a spiritual incarnation after the physical life had ended, and the soothing inner peace she found through meditation—not to mention the emotional anchor her family provided—she might well have gone off the deep end after the death of her father. Tom was wonderful through it all. Although visibly shaken from the gruesome experience of finding Larry's body, after enduring all the questions from the police and the coroner he came home, folded Carol in his arms and wept with her.

In the days that followed, Tom showed Carol the kind of man he could be. He took charge of the funeral services, Larry's cremation and the ensuing memorial service without complaint. He went for long walks with his sons, taking great pains to comfort them over the loss of their grandfather. He brought the boys to see Father Charlie so they would be reassured that Larry now sat at the right hand of God, and he didn't blink (or snicker) when Carol offered her alternative theories to the boys concerning the process of spiritual incarnation as the soul made its journey to the other side.

Tom helped Carol assemble photo and video displays to be exhibited at Larry's memorial, and when Father Charlie offered his services, Tom was inclined to accept until Myrna put her foot down.

"Larry was a lapsed Jew, there's no getting around that," she said wiping a tear from her eye, "but a Catholic funeral will be the first thing he throws in my face when I follow him to the grave, and I can't live with that."

They settled on the Unitarian Church. It was neutral ground and large enough to accommodate Larry's vast number of friends and business associates. At the service Carol could barely make it through her eulogy, breaking down several times. When she had finished Tom walked up to the podium and escorted her back to her seat in the front row. He gave her a long and loving embrace and then went to the podium himself.

"Larry had the biggest heart of any man I ever met, so it's no surprise that's what failed him in the end..." he began and as he continued his eulogy he blended a brilliant mix of gentle humor with pangs of sorrow and loss. He shared wonderful anecdotes of his years working with Larry—his story about tossing a pulled tooth onto Larry's desk to prove his honesty brought the house down—as well as the rapture Larry enjoyed in the company of his grandchildren. Carol wept at every emotional turn in Tom's rendition of Larry's contribution to their lives, and felt a giant throb of relief at the end when she realized he had finished without once attempting to frame the communal grief in the cloak of a cheesy golf metaphor.

It was months before the dark cloud of grief began to lift from Carol's daily life. Larry had passed in the early Fall and thankfully, even though the golf season was far from over, Tom was quick to put aside his compulsion and instead immersed himself in the daily running of the family business. The ownership of the company had passed to Carol's mother, Myrna, but she knew little or nothing about it and ceded all business decisions to her son-in-law. For his part, Tom seemed determined to take the company to new heights. He devoted a tremendous amount of time overseeing the creation of an on-line product catalog and told Carol he was hoping to take the company's market reach to a national level, maybe even global.

It was during this post-funeral period that Tom came home from work one night with a grand idea. He decided he needed to take up another sport for the winter months, one the entire family could enjoy. Carol liked the idea but hadn't a clue as to what activity that might be. The boys suggested snowboarding but Carol vetoed that idea. "It's too cold, too costly, and too dangerous." In the end, Tom settled the issue. On Christmas morning, under the tree were four brand-new tennis racquets along with membership cards to the local indoor tennis academy, lessons included.

The holiday season came and went. By the first week of March the winter began to wane, the first buds of crocus spearing through the snow. The boys were busy in their junior year of high school, taking the SATs and exploring prospective colleges. Most weekends were spent visiting different institutions all over the eastern seaboard, letting the boys get a feel for what kind of school they might enjoy and benefit the most from. It was a busy time for the family and Carol was grateful for it.

While a chicken roasted in the oven she sat at the kitchen table with her laptop, putting finishing touches on the family's spring vacation plans. She was looking forward to the trip after all the running around and it might be their last trip as a family before the boys went off to college. She was in the process of booking flights when she heard the garage door open and Tom's car pull in. She glanced at the clock on the stove and smiled. He was home early.

Tom looked tired when he came into the kitchen, gaunt almost, the look of a long day hanging on him. Although he was bald on top, the hair on the sides of his head was entirely askew, as if he'd been standing in a windstorm. His face was flush. For the first time, Carol thought Tom was beginning to look his age. He smiled when he saw her, walked over and kissed her on the back of her neck. With her head bowed, she glanced at Tom's shoes, and stiffened. She looked up into Tom's face. "Your pant cuffs are all wet and they have grass on them."

Tom's eyes tightened for a moment, then relaxed. "All right, all right, I hit a bucket this afternoon." Tom blinked and added, "I had to drive past the course today and the urge to hit a few overpowered me."

Satisfied with his honesty, Carol nodded once, putting an end to it. His golf clubs remained in the garage and, as far as she knew, Tom hadn't been out on the course since that transformational day of Larry's incarnation from physical form to pure spirit energy. He had earned her trust and she was in no mood to chastise. She turned back to her computer.

"What are you up to?" he asked, walking down the hall to the closet where he hung up his overcoat.

"I just booked our flights for spring vacation," Carol said, turning off her laptop and snapping it shut.

Tom came back in, walked to the refrigerator, took out a can of club soda and popped the top. "Where are we off to this time?"

"I booked us for a week at Caneel Bay Resort on St. John's. Larry used to take us there when I was little. I'd love to see it again and thought it would be nice to share it with the boys. They'll go crazy for it. It has fantastic snorkeling and great hiking trails." Tom nodded in agreement, then froze mid-sip. Carol watched his eyes narrow and his lips tighten. "What?" she asked.

"There's no golf on St. John's, Carol. Not even a pitch and putt."

Carol closed her eyes and breathed quietly through her nose for a few moments. They were right back where they'd left off on the day her father died. It was only her mother's desperate call that had prevented a major blowout.

Carol opened her eyes and looked up at Tom. "It's a family vacation, Tom. I thought we could spend some time together, not just during the evenings after you come staggering off some golf course." Tom was about to protest but Carol cut him off, changing tack. She reached up and took one of Tom's hands in hers. "After the last few dreadful months, this will be healing for me, Tom, for all of us. Maybe you and I could even spend a little romantic time together, does that appeal to you?"

Tom looked down at Carol, his eyes flat and cold, void of expression. The very eyes he had looked at her with that night in the garage when Tank had shut the door on her. "And what am I supposed to do with myself after that magical half-hour?" he said.

With an agility and speed Carol didn't know she possessed, she flew out of her chair and slapped Tom across the face as hard as she could. The sound of the slap reverberated like a gunshot in the confines of the kitchen. Carol stared at her hand as if it were a foreign object that had acted completely of its own volition. She looked up at the red stain blooming on the stunned face of her husband and tears shot down her cheeks. "Oh…oh…oh," was all that would come out of her mouth. She repeated that sound over and over as she fled out of the kitchen and down the hall before turning into the den and slamming the door behind her.

Carol sat on the sofa, shaking, grieving over what she had done. She knew that she'd harbored anger and grief and possibly a subliminal dose of jealousy towards Tom's devotion to golf for many years. She should have put her foot down about it ages ago but she hadn't; instead, by using her vast array of Spiritual Skills to keep her emotions in check, she had allowed her anger to fester deep inside. There was little doubt that this infection of spirit had put her off balance.

Far too agitated to meditate, the best she could manage was to sit with closed eyes on the sofa, counting her breaths with her arms wrapped around her. In the silence she heard the basement door open,

then Tom's recognizable cadence going down the stairs. Beneath her she heard the sharp click of the padlock coming off the bunker door, followed by the thud as Tom closed it behind him.

* * *

Tom sat under the light of the bare bulb in the bunker, mechanically rubbing the sting out of his cheek. He deeply regretted what he'd said to her with all his heart and was on the verge of tears. He knew what had driven him to be so callous, and it had nothing to do with Carol. Well, almost nothing.

He hadn't held a club in his hand for almost five months. Looking back, he realized he had been proud of himself for not golfing, not hitting even a single bucket. He needed to be strong for Carol and the boys, and he had been strong. Assuming command at the office during the day and researching colleges with the boys at night had consumed him. Every now and then, though, something would set him off and a terrible urge rose up in him to tip a bucket of balls at his feet and go to work on them with a 6-iron. Sometimes it was a golf-themed advertisement on television, or sometimes the simple act of passing a driving range on the road. He had successfully banished Hogan from his car, almost completely from his thoughts even, but now and then he imagined he caught a glimpse of the great man blowing smoke at him out the window of a passing bus or waving from amidst a throng of shoppers at the local mall. How Hogan got away with lighting up on a bus was a mystery to Tom, but whenever he spotted him his heart would flutter and the palms of his hands would itch.

One of the first things he'd done after Larry's death, a bow to his new found responsibility, was to cancel all of his golf magazine subscriptions; but while cleaning off his desk that afternoon he'd come across an old copy of *Golfsmith* magazine, one that he had used to order parts for his homemade clubs. Instead of throwing it in the trash, which he knew would have been the prudent thing, he'd picked it up and nonchalantly wandered over to the bathroom to be alone with it.

He'd gotten himself all juiced up about golf with that damn magazine, and then, pumped to exploding with a throbbing desire to connect with a low iron, drove like a madman to the golf course. Borrowing a 4-iron from the assistant Pro, he'd walked through frozen slush down to the range where he proceeded to work his way through a jumbo bucket of balls, each swing a jerky signature of bad golf. Lack of practice had robbed him of his nuanced tempo, his fluid release. His once liquid wrists felt wooden and the soft feel he'd spent years developing in his hands was all but gone. By the time he got home, he was feeling anxious and depressed about the deterioration of his swing, coupled with a simmering ache that somehow he was being deprived. When Carol spoke of a weeklong vacation of "healing"—a vacation with no chance of golf—he'd snapped.

"Goddamn it," he said between clenched teeth and felt a blanket of despair descend upon him. He laid his head down on the workbench and sighed. After a while he picked his head up and looked around his tiny kingdom. He hadn't been down here in months and the place immediately filled him with nostalgia.

Walking into the space, the workbench was the first thing that came into view. Built into the wall, it ran the length of the room. On the bench Tom had installed a vise for re-gripping clubs and another series of smaller vises he used when building his experimental clubs. Some of the clubs Tom had made over the years were put together so badly, so amateurish in design and construction, that you could tell just by looking at them they were absolute abominations. Normally Tom would dismantle those mistakes, saving the parts for later use, but occasionally one of his monster clubs would take his fancy and he could not bear to part with it. He placed his most insidious creations in the gun rack hanging on the wall.

There rested his fantasy club, the Devil Stick, the aerodynamically air-foiled CO_2 propelled driver. Then there was the two-headed 7-iron he had made on a whim to see if he could hit two balls at once, the idea being that if you only had time for nine holes you could play two balls simultaneously and still get in a full round. In a nod to the horror films of his youth he had labeled this one the "Franken Club." On the walls were some cheap posters of Jack Nicklaus, Arnold Palmer and Tiger Woods, along with black and white photographs of Mr. Hogan everywhere. Against the wall behind the workbench was a series of little cubbies that held his golf club building supplies: golf grips, tape, solvent, hack saws.

As he inspected the contents of the cubbies, the first thing that caught his eye was the present that Marty had handed him on that glorious day he'd shot his 76. He had left the envelope in the bunker after Larry died and since forgotten all about it. He opened the envelope and shook the contents into his hand. It was an invitation to some kind of private men's golf club, an indoor facility, Marty had said, and along with the invitation came a small brass key. Tom stared numbly at the two items he was holding and the urge to be in the company of his golfing companions rose up in him, the need to slice open the heart of a long par 3 with a ripping 5-iron was so strong he could taste it. He took out his cell phone and dialed Marty's number but stopped himself before he hit the call button. As much as he needed a man sized dose of understanding and compassion, reaching out to Marty would just be another betrayal in Carol's eyes and he could not bring himself to do it.

He had broken Carol's heart and pushed her to an act of violence. He had years of lying and selfish behavior to make up for, and he was of a mind to do whatever it took to make things right between them. Tom felt his heart swell; his resolve stiffened, and he suddenly understood that his first order of business was

to dismantle the bunker itself. Tear it all down. That would please her no end and demonstrate the depth of his commitment.

Putting the invitation and the key back in the envelope and slipping it into his pocket he began the tear-down by pulling an empty cardboard box out from under the workbench and started filling it by emptying the supplies from the cubbies. When that was done he gathered all of his framed Hogan photos off the walls and stacked them on the workbench.

"Ahem."

Tom had company. He heard the scratch of a match strike, followed by a strong sulfur odor and the familiar blue plume of cigarette smoke. Mr. Hogan was leaning against the wall at the end of the workbench, drenched in shadow, well out of the glare of the overhead light and stared at Tom in silence.

"That was a great day, wasn't it?" Hogan said softly.

Tom wondered if Hogan knew what had taken place between him and Carol, but then caught himself. Of course he knew. Hogan was his spirit guide, he knew everything.

"You won't be breaking eighty or joining any secret man clubs any time soon, I can tell you that much."

Hogan added and flicked an ash in Tom's general direction.

"No," Tom replied, "you're probably right about that."

Tom bent down and rummaged around for another empty box. Finding one, he brought it up to the bench and began putting his collection of magazines and Hogan books into it, but after a moment he stopped. A profound fatigue washed over him and he folded his arms on the bench, resting his head on them. He couldn't believe how tired he was, how sad. Then, without remorse, without any shame of behaving childishly in front of his friend, Tom began to weep.

With no sound of warning, he felt himself being lifted up off his stool and slammed up against the wall. The wind was knocked out of him but he managed to open his eyes and saw that Mr. Hogan had grabbed him by the front of his shirt and was holding him a foot off the floor. Hogan had a cigarette clenched between his teeth and murder in his eyes.

"What the hell's the matter with you?" his mentor snarled. "When did you become the woman of the house?" With that, he released his grip and Tom sank to the floor. Hogan retreated to his spot against the opposite wall and took such a long drag on his smoke that Tom could hear the burning ember sizzle.

Tom's legs felt like rubber but he managed to get to his feet and steady himself by holding onto the workbench. After a moment he found his breath. "What am I supposed to do with Carol? What am I supposed to do with the kids?" Tom could feel contempt coming off Hogan like a wall of heat.

"If you can't pull the wool over their eyes, fella," Hogan snarled, "you're not the man I thought you were."

Tom was standing up now. He didn't have to take this. "I can't go back to golf, don't you see that? I'm breaking Carol's heart. My God," Tom whispered, speaking aloud the dark thought that had haunted him for months, "for all I know I killed her father!" Tom was getting his legs back and started jabbing a finger at his hero while he spoke. "And tell me this Ben, what about my job? I have a business to run." Hogan flicked his cigarette directly at Tom's face and Tom had to dodge his head to keep from getting hit with a small fireball.

"You're not getting it, fella. For you to take your game to the next level, to find the swing of a champion, you're going to have to free yourself of all of that."

It took a moment for Tom to grasp exactly what Hogan meant, but when he finally understood, a terrible panic froze his heart. "What the fuck are you talking about?" he pleaded. "I can't do that."

Hogan was panting, his breath coming in deep gasps stoking a rage seething inside the great man, and for the first time since he'd picked up that 7-iron all those years ago, Tom felt afraid. Although Hogan stood in the far corner of the bunker, barely visible in the semi-darkness, Tom was seeing him clearly for the first time. He was no spirit guide, no heaven sent angel, he was a malevolent being and the demon had something in his hands. It looked like a short, knotted whip of some kind but it was milky white. Tom recognized the shape of the thing but he couldn't bring its name to mind.

"What is that?" Tom asked, tensing himself as if he was about to get into a fistfight. "What have you got there?"

Hogan began to advance on Tom slowly and Tom raised his fists in defense. Hogan's eyes were bloodshot red.

"This thing was on the floor and I tripped over it on my way in," he rasped. Tom was backed up against the wall now, petrified. His eyes glued to what Hogan was lifting into view.

"I know what that is." Tom tried to scream the words but they came out in a high pitched squeal, a whimper.

"Of course you do!" the Hogan creature roared as he came at Tom in a blinding rush. "It's your spine."

* * *

Other than two burning lavender-scented candles burning on either side of her, the room was dark. The rhythmic roar of crashing surf played softly on the stereo. Carol had tried to compose herself in the den, but the tortured sounds of Tom's ravings from the basement were frightening so she had fled upstairs to distance herself from the madness below and tried to purge the anger and shame from her spirit. She was sitting in her meditation room in lotus position on her yoga mat, alternating between periods of deep meditation and counting the beats of her heart. She had already decided to make an appointment the next day to see her Energy Healer and have her chakras realigned, when there came a soft tapping on the door. The door opened and Tom stuck his head in.

"May I come in?"

Carol looked at Tom without expression as he knelt down on the floor in front of her, taking her hands.

"Carol, I apologize from the bottom of my heart."

Even in the poor light of the candles, she could see that his eyes were wet and swollen. She nodded, allowing him to continue.

"I've been working very hard since Larry died and between that and not being able to play a single round of golf…"

Carol stiffened at the mention of golf. "So, you're blaming what you said on not having the chance to hit a golf ball, is that it?"

"I'm addicted to it, Carol. I've been fighting it for months as hard as I can, but today it got the better of me."

Carol could hardly believe her ears. Tom was admitting to what Connie and Sue had tried to warn her about, what she had suspected all along, that golf *was* addictive. It *truly was* a threat to the fabric of family and community; it was just as dangerous as drugs or alcohol or tobacco might be. The cold steel in her heart began to soften when she saw the remorse and sincerity in Tom's face, but now was no time to relent.

"I heard you arguing with yourself down there," she said. "It wasn't pretty."

Tom responded with a vivid blush.

"You finally admit then that you have no control over your compulsion to golf?"

Tom nodded solemnly.

Carol waited a moment to let the impact of Tom's admission sink in. "How bad is it?"

Tom's eyes misted again and he had to clear his throat before he spoke. "I can't pass a well manicured lawn without wanting to pull over and tee one up."

"Well then," Carol said, "let's see about getting you some help with that." She clapped her hands once and a light went on at her desk in a corner of the room. Carol got up and went to the desk, returning with her personal phone book. With Tom at her side and phone in hand, she began calling her friends and colleagues, throwing out her spiritual net and gathering advice.

Chapter Thirteen
Rehab

Tom pulled into the parking lot of the Methodist Church that sponsored the golf addiction rehabilitation program that Carol and her spiritual friends had found for him. When Carol had presented him with the idea, he did not hesitate demonstrating his eagerness to go, but as he sat in his car and looked at the group gathering around the entrance, he wished to God that he had.

There were nine or ten people standing out front smoking cigarettes or puffing on cigars. He recognized a couple of them as avid players he'd seen on the course years before, and when they'd disappeared he'd simply assumed they'd moved away - but he was wrong. They had come to this awful place where golfers go to die.

Some of the men standing around looked in the direction of Tom's car and when they recognized Tom they waved, then nodded to one another as if he had long been expected. A couple of guys let out hoots of approval and applauded. He felt himself blush with shame and embarrassment as he started to get out of the car.

"How long does this last?" he had asked Carol when she told him the date of his first Golfaholic meeting.

"As long as it takes, Tom," she'd replied, and after kissing the bald spot on the top of his head, she added, "Who knows, maybe the rest of your life."

Tom stood by his car as several of the smokers came over and greeted him warmly. "All right, Tom! Knew you were going to find your way here sooner or later," one said.

"Yup," said another, "we've been saving a seat for you." A familiar-looking fellow who'd been sitting on the front steps of the building crushed out his cigarette, put the butt in an empty coffee can at his feet, got up and walked over, holding out his hand.

"Remember me?" he asked with a shy grin. "We played together a few years back." Tom almost recognized the face and the voice but couldn't place the name until the guy took a golf stance and pantomimed his take away and follow through. He would know that swing anywhere.

It had to be at least seven or eight years ago since the day Tom and Silverstein had been on the range hitting practice buckets when they noticed someone at the other end with the most graceful swing Tom had ever seen. The owner of that swing was fun to watch even though everything about him made Tom envious. He was young, tall and handsome and when he struck the ball, the crack of impact reverberated down the entire range, followed by an air-splitting whoosh as it shot skyward. As he held his finish pose, he would spin the shaft of the club in his hands like a pro. One after another, the balls would follow the same beautiful arc. Hitting balls next to this fellow was just plain embarrassing. "Who's that guy?" Tom had asked his friend.

"That's Sean McMahn," Silverstein said. "He's here almost every day. He's been trying to break into the acting profession for years now, without much luck." The two of them stood there mesmerized by the young man's fluid motions, his flawless technique. "That," Silverstein said with genuine admiration, "is the swing of the chronically unemployed."

Tom had made a point to seek Sean out back then, playing with him whenever he could, and spending entire rounds just trying to imitate his swing motion. Tom had thought they were on the verge of becoming close friends when, quite suddenly, Sean disappeared. He'd thought perhaps Sean had gotten some kind of acting gig that had taken him out of the area. Whatever the case, Tom had been sorry to see him go.

"Sean McMahn," Tom said, relieved to see a warm and friendly face. Something had happened to his nose since the last time Tom had laid eyes on him—it was bent and broken—but it was Sean all right. "What the hell ever happened to you?"

Sean shrugged, looked around and held his hands out to his sides, palms up, indicating their present surroundings. "I wasn't making it as an actor and my wife got fed up with all my golf bullshit, simple as that. I'm an accountant now."

"Oh," Tom said, trying to sound enthusiastic, "good for you."

An awkward silence followed as the two men stood with their hands in their pockets, both dismayed by their circumstances. Feeling uneasy, Tom broke the silence. "What did you do to your nose?"

Sean turned bright red, pulled a hand out of his pocket and brought it up to his face. "I thought everybody knew that story," he said. He took a pack of cigarettes out of his pocket, shook one out and lit it. Sean spoke quietly for about three minutes. When he finished his story, Tom was standing quite still, his mouth agape. "I honestly don't know what I was thinking," Sean said, perhaps attempting to mitigate the astounding absurdity of his confession.

All Tom wanted to do was get away from Sean as quickly as possible. He was considering a run for his car when the door to the meeting hall opened and a middle-aged woman wearing a golf visor stuck her head out. "We're starting now." Sean took Tom by the arm and guided him toward the door.

Inside were men and women of all ages dressed in mostly pedestrian clothing, but he noticed the occasional golf cap or visor. It was barely eight in the morning and almost everyone in the room was exhibiting some kind of withdrawal symptom. Some of the addicts chewed nervously on golf tees or were flipping ball marker coins in a heads-or-tails fashion. Once or twice Tom spotted someone wearing a golf glove, unconsciously opening and closing the Velcro fastener. One fellow was bouncing a golf ball off the hard linoleum floor over and over again.

What surprised Tom was the number of attendees. "Jesus Christ!" he said to Sean as the room filled up. "I had no idea."

Sitting in the folding chairs around the table were at least twenty-five addicted golfers, as well as a row of chairs around the perimeter of the room, also filling up quickly. As the addicts filed in, Sean filled Tom in on the basics.

"The goal here is not to necessarily quit golf completely, but to get your play down to once or twice a month—recreational golf," Sean said, but then added, "but we all understand that, like drugs or alcohol, it's an obsession. Total abstinence is most likely the only real way out."

The more he looked around the room the greater his sense of shame. These were the same people Tom had sneered at when he'd seen them begging the course starter for a tee time. "Please, please, can't you squeeze me out on the back nine?" he would hear them whine. When denied the opportunity to play, they'd throw a hissy fit in the parking lot like twelve-year-olds; or worse, they'd sit on a bench choking back tears while they called their wives. "The bastards won't let me out, Honey. Come pick me up and we'll go curtain shopping like you wanted to." Here were the maniacs who would go to the driving range on a hot July afternoon and swing themselves into heat stroke because they couldn't control their golf lust. These were the golfers who walked into the pro shop, bought a seventy-five-cent bag of tees, and then pestered the poor golf Pro for half an hour trying to weasel free swing tips. They were, all of them, degenerates. Most of them couldn't break 90 if you put a gun to their heads, and yet here they were. And now, supposedly, Tom was one of them.

Tom turned to share this observation with Sean, who was seated next to him, and saw that Sean had taken out a small tube of sunscreen and was rubbing a dab onto the backs of his hands and sniffing them. He caught Tom staring and quickly stuffed the tube back in his shirt pocket. "I just like the smell of it."

On the walls were little placards with smarmy sayings that were supposedly helpful with keeping your golf addiction in check. "Family First, Golf Second!" one said. "Think before you swing!" announced another. In the center of the table was a small wooden triangle with, "It's not your fault," written on one side and, "Golf responsibly" on the other.

A man seated at the head of the table clapped his hands a few times and brought the room to silence. "That's Gary," Sean whispered. The last of the smokers outside flung their butts into the coffee can by the door and hurried in.

Gary was an older man, somewhere in his sixties for sure, maybe older, it was hard to tell. A thick head of immaculately groomed silver hair was his most recognizable feature but if you looked closely, there was more. From a distance the skin of his face was a beautiful bronze from all his years out of doors. He was dark and manly. But if you stood right next to him, you saw there were hundreds and hundreds of small whitish marks on the surface of the skin where a dermatologist had blasted away small basal cell cancers from his face with a canister of liquid nitrogen. His flesh tone seemed to dissolve into a thousand dots and his features melted into an impression of a face, like what happened when you walked up close to a Monet painting. Gary looked his best standing in soft shadow from a distance of about ten feet.

Gary's story was, depending how you viewed these sorts of things, either a spectacular high or a vile low note in golfing depravity. He opened his remarks with a litany of his accomplishments. "If I'd taken the game up as a teenager I might have been low state amateur, maybe a pro…" Tom was impressed with Gary's golf resume, but due to the deep and preacher- like sincerity of Gary's voice, Tom drifted in and out, only picking up the main points. Jobs were lost to golf, many career opportunities squandered and of course several marriages along the way. The high point of the saga came when Gary admitted to slipping his girlfriend's infant son into the side pocket of his golf bag and sneaking out onto the course for a quick nine instead of staying home and babysitting like he'd been asked to do. He got caught when an errant golf ball bounced into his bag and the baby let out a shriek on someone's back swing. He was led off the golf course in handcuffs and ended up doing prison time. Repentant and shamefaced he ended his story like the crescendo of a Sunday sermon, "What I did was wrong, I admit it, but it's not my fault," Gary pointed to the sign on the table, "I have a disease."

"I've heard of you, Tom," Gary said when Sean introduced the two men after the meeting. Gary's eyes were open a little too wide and his smile a bit too eager, which gave Tom the unsettling feeling of being in the presence of a Born-Again, a zealot. Gary also was a toucher. He used both hands in greeting and held on for way too long, then grasped your elbow or had his arm around your shoulder through the whole conversation.

Inside, Tom cringed. Extended time with Gary would almost certainly involve full frontal embracing.

"Let me help you Tom, before it's too late," Gary said. "My ultimate goal is to get the federal government to register golf as a controlled substance like narcotics, tobacco or alcohol." Gary pointed to several teenagers in the room. "My God, they let children play."

"Sure thing," Tom said, just wanting Gary to let go of his arm.

On the way home Tom caught Hogan grinning back at him in the rearview mirror.

"Wow," Tom said, hoping like hell Hogan wouldn't make fun of him for going to the meeting. "That Sean's a mess, isn't he?"

"Fella," Hogan said, never seeming to remember Tom's first name, "I've heard some hairy stories in my time, but that guy's plumb loco."

What Sean McMahn told Tom in the parking lot was the strangest tale Tom had ever heard. The fact that Sean would share that story with anyone, ever, was astonishing in its own right.

"One day I went out on the course," Sean began, "and somehow, on the second hole, I completely lost my swing."

"Oh Jesus," Tom nodded his head in sympathy, "what a nightmare."

"I was hooking every shot and when I attempted to fix it I immediately got a case of the shanks." Sean's body shivered at the memory of it. "It was a disaster, and nothing I tried seemed to help. I carded an eighty-nine that day and I was grief-stricken."

"Been there," Tom said.

"After my round I went to the men's room to take a leak. I was all fucked up in my head, you have to understand that," Sean continued. Tom was having a little difficulty hearing the words because Sean had brought his volume down to a confessional whisper. "I was standing at the urinal using both hands when suddenly I had an epiphany. It was my grip. My grip was all wrong. I took my hands off my pecker and then put them back on. I did that for a few minutes, on and off, on and off, adjusting my grip each time. I had figured it out and I was ecstatic."

Sean's re-enactment in the parking lot, the mime show of gripping and un-gripping of his penis was revolting. The whole thing made Tom feel dirty and anxious.

"Another guy stepped up to the urinal next to me and couldn't help noticing that I was doing something weird with my hands. 'What the hell are you up to?' the guy asked me. So there I am, holding my dick like a 4-iron and I say to the guy, 'It's my grip. Can you see it? My grip was all wrong.' Like an idiot, I turned to the guy to show him, but unfortunately all that hand action had given me an erection. A big one. I took a few swipes with my rod in this guy's direction and the next thing I knew I was on the floor with a broken nose. When I finally confessed to my wife what happened, she made me take my clubs down to the harbor and throw them off the pier."

"Jesus," Tom said to Hogan as he pulled into his driveway, "How am I supposed to cozy up to people like that?"

* * *

Thrilling was the only word to describe the changes taking place in Carol's life. Spring arrived without a hint of golf. When Tom wasn't traveling he was teaching the boys to drive, and actually found the time to paint the entire exterior of the house and garage.

During the same period, Carol crammed for her real estate license and after passing the test she was immediately hired on a part-time basis by an old high school friend who ran the largest real estate office in town. When she came home from her first day on the job, a certified pre-owned black and silver (Tom joked it was color coordinated to go with her hair) BMW sedan was waiting for her in the driveway.

Like Lazarus, when Tom emerged from his hidey-hole in the basement that dark night months before, it was as if he had been resurrected; he was a changed man. Free from the shackles of his golf addiction he walked taller, with more confidence than ever before. Gone were the flushed cheeks of excitement over how many shots he'd taken on each hole and the breathless descriptions of the various courses he'd played. Best of all, the lying had stopped. The evening of the slap seemed in the distant past and for the first time in Carol's memory, Tom was constant in his straightforwardness about where he went and what he was doing. A peaceful calm had come over him, a quiet deliberateness in his actions that impressed Carol. Nothing he said or did was rash or compulsive in nature. Each evening when Tom walked through the door and came to her for a kiss, Carol inhaled through her nose, and then smiled blissfully inside. He smelled clean, wholesome. *Oh my God in heaven*, Carol thought. *I should have slapped him years ago.*

One evening, Tom and Carol were sitting on the sofa in the den watching television when Carol clicked through the channels and settled on Olympic ice dancing. While Tom normally ran from glitzy spectacles of this nature, this night Tom sat still and said nothing. "Really?" Carol asked as she pulled him close, "You don't mind?"

Tom held her tight and whispered in her ear, "I'll be with you, won't I?" But after a half-hour of watching in silence, Tom could no longer contain himself. "Jesus Christ."

"What?" Carol asked, giving him an annoyed elbow to the ribs.

Tom pointed to the set. "Look at the outfits on these guys. I don't care what a guy does for a living, but no self-respecting man can show up for work wearing a pink boa with a matching sequined codpiece."

Carol rapped a knuckle on the top of his head and pushed him away from her. "If you can't behave, go watch something upstairs."

Tom pulled himself closer to Carol and put his arm around her. "I'm not here for the skating, honey, I'm on a date." Carol glowed inwardly and for the first time in too long they kissed like lovers. Tom pulled an inch away from her face and started to slide his hand up the inside of her sweater, when the phone rang. In the corner of the television screen the caller ID appeared showing Tank and Connie's number. Carol went cold and broke their embrace.

Tom winked at her, picked up the phone on the side table and pressed the speaker button. "Tank," he said, "long time no see. What's up?"

"Hey, Tom," Tank started, "are you alone, can we talk?"

Tom grinned at Carol and raised a finger to his lips. "Yes, Tank. I'm alone."

"What gives, Tommy?" Tank growled. "I've been trying to get a hold of you all week. I left half a dozen messages at your office."

Tom made a grimace and then shrugged. "Sorry Tank. I've just been busy as hell. What can I do for you?"

"Silverstein, Father Charlie and I are in the opening tournament on Saturday and your replacement just crapped out on us." Tank dropped his tone to a whisper. "Think you can sneak in a round behind you-know-who's back?"

Tom covered his laugh with a cough and then mouthed the words "you know who" and pointed at Carol. "No can do, Tank, sorry. Weekends are family time around here now. We've got tennis in the morning and in the afternoon Carol's taking me to a yoga class."

"Tennis? Yoga?" Tank shouted into the phone. "Jesus Christ, Tommy, are you kidding me?"

Tom was playing it straight faced while Carol buried her face in a cushion to smother her giggling. "No, I'm not kidding. The tennis is hell on my knees but you-know-who and the boys love it."

Over the phone they heard Tank rattle a glass full of ice, then slurp a swallow. "I can't see you in tennis whites, Tom. I bet Carol looks nice, though."

Carol's eyes were saucers. "Thanks, Tank," she blurted out, "You're sweet."

There was a pause and Carol looked to Tom, both of them fighting a losing battle to remain composed.

"Oh," said Tank. "You have me on speaker? That's cute, Tom."

"Anyway, I'm sorry, Tank," Tom replied with a shrug at Carol, "but I'm done with golf for a while. Maybe for good, I don't know."

Tank was quiet for a moment and finally said, "I see."

"Oh, and Tank, do me a favor would you? Don't call me on the office line anymore. I've made it company policy not to use the office phones for personal use. It sets a bad example. I won't even let you-know-who call me there. If you need to reach me for something really important, an emergency or something, call me on my cell. Can you do that?"

Carol sat still, biting her lip as she heard Tank grunt and rattle his glass one more time. "Yeah, sure thing, Tom, I can do that." With that the line went dead.

Tom turned the phone off and looked back at Carol. She slid over to him and kissed him hard on the mouth, flicking her tongue over his upper lip as she pulled back. After gazing into Tom's eyes for a moment she got up, went to the den door, closed it and turned the lock.

The next hour was a revelation for Carol. She felt as if she had never had sex with this man before. Instead of his usual adolescent rush to get both of them to climax as quickly as possible, he was slow with it now, deliberate and careful. After an extended period of delicious foreplay, Tom pulled a blanket off the sofa, spread it on the carpet and rolled onto his back. Just as Carol mounted him, Tom did something playful. He reached up with one hand and gave her a smarting slap on her backside. She looked down in surprise at his closed eyes and he moaned in a whisper, "Git along now little doggie."

Chapter Fourteen
The Chosen

Two weeks after he began attending the Golfaholic meetings, on a cold, damp spring evening Tom stood across the street from a small warehouse structure in the middle of an industrial park on the outskirts of town. There were half a dozen cars parked on the street in front of the building, but the rest of the complex looked deserted. Tom was so excited, his breath was catching in his throat and he could feel his heart pressing against his ribcage with every beat.

In his hands he held the contents of the envelope that Marty had presented to him on that fateful day when he had first broken 80, at probably just the same time his father-in-law's heart had given out. The envelope contained two items. In one hand Tom held a plain, unlabeled door key while in the other hand was what, at first glance, appeared to be a business card of some kind, but it wasn't that at all. It was in fact an invitation to membership in a special fraternity.

The Under 80 Club
Be a Master!

He crossed the street and approached the warehouse, careful to match the address on the back of the card with the door of the building in front of him. By the time he reached the entrance he could hear the loud thump of a bass line beat pounding through the walls. There was no doorbell so he pounded his fist on the metal door, but got no response. Feeling like a spy, he looked both ways down the street first, and only then did he try the key. It turned easily in the lock and he pulled the heavy door open.

There were very few times in Tom's life that he had been stunned into silence, but this was one of them. Marty and Tank were waiting for him on the other side of the door, greeting him with stinging high fives. *Born to Run*, a Springsteen song that had rocked Tom to his roots in his college days, was blasting from speakers over raucous yelling and bursts of laughter. Someone thrust a cold bottle of beer into his hand.

Tank talked in Tom's ear over the racket. "Don't ever knock, Tom. It makes us a little jittery because that means whoever's out there doesn't have a key and it might be somebody's wife." Tom nodded like he understood, but he'd barely heard him. The place was overwhelming and he couldn't take it all in at once.

The large warehouse space had been divided into two sections. On one side was a beautiful, fully stocked mahogany bar long enough to accommodate the eight bar stools lined up in front of it. The bar was tucked under a low-slung ceiling with muted, recessed lighting creating an intimate mood. In front of the stools were several felt-covered card tables with comfortable looking armchairs, and on the tables were bowls of nuts and open boxes of pizza. At the near end of the bar was an old-fashioned jukebox, lit up and pounding out one classic rock tune after another. Mounted on the wall next to the jukebox Tom spied a professional dart board, and two flashing pinball machines just beyond that. At the far end of the bar, in a corner that was lit by a strobe light changing color every few seconds, was a shiny chrome pole that ran from ceiling to floor. Working that pole was one of the prettiest, most energetic and totally naked strippers Tom had ever seen.

On the opposite side of the warehouse were two large stalls bisected by mesh netting. Floor to ceiling screens at the back of each stall projected lush, color images of various golf holes. In each stall were golfers, several of whom Tom recognized as some of the better players at the course, hitting balls off Astro-Turf mats into the screens. Everyone held cigars and beers, and every man was wearing an emerald green vest. It was all a wonderful blur. Whatever a man might want in life, it was all here. As Tom stood there taking it in he felt a pang of regret that Larry wasn't still alive. He wanted nothing more than to drag his late father-in-law to the very spot where he was standing and show him that he had done the impossible and found a way to step back in time. He had returned to his college frat house.

Tom leaned in toward Marty and shouted, "Where am I?"

Marty put his mouth to Tom's ear. "Welcome to the Under 80 Club," he shouted, then pulled Tom over to the bar where it was a little less raucous. On the bar was a flat cardboard box with Tom's name on it. Marty slid the box over to Tom. "This is yours if you want it. You earned it." Tom opened the box and nestled in a layer of tissue lay a green vest. "You're a medium, right?" Marty asked. Tom nodded and took the vest out and held it up in front of him. "Everyone who has broken 80 at the course and who's not a total asshole gets invited. Not everyone accepts, but most do. If you decide to join us, you pay $100 a month in dues. That's how we afford this place. It's perfect. We can make as much noise as we like, especially at night because it's an industrial park and there's no one around. We run a night league here year round and use both stalls. At any given time we have two foursomes playing virtual golf on all the great courses like Pebble Beach, Crooked Stick, and Wingfoot."

Tom was awestruck and elated. He was so excited, his hands were shaking as he slipped on the vest. This is what it must feel like to win the lottery, was all he could think.

"Any questions?" Marty hollered.

Tom raked his eyes across the entire space again and stopped at the stunning beauty riding the pole. "What's with the stripper?"

Marty threw a glance to the far end of the bar and then looked back at Tom with a frown. "You got a problem with that?"

What an idiot I am, Tom thought and shook his head no.

Marty gave Tom a light punch in the shoulder. "Come on over then and I'll introduce you," he said. "She's a great kid."

Journal Entry #410

So...Larry was going to sell the company. Well, well. It's course management time. There's an opening here. Think it through!

Several days later Tom stuck his head into the doorway of Marty's office, a tiny room tucked away in the storage space in the rear of the pro shop. The room was cramped and filled with golf paraphernalia. Sample golf clubs from various manufacturers were lined up against the walls as well as stacks of boxes containing the latest brands of golf balls. Pinned to the walls were photos of Marty with golf cronies, past and present, along with framed certificates of qualification from the PGA. Although there was a second chair next to Marty's desk, Tom had never seen anyone but Marty use it.

Marty looked up at Tom from stacks of paperwork that cluttered his desk. "What's on your mind, Tom?"

Tom regarded his mentor for a long moment and said, "I have come to a decision, my friend. I need your guidance."

Marty contemplated Tom's face for a second, then pointed Tom to the empty chair. He got up, went to the door, and after making sure no one was loitering about, closed it.

*   *   *

Summer came and went. As the boys entered their senior year in high school, Tom had become a model husband. Other than the hectic travel schedule required by his decision to take the company to a national stage, he spent all his time with Carol and the boys. On weekends the whole family would rake leaves or go for bike rides, and there was always tennis. In the late afternoons Tom and the boys would hole up in the den and watch baseball playoffs or the early part of the football season. As they screamed and yelled at the set, Carol listened with glee and made them snacks. *This was the way it was supposed to be,* she thought, *the way God intended it to be.*

The only thing that made her life imperfect was the nagging worry that golf could rear its ugly head at any time. Over the years she had developed an internal lie detector when it came to Tom and golf, and she'd found it hard to let her guard down. Just the other day he'd missed dinner with the family because he was late coming home from a client meeting. When she greeted him with a hug, he positively reeked and she called him on it. "Why do you smell like sunscreen?"

Tom stepped back and regarded her with that little boy grin of his. "Oh, it's Detective Carol on the job, I see." He laughed and pulled her in close. 'My dermatologist wants me to put it on every day, even if I'm only outside for a couple of minutes. All those years in the blazing sun on the course and driving range have put me in jeopardy of skin cancer. You don't want me to get melanoma, do you?"

Carol laughed back at him. "No, Tom, I don't want you to get melanoma."

He started to head upstairs to change, but Carol was not through. "Why so late, honey?" Tom froze on the landing at the bottom of the stairs, then slung his jacket over the banister and went back into the kitchen.

"I had a meeting with our website guy. If we go national most of our product will be sold directly online, so we had to go over a hundred details. This isn't going to happen for a while yet, but one day, Carol, the entire business will be done over the internet. No more long days at the office, no more sales meetings. I'll be able to work out of the house for the most part. Think of it. It'll be just like the old days before the boys were born. Make a few phone calls, have some sex, check the website orders against inventory and then have sex again."

"Gee," Carol said, mugging a face at the prospect. "I can't wait."

Seasons came and went without a hint of golf. Over the last year Tom had spent any free time teaching the boys how to drive and now that they had their licenses, the only discord in the house was who was going to get the car for the weekend. Tom's travel schedule continued to be intense. He was usually gone three days a week, sometimes more, and most weekends Tom worked in the yard or tended to general maintenance of the house. Meanwhile, Carol worked hard at establishing herself as a trusted and reliable member of the real estate community, spending most of her time in the real estate office or out showing properties. Before she knew it, another year without golf had come and gone. She blinked…and the boys had packed up and gone off to college.

Chapter Fifteen
Destiny

The greatest source of stress in Tom's life was his cell phone. That was a hard fact. It was like having a bloodhound in your pocket. Every time the phone rang, whether he was in the car on the way to a golf course or at a driving range, he could hear the prison dogs braying in the distance, tracking down the escapee.

In the old days, before cell phones, if Carol wanted to know where he was or what he was doing during the day, she either had to catch him at the office or wait until he got home. Now he was wishing he had a straight two-foot uphill putt for birdie for every time she buzzed him on his backswing. He harbored suspicions that Carol might have put a tracking device on his car or golf bag, because it seemed every time he stepped onto a driving range mat or walked out to the first tee on a course, the damn thing would start buzzing like a giant wasp was trapped inside his pocket. It was uncanny.

Playing out of town, under Carol's radar, Tom got in two or usually three rounds a week, and there wasn't a day that passed that didn't find him on a driving range somewhere in the county. If Carol called him on his cell while he was playing or at the range, he ignored it. Initially he felt a twinge of guilt when he let her calls go to voice mail, but after more than a year and a half of subterfuge, he was numb to it. Later, if she pressed him, he could cook up some story about being in a meeting or on the road. He had told her more than once that he didn't take calls on the highway. Ever! Ironclad rules like that came in handy.

On this particular day he was at a driving range thirty miles out of town. He was at ease; he didn't know a single person there and they didn't know him. Most of the guys on the range were dressed in shirt and tie, taking their lunch al fresco and working diligently on their swings. When someone's cell phone went off they would immediately cut off the ringer, look at the caller number, and either let the phone take a message or answer it while quickly jogging out of earshot so as not to disturb their fellow golfers. For the average Joe in today's society, etiquette and consideration are a lost art, but a serious golfer lives by it.

Tom was halfway through a jumbo bucket of balls, finding a wonderful tempo and rhythm that made his 5-iron feel like a perfect extension of his hands. He was ripping bullets with it, drawing and fading the ball at will, when, in the span of five minutes, the giant bug in his pants buzzed his nut sack four times, ruining his swing. Each time it was Carol. He was determined not to pick up, but on the fifth flutter the damn thing felt like it was trying to crawl out of his pocket, and he panicked. She never called him five times in a row; maybe there was some kind of family emergency. Had Zach or Max had been in an accident? His resolve broken, and holding his phone in the air, he ran down the length of the range asking everyone to stop hitting.

"Hold up, fellas," he cried out. "It's my wife!" Immediately everyone stopped hitting, waiting until he was out of earshot so his wife wouldn't hear the telltale whack of a golf ball being struck. It was all about the etiquette.

By the time he'd bolted off the range and into the parking lot Tom was panting and he took a moment to gather himself. Over the years some of Carol's meditation skills had rubbed off on him. When he was having trouble sleeping or anxious about an issue at work, she'd shown him how to calm himself quickly by taking a few deep, controlled breaths. He did that now until his pounding heart quieted before hitting the talk button on his phone. "Be casual," the Hogan voice warned. "Be warm."

"Hey, Carol, what's up?" He hoped he sounded light and smooth.

Something was wrong. He could hear her fighting back tears before she spoke. "I've been calling and calling! *Where are you?*" she finally got out.

"I'm driving back from a meeting, honey. I had to find a place to pull over. Is everything alright?"

"No, Tom. Everything is not all right." Carol started to cry uncontrollably now and he felt his afternoon practice session slipping away.

Hogan's voice interceded, "Don't get testy," it warned. "Be there for her."

"Carol, sweetheart, you have to tell me. You're scaring me to death."

When she was able to catch her breath she said, "I told you I had a physical scheduled for today, didn't I?"

Tom vaguely recalled information of that sort floating in one ear and shooting out the other over breakfast. They had been married so long, sometimes Tom noticed he would see Carol's lips moving but wasn't grasping a word of what she said. Her voice, her tone, had become ambient noise. "Of course, I remember."

"I just got back from the doctor's," she started, a weepy tremor rising. Once Tom had picked up Carol's call he'd continued to walk the phone further and further out into the parking lot to make sure she couldn't hear any driving range sounds—the crash of the ball machine dispensing buckets of balls was a dead giveaway—and while she tried to compose herself, he turned back toward the range and admired the flight of yellow range balls soaring into the sky. "And?" he asked, coaxing the narrative along.

"Doctor Delany says…..they found….a lump."

Carol's internist had then referred Carol to a surgeon and the surgeon in turn told Carol that he wanted her in his office for a consultation the next morning.

"I have to stop for gas," he said, buying himself a little time, "Then I'll be home as soon as I can get there. Don't be afraid, Carol. I love you." Tom blew her a kiss and hung up. He slid the phone back into his pocket and took a moment to assess. *Carol needs me now,* he thought, but then his lips moved and he heard the Hogan voice. "You haven't nailed down your fade yet. Ten minutes is all you need."

Arriving home, he found Carol sitting at the kitchen table with red puffy eyes and a pile of tissues in front of her. She said she was too agitated to meditate, instead asking Tom if he would go for a walk with her. Carol wanted to talk about the possible outcomes that lay ahead and Tom had the good sense to let her vent. They walked hand in hand while she tried to make clear to him that if she were terminally ill, no extreme measures were to be taken to extend her life. "Let me go to the other side with dignity," she stressed.

She also made it very clear that should she not survive this calamity, Tom absolutely had to remain golf free so he could devote his full attention to the business and the welfare of their sons. Both boys had gone to the same school, even lived in the same dormitory at Connecticut College, but it wasn't that far away and they'd be home often and over the summer. "You'll be captain, cook and chief bottle washer," she said over and over. "They will need you to be here for them."

Tom put his arm around her as they walked back up the driveway to the house. He was doing his best to comfort her and stay in the moment, but it was such a beautiful afternoon for golf he could almost taste the first tee on the tip of his tongue. "Be patient," the Hogan in his head whispered. "If she decides to take a nap you still might be able to sneak out for a quick nine holes."

Tom knew better than that. Trying to sneak out for a few holes at this juncture was just inviting disaster. This was no time to get sloppy. The last time he'd gotten sloppy—muddy shoes and pant cuffs covered in grass like an amateur—had earned him a slap in the face and a lifelong sentence to those ridiculous Golfaholic meetings. Hogan was right about one thing, he'd need to be patient and focused. *You'll get out* he told himself over and over, *just don't force it.*

Calmer after their walk, Carol went upstairs to meditate under her healing pyramid but surprised Tom by coming back down a short time later. Tom was watching a bikini-clad Natalie Gulbis slip into a hot tub on the Golf Channel when he heard a step on the stairs and switched to a news channel just in time. She sat down on the sofa next to him and put her head on his shoulder. "I want you to promise me that if I die before you and you meet the right woman, you will let yourself fall in love again. I don't want the memory of me to stand in the way of your happiness."

"Let's not rush things," Tom said, giving Carol a gentle squeeze. "I'll tell you what—let me check out your nurses before I commit one way or the other." She shoved him away but at the same time she snorted a little laugh and he felt the tension begin to melt out of her.

As they sat there Carol fantasized out loud about what the future might hold for her family after she incarnated on the other side. "God," she said, "I hate the idea of not being around to see the boys graduate from college, what kind of careers they'll have, or the girls they'll meet and marry."

Tom came back with a line from Carol's New Age philosophy, a line she had thrown at him many times over the years; it was tattooed on his brain. "Don't project, sweetheart," and then almost added, "Let's just play it one hole at a time," but he was able to catch himself.

He would never admit it in confession, or anywhere for that matter, but sitting there with a consoling arm around his wife Tom was conjuring a few fantasies of his own. "With Carol out of the way," Hogan hissed in his ear, "you could play golf anytime you want; the kind of golf the Pros play, free from constant nagging, unfettered by a guilty conscience and the constant interruption of cell phones." The seducer in his head, taking full advantage of this grotesque and tragic scenario, went so far as to whisper that with the boys away at school he could start playing courses all over the country, all over the world. "You'd only have to be home to cook turkey for the holidays," the voice intoned. "You'd be a scratch golfer, that's for damn sure."

Jesus, Tom thought while absently caressing the tension out of Carol's neck and shoulders, *if Hitler had been a golfer he'd have had thoughts just like these.*

"Florida," Hogan continued to moan, "Bermuda, Spain, California, Scotland…"

That night in bed Tom and Carole snuggled in the dark. The moment was so quiet and sensitive that while holding Carol in his arms Tom thought of suggesting that this might be their last chance for healthy sex, but he held back. The impetus for that probably needed to come from her.

"I'm not going to sugar-coat this, Carol," Dr. Sullivan said. "You have a growth, a tumor or cyst of some kind right under your left armpit." Tom gave Carol's hand a squeeze as they looked across the doctor's desk. "Here's what I'm going to recommend."

The appointment with the surgeon had been scheduled for ten a.m., and the hours prior to the meeting had been the hardest for Tom. He'd shackled his golf lust in order to concentrate on Carol's dilemma, but it was one of those warm, sunny mornings that screamed *PERFECT GOLF DAY*. It was all he could manage to stay focused on the situation at hand as the golfer inside him tugged at the restraints.

Dr. Sullivan put up the x-ray and with some kind of science ruler began to measure a shadowy spot that he claimed was the tumor. Carol sucked in a sharp breath and grimaced when she saw the measurement to be about the size of a nickel.

Tom often suspected that Carol's ongoing search for a spiritual identity was her attempt to fend off a midlife crisis. He often wished that she'd just go out and buy herself a smart little sports car like everyone else; but every now and then she would say something spiritual that actually resonated with him. Once, years ago, when he was just coming into his own as a golfer, frustrated with his swing and ranting about it in the house—he claimed he was swinging as hard as he could but still wasn't getting any distance—Carol had stopped him with a hug and said something in his ear that brought him up short.

"It sounds to me like you're trying to force it, Tom. Just let it go." She'd whispered it like she was passing him a secret message, a mantra. "Learn to relax and let it come to you." She was right, too. The moment he started to relax with his swing, the more he could let it go, the more distance he achieved.

That's what he was trying to do now, let it go. The golfer inside him was itching to smash a golf ball with a stiff-shafted block of forged titanium in the worst way but he knew that if he could just relax, the moment would come to him unexpectedly.

"The first thing we have to do," Dr. Sullivan continued, "is to go in and cut that tumor out of there." Carol sobbed at the dual vision of 'cut' and 'tumor.' Tom reached for a tissue box on the doctor's desk and handed her one.

He had been in the surgeon's office for five minutes, and like a good husband he was working hard to keep his focus on Carol and nothing else, but while Carol blew her nose and took a few moments to compose herself, he was able to relax his concentration and begin to see the room clearly for the first time. Right off he noticed the shelves behind the doctor's desk were filled with the standard array of medical texts and a series of photographs. As he studied the photographs more closely it dawned on him that the pictures had been taken of the doctor on various golf excursions all over the world. In one picture the doctor had his arm around Jack Nicklaus and in another he was with Hale Irwin. There were also golf trophies on the shelves, a lot of them. He jerked his head to the left and then the right, performing a deft scan of the walls. Sure enough, to his left there was a small, elegantly framed poster depicting the layout of the Old Course at St. Andrews. To the right, a sequence of glossy photographs exhibiting the glorious holes that made up Amen Corner at Augusta. Had Dr. Sullivan actually played there? On the desk he spied an elegant ceramic bowl full of golf tees and a small crystal cube encasing a golf ball autographed by none other than Arnold Palmer.

Finally, Tom examined the medical man in front of him. He was a tall character with an easy charm. He exuded confidence, the kind that Marty had, a projection that made you feel that whatever might be wrong with you, he would be able to fix you up in no time. Then there was the healthy bronze of his skin. It had golfer written all over it.

A thunderbolt exploded in Tom's mind. *Holy shit*, he thought as the flash of light behind his eyes faded and the picture became clear. *This guy is a player.*

"Now Carol, I want you to remain calm and stay positive," Dr. Sullivan said. "Chances are ninety-nine percent that this is a cyst of some sort, a completely benign growth. You have no family history of this kind of thing and that's a good sign. " Tom patted Carol's arm, an unconscious act of sympathy, but inside he heard the rattle of chains, there was something clawing to get out.

"I've scheduled a surgical procedure for you tomorrow morning. We'll remove the growth and test it for malignancy then and there, while you're still on the table. If it's benign, which I think it probably is, I'll sew you back up and that'll be the end of it. If it's malignant we'll excise additional tissue around the tumor and in a few weeks start you on a round of chemotherapy."

At the mention of chemo Carol sobbed and, turning to Tom, buried her face in his shoulder. Tom rubbed Carol's back and leaned his head into hers but his eyes never left the surgeon's face. Dr. Sullivan, who had been through thousands of emotional moments like this, didn't miss a beat. He glanced at his watch and continued. "The surgical procedure is not very invasive and you won't be under anesthesia for more than two hours."

Another electrical synapse detonated in Tom's head. He actually saw stars, then heard or felt a snap behind his eyes as the beast inside him broke free of all restraints and flew to the surface. The doctor was talking about time and time was just what Tom was looking for. With Carol's face conveniently tucked into his neck, Tom raised four fingers of his free hand and locked his glare directly into the surgeon's eyes, mouthing the words, "Can you make it four?"

It was a wild and dangerous gamble. A non-golfer would not remotely understand what he meant by waving those four fingers, and if by chance he did know, he most certainly would be appalled at anyone's desire to have his wife held under general anesthesia unnecessarily for an extra two hours. A non-golfer like that would most likely blow the whistle on Tom right then and there, but a player, a real player like this sharp looking fellow in front of him, would grasp Tom's meaning instantly. He would be sympathetic.

Tom held his breath while Dr. Sullivan took a long moment to digest the meaning of his four-fingered salute. Then, without the slightest change in expression he mouthed the magic word, "Golf?" Tom lifted his left eyebrow half an inch. A professional man like this would require nothing more. The smile that creased the corners of the surgeon's mouth was almost imperceptible, but to Tom it was a beacon, the shining, full toothed grin of a brother. The surgeon raised a hand, executed a deft a-okay sign and the deal was done. Tom gave Carol' shoulder a gentle squeeze. "Don't worry, honey, I'll be with you every step of the way."

That evening while Carol was ensconced in her sanctuary with a posse of her psychic friends performing some kind of holistic, spiritual preparation for her surgery, Tom texted Tank a cryptic spray of words—Carol…tumor…surgery…tomorrow…tee-time. In a moment came the response.

"Done."

Good old Tank. The Tankster was not one to let a little cancer get in the way of a round of golf.

Early the next morning, as Carol was being wheeled into the O.R., Tom walked beside the gurney holding her hand, speaking in encouraging tones right up to the operating room doors. Carol was usually the most centered person in the world, but this thing had her rattled and he was happy to be there for her.

"Tell the boys I love them with all my heart," she said. Then, giving his hand a final squeeze she added, "You're my rock."

The orderly pulled the gurney through the doors and she was gone. Tom stood by the entrance to the O.R. for a moment having a final inner debate about what he was planning to do. Sneaking in a round of golf while Carol was under the knife had an unusually high-risk feel to it; the smallest drumbeat of anxiety was beginning to echo deep inside, but Hogan was adamant. "There's nothing you can do for her pissing away the hours in some dingy waiting room," his secret friend shouted.

As sensible as that sounded, Tom remained torn. There was still a part of him that loved Carol deeply, a part that was terrified of losing her; and there was another part too, a part that feared Carol's wrath, a part of him that knew full well that should Carol discover that he'd gone out to play while she lay cut open and bleeding on the operating table, there'd be consequences, frightening ones. Merely attending the ridiculous Golfaholic meetings would not be enough if his secret trysts were exposed. Tom could see the unholy specter of marriage counseling, even divorce, rising before him. Getting caught with a golf club in his hands today would force him into a plan of action that he had thought about, planned for even, but for his marriage it would be an unmitigated disaster. He leaned against the wall outside the O.R. feeling perspiration gather at his temples, trying with all his might to keep the voracious appetite of the beast within from interfering with sound judgment. The Hogan voice offered a final rationale. "You heard the doctor…"Ninety-nine percent it's nothing serious," the voice whispered, "…like having a tooth pulled." Tom could feel whatever resolve he had for staying put begin to melt. "For God's sake," Hogan added, "what are the odds of her ever finding out?"

Just then Dr. Sullivan strode by in his scrubs, and seeing Tom, paused. Pulling down his face mask, he offered Tom a warm smile and a wink. "Hit' em straight, my friend."

Tom arrived at the course just in time, only minutes before he was supposed to tee off. He was uncomfortable rushing out to the tee without a proper warm-up—a bucket of balls and ten minutes on the practice green was his usual routine—but under the circumstances, what could he do? Most of the golf Tom had played over the past year-and-a-half was on courses where there was no chance of being spotted by Carol or any of her friends, so today he was thrilled at the prospect of showing off his growing prowess in front of Tank. Being on his home course made it even sweeter. Before he knew it, he and Tank were out in the fairway, enjoying the warmth of the morning sun on their faces, listening to the clatter of their clubs slung on the back of their golf cart as they headed toward the first green.

Aware of Carol's health crisis and thoughtful of Tom's possible emotional state, Tank brought some delicious cigars and a six-pack of ice-cold breakfast beers to cheer him up. It worked, too, because by the time they reached the back nine Tom was in excellent spirits and playing very well. He was in the zone.

* * *

The coin-sized lump of gristle that Dr. Sullivan eviscerated from Carol's armpit had been whisked out of the O.R. and was on its way to the lab for testing.

The surgeon and the anesthesiologist chatted over the patient's prone form while waiting for the results.

"Dr. Wang," Sullivan began, "I don't suppose you know this patient's husband, do you? Did you meet him?" Dr. Wang looked over the rim of his glasses at Dr. Sullivan while keeping one eye on the monitors at his side.

"I don't know him personally, but I've seen him around the driving range for a number of years. He plays out at Rocky Shores."

"No kidding." Dr. Sullivan picked up a hemostat that was lying next to Carol's head and scratched the tip of his nose with it. "He gave me the impression that he belonged to a private club."

"Oh, I don't think so." Dr. Wang shook his head. "He's a salesman of some kind. With kids in college, he doesn't have that kind of money."

"Really," Dr. Sullivan said with genuine surprise. "I had no idea." He was silent for a moment, rubbing his nose and thinking things over. "So...he's strictly municipal? Is he any good?"

"I've only seen him on the range. He's not bad from what I can tell, got a reasonable swing. Funny thing, now that I think of it."

"What's that?"

"He's one of those wacky guys who talks to himself through a practice bucket, you know what I mean? Waving his arms around and yelling like he's working with an invisible swing coach - it's kind of creepy. Why?"

"He asked me to keep his wife conked out for an extra two hours so he could sneak in a round."

Wang threw a glance at the clock on the O.R. wall and then back at Doctor Sullivan. "I've got her just beneath the surface. You really want me to hold her here for another three hours? For that guy?"

*   *   *

Carol came to the surface and opened her eyes. The anesthetic had knocked her for a loop. She felt drunk and was having difficulty focusing her vision. Her eyes flitted around the room until she remembered where she was. She tried sitting up but her head began to spin and she had to fight the urge to vomit. She closed her eyes and concentrated on her breath. *I've been operated on. Yes, that's where I am, the hospital.* There was a fleeting memory of a nightmare; the doctor whispering to someone, a nurse perhaps, words like "time" and "Tom" and "golf." A while later as the fog cleared, a surge of panic threatened to overwhelm her. *Do I have cancer or not?* her mind screamed. *Where's my Tom? He should be the one to tell me!*

She heaved to rise up on her elbows, but her head started to swim again. Carol lay back against the pillow, closed her eyes and began silently mouthing her mantra over and over. The dream came back to her again, clearer somehow—and filled her with dread. She felt a fumbling at her arm and saw that a nurse had come in to take her blood pressure. When the nurse placed the cuff on Carol's arm, she opened her mouth and tried to speak but her throat was dry and her tongue was plastered to the roof of her mouth. She pointed to a plastic cup with a straw that sat on the swing table next to the bed. The nurse propped Carol up on her pillow and handed her the cup. Carol took a sip, coughed a speck of dry phlegm from the back of her throat and then looked up at the nurse. "Where's Tom?" she whispered.

The nurse leaned in close. "What's that, honey?"

Risking another attack of vertigo, Carol forced her back up onto the pillow. "My husband," she croaked, "where's my Tommy?"

* * *

Tom and Tank heard the car roaring down the access road to the park from a long way off. The road, which passed behind the fourteenth tee-box that the two men currently occupied, curved a good deal. From the screech of rubber, someone in the distance was approaching at a breakneck pace. They were smoking cigars and had just cracked the last of their beers, their feet resting on the dashboard of the golf cart, waiting for the fairway in front of them to clear. Tank was regaling Tom with the latest gossip he'd picked up from Father Charlie and Silverstein, a tale that blended a teenage girl on the field hockey team with an exotic gynecological trait and the name of a local politician they all knew well. The story had everything - sex, ambition, sports, politics, impending disaster. Tom was enthralled.

They had already turned their heads to the sound of dangerous driving when the responsible party rounded the curve behind the tee box. The two men sat frozen, watching over their shoulders; the black and silver BMW slammed on its brakes, fishtailing to a screeching, rubber-burning halt directly behind them.

"Holy shit!" Tank said.

Tom watched wide-eyed and filled with horror as the car rocked itself to a standstill with pale blue smoke pouring off the tires. The door to the sedan popped open and Carol slowly extricated herself from the vehicle. She was still wearing her hospital gown and had a band-aid over the spot on the back of her hand where the I.V. had been. Even from this distance they could see a blood stain blooming under her left arm.

"It can't be," Tom said, as the small flutter of panic he had felt at the hospital returned, then mushroomed into unbridled terror. It was a level of fear he was so unfamiliar with that his beer-swollen bladder squirted a hot stream of urine against his thigh. Acting instinctively, Tom tossed his cigar to the ground and handed his beer to Tank. Carol approached the stone wall separating the tee box from the street. She was visibly shaking. Tom sensed that it was not fatigue from her surgery making her vibrate, but a deep seeded, blinding rage devouring her shell of serenity and breaking free. This rage was so intense, so beyond his experience, that he felt dwarfed in its presence. The rage before him was a living thing; a seething beast. This creature would not listen if he attempted to speak to it, touch it or soothe it with a hug; it would bellow fire and dissolve him.

As he got out of the golf cart he realized he was shaking. His knees felt useless and numb. Urine dribbled out of him, threatening a gusher, but he was just stable enough to clamp it off.

When Tom was a boy and he got caught in a lie, or was accused of breaking a neighbor's window, or when his mother held up a copy of some porn magazine she found under his bed, his immediate reaction was always the same. The jolt of fear that ran through his body acted as a circuit breaker and shut his brain down for a few seconds. He would stand in front of his accuser slack-jawed and blank-eyed, blinking at nothing for a second or two. Then, one by one the lights would come back on as his brain re-booted, and a flurry of words, lies usually, would start forming on his lips.

This time was different. When the switches in his brain snapped back on there were no words, only a thick wedge of panic lodged in his throat. His brain offered no excuses, no answers, only questions. How the hell did she wake up? How did she get out of the hospital and find her way home? He glanced at his watch. She was supposed to be unconscious for at least four hours and only about three hours had gone by. Although Dr. Sullivan did not strike Tom as the irresponsible type, someone had clearly dropped the ball. Whatever had happened, Tom now found himself living his worst nightmare. Somehow, Carol had awoken in recovery, escaped the hospital, gone home, retrieved her car and come here. She found him drinking beers, smoking cigars and playing golf. If she had awakened in her hospital room to find Tom having sex with a naked young nurse in the next bed, he would have been on firmer ground.

As Carol approached them, Tank, perhaps sensing that he too might be in some kind of physical danger, started inching away from Tom. He spoke to Carol in the soft alto of an adolescent, as if trying to make friends with a vicious dog.

"How'd the operation go, Carol?" It came out sounding like someone was squeezing his testicles.

As Carol inched toward the stone wall she was a terrible sight to see. Sweaty, damp hair was matted to her head, her face vampire white. With her halting gait and dressed in the green, bloodstained hospital garb, she reminded Tom of a zombie out of some B horror film.

"You shut the fuck up!" Carol shrieked at Tank, with a volume and tone sharp enough to stop the next foursome approaching the tee box dead in their tracks.

The startled golfers wanted no part of the unappealing scene unfolding before their eyes. Carol had left her car running, parked diagonally across the road, effectively blocking traffic in both lanes. Impatient drivers were leaning on their horns and shouting obscenities out windows. Every golfer within a hundred yards had stopped what they were doing to shoot Tom dirty looks. Bringing a domestic fracas of this scale into the middle of an active golf course was a grotesque breach of etiquette. There would be an outcry of some kind followed by a letter of reprimand and possibly a suspension of privileges. He would be a laughing stock, a pariah. Tom raised his hands in the air, a gesture of surrender or an attempt to get Carol to stop, he didn't know which. His lips were starting to form a word, but Carol cut him off with a howl.

"Don't you speak one word, you bastard. Just don't."

Carol had reached the stone wall and stopped. She and Tom locked eyes for a moment and then Carol said loud enough for anyone within fifty yards to hear, "Get in the car, you son of a bitch."

Tom looked around searching frantically for something, someone to make it all stop, but there was nothing. Hogan, his golfer brain, his support beam, had left the building.

"I've already ripped open my incision getting here, Tom." Carol was pointing to the gob of red still growing at her side, as if offering evidence to the gathering crowd. "If you make me climb over this fucking wall I will kill you. Make no mistake, I will kill you."

The whole scene was becoming too much for Tom. His thoughts were blurry, making him feel disoriented. Was the urine stain on his kakis noticeable? He had a pretty good round going. What a shame not to post it. Was he breathing? His head was spinning and he was suddenly gripped with the notion that he might faint. To his knowledge, Carol had never dropped the F-bomb in anger before and its effect was shattering. His heart skipped a beat as her hand touched the stone wall and she lifted her leg in an attempt to mount it. Her hospital gown slid above her hips and like everyone else in a twenty foot radius, Tom gasped and averted his eyes. He felt a hand on his shoulder and turned to see a round, jovial face, a local rabbi he remembered playing with several times. This was a fellow golfer, a man of faith and understanding; help had arrived.

"This has to stop, Tom, you'd better go with your woman." Tom looked into the rabbi's face, a bowl of compassion. "Go on, son." the rabbi urged.

Suddenly Tom stood up straight as if he'd been slapped. He offered the rabbi a curt nod, then shrugged the man's hand off his shoulder. With a last glance at the creature straddling the wall, Tom turned abruptly and strode over to his golf cart, unstrapped his clubs and slung them over his shoulder. Then he turned and ran.

Chapter Sixteen
A Man on the Run

Later that night as Tom drove past the night-lit skyline of Washington, D.C., he felt giddy. Like a secret agent finally able to step into the light of day, he felt like a great weight had been lifted from him. Up until now he believed the subterfuge he'd been perpetrating for almost two years had not been all that difficult, but he as he drove through the night he felt the stress of it melting away, and acknowledged that it had indeed taken a toll. He had known all along that sooner or later Carol would discover his ruse—the hospital event only expedited it—but now that it was all out in the open he felt relieved, grateful even.

He was thankful that he'd had Tank and Silverstein to share his secret with and from the start they'd both been supportive and understanding. When he'd asked them to repeatedly call him at home so he could blow them off in front of Carol, they didn't flinch. When he told them he would be playing most of his golf away from their home course or out of state, they took it well and often joined him when they could. They had all hoped that Carol would warm to Connie and Sue so the women could create a social life among themselves, having their lunches and shopping together and whatever else women do to occupy themselves - but it was not to be and Tom should have guessed that it wasn't going to work out. Connie was abhorrent, both physically and in temperament, and Sue was in such a state of arrested development that simply giving her a light hug made you feel like a molester. They were not Carol's kind of people, even under the best of circumstances.

It was unfortunate that Father Charlie had to be left out of the plans that Tom was making, but he knew the priest was too much of a risk. Charlie was a good friend and a wonderful storyteller, but Tom knew, as did Tank and Silverstein, that if the Priest couldn't keep a confessional secret under the sanctity of the Holy Church, the odds of his keeping Tom's plans to himself were next to none.

In the end, though, the foundation of Tom's support—besides the rigid backbone of Hogan inside him—his real anchor had been Marty. When Tom made the decision to follow his late father-in-law's lead and wash his hands of the day-to-day supervision of the business, he'd gone to see his mentor for guidance and Marty had jumped in with both feet. "There's no question that your swing will improve if you're not wasting precious time working a nine-to-five job," Marty'd said.

The first thing Marty had done was put aside a special time once a week when they could continue lessons in secret at the Under 80 Club, hitting into the indoor screens and at the same time formulating a plan of action. After a vigorous hour's lesson of hitting on the computer-generated driving range, Marty and Tom would sit talking at the bar. It was the middle of the day and they had the place to themselves.

"I admire your courage, Tom," Marty said. "Very few men have the spine to walk away from their comfortable suburban lives and devote themselves to capturing the best possible swing." Tom supposed that Marty's own disastrous marital experience had drained any empathy from him when it came to another man's spousal situations, but Tom loved the fact that Marty didn't judge him one way or the other when it came to his deceiving Carol. If anything, he was encouraging.

Once Tom extricated himself from the workaday drain of running a business, (he'd converted the entire business to an online click-and-shop-enterprise, then hired a consulting firm to manage it from a shipping warehouse in the next town over - two or three phone calls in the morning and he was done for the day!) he & Marty had decided that Tom should go on make-believe business trips once a week. In this regard Marty's guidance had been instrumental.

"First off, you don't want to be seen playing here in town if you can help it. Sooner or later someone will see you and mention it to Carol. The longer you can play without her knowledge the better you'll get, so don't get sloppy," he'd warned. He then pulled out a sheet of paper and handed it to Tom. "I've drawn up a list of courses here in Connecticut and a few in New York that you need to start playing whenever you can. They're much more challenging than our simple track. Let me know when and where you're going and I'll contact the PGA Pro at each course. They'll take care of you."

Tom crossed his fingers. "Would you be able to get me resident rates?"

"Of course resident rates. You'll be my ambassador, Tom."

Without ever saying it out loud, they'd both understood that sooner or later Carol would discover Tom's secret. It had been on Marty's advice that Tom plan extensively for that unfortunate day. They'd spent a good deal of their time together plotting his escape plans. "Remember to use cash with all of your expenditures." Marty had been insistent on this point. "If Carol hires a private dick to find you and you're using credit cards, you might as well not go at all."

Tom agreed. "I have plenty of cash socked away, but I'll need some kind of fake ID, won't I? Even the cheesiest of motels will want to see a credit card or a driver's license."

The pro had slipped a card out of his wallet. "Call this guy when you get a chance and mention my name. He'll set you up."

Marty brought maps to their sessions and he and Tom scoured them over cold mugs of beer and tasty cigars. "I'm circling the most important courses in South Carolina, Tom." Marty said. "These are premier courses that will test you. Each one will improve your game in one way or another." Then he gave Tom a list of names and phone numbers taken from his private rolodex. "These are the names and addresses of men who have gone before you. You can use them as contacts when you get down there. For the most part they're all hiding from their wives, so I imagine they'll be understanding and supportive."

Tom couldn't believe what he was hearing. "You've helped other guys get down there?"

"Sure," Marty said, a conspiratorial edge in his tone. "All the PGA guys are involved. It's like the underground railroad…only different."

"Anyone I know?"

"I don't think so," Marty said, "But you'll like them. They're just like you." Marty profiled the other escapees, told their stories and described their swings. "It's an ultra-secret network, Tom," Marty had leaned in close and clapped a hand on Tom's shoulder. "Now you're a part of it."

Sometimes they'd just sit back, put their feet up on the bar and bullshit. "You're to be envied, Tom," Marty said, holding a match to Tom's cigar. "You've learned how to play golf unburdened by the guilt that plagues most ambitious golfers. I've seen guys in the middle of shooting a sub-par round walk off the course at the sixteenth hole because they might be late for a parent-teacher conference or a cub scout meeting. I've watched talented golfers shoot tremendous front nines only to fall apart on the back because they're worried their wives will be upset that they're late for supper. I mean, really? What the fuck is that?"

Tom was in the middle of puffing on his cigar and choked on a mouthful of smoke. "I've been there, believe me," he sputtered.

Marty got up, walked behind the bar and cracked open another round. "Yes, we all have; but the day you decided to put golf over a family gathering because you were in the middle of a transformational lesson, I knew you were made of special stuff. It's the same stuff all great golfers have. Tiger Woods has it."

"Stop it," Tom said and gave Marty a sock in the arm. "Let's be clear, I'm no Tiger Woods."

"I know that," Marty grinned. "None of us are. But you do have something in common with the great man. You play golf unfettered by guilt. Look at what Tiger can do. He wins tournament after tournament with the weight of fifteen or sixteen mistresses on his conscience. It's amazing. If his wife had been chasing him down a fairway waving that 4-iron over her head, the son of a bitch still would have birdied the hole."

One day, after a grueling session of learning how to hit a knock-down seven iron, they sat at the bar working on a pair of cold ones. For the first time since Tom had been a member of the Under 80 Club, he noticed a row of framed photographs, almost hidden in shadows above the expansive mirror behind the bar. Tom turned on the lights over the bar, then stepped back to inspect the pictures more closely. It was a rogue's gallery of golfers, many of whom had come and gone before Tom's involvement in the game. A lot of the photographs could be dated by the long hair, handlebar mustaches and wild outfits indicative of the seventies and eighties. Others however, were more recent faces that Tom half remembered from his early years on the course. All of the photos had one thing in common; each of the men wore a joyous smile.

Together they looked like a row of happy orphans on Christmas.

"Who are those guys?" he asked Marty.

"Those are former members of the club. Most of them have passed on to the great clubhouse in the sky."

"And the others?"

"The others are guys like you, Tom, golfers who have moved on in an attempt to push their game to another level. A couple of them are on that list I gave you, living the golfer's dream, working on their game year round in the warmth of the southern sun."

One photo at the end had a black sash across it, covering the image of the former member. Tom pointed to it. "Who was that guy?"

Marty got up from his stool and stood next to Tom, the two of them staring at the shrouded photo.

"That's your friend, Gary," Marty said. "After the stunt he pulled with that baby on the course he was banned for life."

"No kidding," Tom said. "Gary didn't come right out and say it but he intimated he quit the game of his own volition."

"Horseshit," Marty scoffed. "His picture is on file at every public course in the state. If he so much as shows up in the parking lot of a golf club he gets the boot."

"Oh my God," Tom said.

"In all honesty, Tom, none of us gave a hoot one way or the other that he stuffed an infant in his golf bag and snuck in a few holes. I mean, it was a bold stroke when you think about it."

Tom felt he could argue this point with Marty, Gary had done prison time for it, but instead he just nodded and shrugged, "So what's your beef with the guy?"

"Gary getting caught like that put a harsh light and intense public scrutiny on the golf world. Nobody, I mean nobody wants that. It's unfortunate, but the non-golfing world hates golf, Tom, that's just a reality. For a while there Gary became a lightning rod, a poster boy for all those nit-wits out there with an ax to grind against the game. Tree-huggers write editorials in the local paper every year saying we fertilize too much and we're responsible for every algae bloom that crops up. It might be true, but hey, who wants to play on a brown course? When there's a drought, we have to sneak around and water the fairways and greens at night so we don't get called on the carpet for wasting community resources. If we didn't have devoted golfers planted on most of the town committees, we'd be playing half the season on burned out hardpan."

"Yeah," Tom said, "I've heard those complaints."

"But there's a more sinister, underlying threat that we always have to be on guard against."

"What's that?"

"The civilian population is afraid of golf. It's an unspoken fear, but we all know it's there. They think it lures otherwise responsible men and women away from their families and their jobs, that it robs people of their sense of community; and that makes society nervous. They don't understand that dedication and self-sacrifice are precisely what it takes to get good at golf. Those of us in the business are fully aware that if public sentiment were to turn against us, there's no telling what might happen. For all I know our friends in local government could get overruled, the town's board of finance could decide to pull the plug on the course tomorrow, and develop the property into…I don't know what… condos or low-income housing… Can you imagine that?"

The two men continued to stare up at the face behind the black cloth.

"So, Gary can never come back?" Tom said, stricken by the finality of it.

"Never," Marty replied. "He's dead to us."

As Tom drove deeper into the South he reached into his jacket pocket and pulled out a pack of non-filtered Camels, coaxed one out of the pack and lit up. Ever since the night Mr. Hogan had accused him of cowardice in his basement bunker, his old compulsion to smoke had come back with a vengeance. Carol had forced him to quit right after they'd met and he had been glad of it, but now he'd fallen off the wagon, big time. There had been other changes, too. He glanced in his rear view mirror and admired the smart little golf cap he had on, along with a matching cardigan sweater. Not long ago he would have deemed that look too old-school for a man his age, but now he thought he looked just dandy.

When Hogan entered Tom that night in the basement and re-inserted his manhood—there simply was no other way to describe the event—Tom had felt an immediate change come over him. His first reaction was fear, of course, but almost instantly the fear had given way to excitement and glee. Within seconds of Hogan melting into him, Tom felt a series of brand new sensations. A surge of confidence spread through him like he'd never felt in his life. He suddenly knew for certain that he *was* the man. He possessed the secret of the golf swing. Screw everyone else. And it wasn't just the incredible newfound feeling of self-respect; it was more visceral than that. It was guts, the guts to make the shot. If he wanted a smoke, who was going to tell him he couldn't? It took guts to put on a suit every day and pretend to go to your job like other people. It took guts to chuck the business and go to the driving range or the course and work on your game instead. Tom could feel that sense of determination, manliness throbbing in his veins, and it thrilled him. Carol had even noticed the change in his physical presence, he was sure of it.

He had to be careful with Hogan though. Sometimes it took a conscious effort to keep him from taking over completely. When he was around Carol and the boys he'd had to shove that part deep down inside him so that nothing overtly Texan leaked out. Luckily, around the house or out socially Hogan was usually obedient and didn't interfere with Tom's personality, except during golf situations. The only time Hogan had caught him off guard and showed his hand was during the occasional tryst with Carol. All Carol had to do was gloss her fingertips under his pajama top at night and Hogan would start clawing and scratching his way to the surface. It took every ounce of strength to keep the beast from popping out, grabbing the reins and "taking her for a ride," as Hogan had put it to him. Sometimes while making love it felt like Hogan was right beside him, whispering lurid suggestions in his ear. Those moments left Tom with the unsettling sensation of being in a ménage à trois. Once, when Hogan did make it to the surface, he did something that was totally out of character for Tom. He gave Carol a smart slap on the butt and said something insane like "gitty up now, little doggie." He didn't remember Carol yelping at the time, but it must have stung. The memory of that moment still made him shudder and blush.

In spite of the strange and sometimes unseemly sensations he felt with another spirit inside him, Tom had thrilled to the pulse of the Hogan creature coursing through his veins. Hogan possessed a comfortable manliness that Tom had never known. It was in the way he carried himself, more erect, longer strides. He caught people gawking at him when he walked by. Best of all, when Hogan guided him on the golf course Tom's head became perfectly clear. Hogan allowed no distractions and his focus was dead-on. Now and then, when Hogan edged Tom aside and put both hands on the club, it was a magical experience to be a part of.

The things that man could do with a golf ball were astonishing. It was said that you could never hide the pin from Hogan and it was true. He could cut or draw the ball at will. He could hit low trajectory power fades into the wind that astonished Tom's friends. The only nagging worry was that he knew from his years of research that Hogan had never been much of what you'd call a sharer, and Tom wondered how much of that swing was actually rubbing off on him. One day down the road he'd find a way to get the Hogan thing out of him completely, and when that happened Tom hoped with all his heart that Hogan's swing, or at least a part of it, would remain with him.

* * *

Carol stood at the locked entrance to what had once been her father's thriving office space, staring through the glass door at the empty rooms within. Gone were the desks and computers. The walls, once cluttered with photographs of her father and dozens of plaques honoring him, were barren. All that remained was the carpeting, dented from the weight of furniture, and snakes of dead cable wire hanging from dormant outlets.

It had taken Carol three solid days of sleep, prayer and meditation in her sanctuary to recover from her surgery. When she felt well enough, she went back to manning the phones at the real estate office. Linda Shaw, the high school friend who had helped her through the process of getting her license and then hired her as a part-time agent and office assistant, was very sympathetic. Everyone in the office had heard about Carol's ordeal at the hospital, mostly because her wretched 'zombie walk of death' at the golf course was captured on some golfer's cell phone and the grainy video had been posted on You Tube under the title, "Classic Buzz Kill."

"He's run away, Linda. None of his friends claim to know where he is." Carol was doing her best not to become emotional in front of her employer and friend.

Linda was a tall, sinewy woman; muscular, with short, cropped blond hair. A combination of age and a no nonsense business persona had chiseled some hard edges into her face. She had been married, gone through a bitter divorce and built a successful career for herself, all in the span of five years. When it came to a husband's philandering, whether it was with another woman or with golf, she responded in absolutes.

"Whether he comes back or not, Carol," Linda preached while she checked her make-up in a corner that housed the coffee maker and a discreetly positioned mirror, "you absolutely have to divorce the bastard. Leaving you at the hospital like that to go play with his man friends is despicable, unforgivable."

Carol winced at the word divorce and started choking back tears.

"Have you tried his office?" Linda came over and sat on the corner of Carol's desk, a coffee in one hand and a tissue for Carol in the other.

"I tried, but got a recording that the number was disconnected."

"Well, that can't be right," Linda said, and slipped off the desk, heading to a bookcase by the door. "What's the business address?" she asked. She pulled out a directory, a master list of commercial real estate in town, and when Carol gave her the address Linda began rapidly flipping through the pages. After a few moments of searching she stopped abruptly and looked back at Carol.

"What is it?" Carol asked.

Linda walked back to Carol's desk holding the directory in her hands and planted it in front of her.

"Oh, Carol," she said, with her finger pointing to a listing on the open page. "that office space has been on the rental market for over a year."

"Oh my goodness," was all Carol could manage to say. She stood up and said, "Excuse me for a moment," then ran for the office bathroom. She entered a toilet stall while a bell was going off in her head. *"If you need me, call me on my cell phone,"* Tom had insisted, *"not on the company line."* Placing both hands on the sides of the stall for support, she bent over and threw up.

Now, standing outside Larry's old business address staring vacantly into the dim light of the empty space, Carol began rocking back and forth, tapping her forehead on an index card taped to the dusty glass of the door. On the card someone had typed, 'Kymer & Son Medical Machines has moved! Visit www.kymerandson.com. Your medical solutions are just a click away.' She tapped into the internet via her cell phone and while scrolling through the web site she was peppered by a rapid fire assault of truths; some that Linda had fed her and some she was just finding out for herself. Each truth hit her like a bullet, each one stinging her deeper than the one before. Tom hadn't sold the company; he couldn't have because the company remained in her mother's name. He'd slowly disposed of an office full of longtime employees, moved the entire operation to some giant mail-order warehouse on the outskirts of Bridgeport, and hired a consulting firm of strangers to run the family business. Then for over a year and a half, her husband, the love of her life, had pretended to go to work every day. Carol had a memory of him whistling as he walked out of the house in a suit and tie, briefcase in hand, then driving off into the sunrise. Every night, with a haggard expression plastered across his face, he'd stagger in the door, letting himself be soothed with hugs and kisses as if he'd earned it.

Carol had to fight for breath as another thought hit her and twanged her solar plexus. *"All that travel to conventions and warehouse sites…it was all just golf."*

Carol rocked more forcefully, rhythmically banging her forehead against the glass door while forming the words of a brand new mantra. "You rotten bastard," she said over and over again, "You dirty rotten bastard."

Chapter Seventeen
On Holy Ground

Tom crossed the border into South Carolina and headed straight for Myrtle Beach, the Mecca of year-round golf. He found a cheap motel near one of the courses Marty had circled, checked in and immediately conked out. As tired as he was, he'd remembered to use his fake ID— he'd chosen the alias Homer, because he too was on an epic journey. He also paid for everything in cash, as per Marty's instructions. He was on the run now and he'd have to stay on his toes. Keeping a low profile was crucial. By midday Tom was up, sucking down a cup of coffee and working the phones.

At first he was afraid that Marty had made some kind of mistake, because after calling almost all the numbers on the "underground roster" he discovered to his dismay that every number had been changed to unlisted or was no longer in service. He was about to give up and go it alone when he finally reached a guy who Marty claimed was rock solid. The name on the list was Tony, but when Tom got him on the line he insisted on being called Lester. *Cool*, Tom thought, *he has an alias too*. He gave Lester the short version of his story.

"The first thing you're going to want to do is get a round in," Lester offered.

Tom was so excited he heard himself talking like a kid setting up his first date with a real live girl. "Gee, that would be swell," he said. He pulled out Marty's map and suggested the closest local course that was circled.

"Oh, yes," Lester said after a pause, "I used to play there quite a bit."

Tom sat in the grill room of the clubhouse waiting for Lester, tapping a light drumbeat on the table with his index fingers. The idea of meeting a fellow escapee was thrilling. People were passing Tom's table heading out to the range or the first tee, but none of them fit the description Marty had given. Tony/Lester was "fat and happy, like Tank," Marty had assured him. Just then a slender, nervous-looking man peeked through the entrance and stopped, scanning the room. Looking directly at Tom the man mouthed the word, "Homer?" Tom started to look away but then remembered he *was* Homer. He looked back and nodded. The man rushed to the table and sat down, then reached a jittery, pale hand across the table. "Hello, Homer" he said, "I'm Lester."

Lester's hand was a grimy, sweaty sponge that would've had filth under the fingernails if they hadn't been chewed to the nub. "Hello, Lester." Tom said, forcing a warm smile. "It's good to see a friendly face."

There was a passing awkwardness as the two men sized each other up. Breaking the silence, Tom proclaimed, "Lunch is on me," then instantly regretted it when Lester asked for a full steak dinner with an extra order of fries on the side. While they waited for their food, Tom told Lester about his trip down and detailed his plans. Lester listened politely. When Tom asked Lester to share his experiences in the South, Lester hemmed and hawed.

"Well…" He cleared his throat a few times, and finally shrugged. "It started out good, that's for sure."

With that, Lester drifted off, offering no further specifics, forcing Tom to change the subject. "Has Lester worked as an alias for you so far?" Tom asked as their food arrived. "Has anyone from home been able to track you down?"

Lester grabbed his fork and knife, cut a large piece of steak and crammed it into his mouth. His words were garbled with the voracious chomping of meat while red juice collected in the deep crevices of his chapped lips, then dribbled down into the stubble on his chin.

"I'm sorry, Lester," Tom was straining to hear, "Did you say something about the police?"

"I had a little run-in with the law down in Charleston," Lester said almost choking on his enormous mouthful, "Don't need anyone poking around here for someone named Tony, know what I mean?"

"The law…?" Tom started, but Lester dismissed it with a wave of his fork.

"Stupid shit, that's all."

Tom was mesmerized by Lester as he watched him ravage his plate of meat. What he saw was worrisome. Lester had clearly lost a good deal of weight and the loose flesh hanging off his face gave him a pained, hound dog appearance. His eyes were red and watery and he needed a haircut and a shave. This guy was at least sixty years old, had been a banker in fact, and his hair was so long he could have tied it back in a pony tail. He had a five-day growth on his face and even in the dim light of the lounge Tom could see that his teeth had an unhealthy, gray tint. Finally, the guy needed a shower. Tom could smell him from across the table. If asked to describe Lester in one word, Tom would have said stumblebum or hobo.

They ate their meal in silence while Lester kept looking up furtively whenever someone entered the lounge. Lester asked for a doggie bag as their tee time approached and clutched it to his chest as if someone were ready to snatch the parcel from him as they exited the restaurant.

Minutes later, standing at the ticket window to pay their greens fees, Lester slapped his forehead and claimed he'd forgotten his wallet. *Jesus, he's putting the squeeze on me,* Tom thought, and while he forked over the cash, his suspicion was confirmed by the nasty vibe coming from the starter behind the window. The man's disgusted expression confirmed this was not the first time Lester had pulled this sort of thing.

The round turned sour right off. Tom hit a bomb right down the middle, but Lester, who according to Marty was an excellent golfer, swung spastically and topped his ball. It dribbled into the rough about fifty yards in front of the tee, never even making it to the fairway. Lester threw his driver down on the tee and clapped his hands to the sides of his head, screaming at the top of his lungs, "CUNT!"

Tom was appalled. In all his years of playing he had never seen such a lack of decorum. Hogan, who always surfaced when they were on a course, took Lester by the arm and shook him. "If you're going to use language like that you won't be playing with me, fella."

Teary-eyed, Lester apologized to Tom, picked up his club and bag and shuffled to his ball.

A few holes into the front nine, two men on an adjacent fairway drove by in a golf cart. One cupped his hands and shouted at Lester in a southern drawl, "Hey fuckhead, you still owe me fifty dollars." Lester cringed like a whipped dog and didn't even bother to look up.

For a course that he'd never played before Tom was satisfied with his game, but Lester's play was so wretched he tore up his scorecard after the sixth hole. By then Tom had seen enough. He just wanted to get away from the man as quickly as possible.

At the halfway shack Tom bought iced tea for both of them and sat at a picnic table with Lester while they waited for the tenth tee to clear. They sat together in silence and when Tom lit himself a cigarette, Lester asked for one. Tom placed one cigarette and a pack of matches on the table between them.

"Lester, what the fuck happened to you? You're supposed to be down here having the time of your life and even an idiot like me can tell you're miserable. What gives?"

Lester lit his smoke, rubbed the fatigue out of his bloodshot eyes, and then looked up at Tom. "I live in my car now, did I mention that? I came down here just like you. I left the life I had behind me in search of some kind of fulfillment, a better game maybe. Fuck, I forget. At first things were really great. I golfed every day, usually thirty-six holes. Every night I played cards and slammed back six-packs with new friends. I was having the time of my life. I know you won't believe it from the display I'm putting on today, but just a few months ago I was playing scratch golf, Tom. Scratch golf!" Lester flicked his butt into a tall stand of fescue and exhaled the smoke on a long sigh.

"Then my money started to run out. My wife cancelled all my credit cards and emptied our checking account and the next thing I knew I was flat broke. That's when my swing went south. I've been trying to fix it ever since, but…" Then Lester just shrugged and drifted off again, picking at his teeth with the matchbook cover. "Hey," he asked offhandedly, "You don't have any dental floss on you, do ya?"

Tom shook his head no and wished he could get away. Just sitting near the man was making him nervous. Couldn't you get a job?"

Lester laughed weakly and ran a hand through his greasy hair. "You'll learn pretty quick down here that the people can be very charming and warm, but when the money runs out you're just a damned Yankee, and if you hold your hand out for help they'll snap it off."

Lester was getting red in the face and starting to shout. Tendons were straining the flesh of his neck.

"I did get a job on one of the local courses running the range ball picker, but once the locals got word that a

Yankee was in the picker, it was open season. It's one thing to have an occasional ball hit the cage when you're driving around the range, but every two seconds was more than I could take. 'This one's for General Lee,' they'd shout and then, wham! I lasted six weeks."

Lester held up a hand and they both watched it quiver and shake.

"Why don't you just go home?" Tom offered. Lester stiffened and for the first time showed a little backbone.

"Go home? Go home to what? Every time I call my wife and tell her that I'm broke and I've lost my swing, that I'd like to come home, she just laughs. No words of comfort, just peals of high-pitched, shrieking laughter. Would you go home and live with that for the rest of your life?" Lester had leaned forward into Tom's face and Tom could feel the fear coming off him like waves of heat. "Would you?"

After they putted out on the eighteenth hole, Tom gave Lester the customary handshake and "nice playing with you." Then, before Lester could ask him what his dinner plans were or where he was staying or when they might meet again, Tom turned brusquely and walked away as if Lester was carrying a contagious and fatal disease.

Back at the motel Tom asked where he could get a web connection and shortly found himself ensconced in the reference section of the public library, surrounded by a throng of teenagers doing homework. He opened his laptop and logged on to his secret "wedge accounts." This was money he'd put aside whenever he felt he could sneak it past Carol's watchful eye. Over the years he had accrued over twenty thousand dollars in emergency golf funds. These accounts remained undetected, but when he checked his joint bank accounts, where his salary from Kaymer and Son was still being sent, he found that all were empty; Carol had wasted no time.

It nagged Tom that in his haste to put physical distance between himself and Carol's murderous rage, he had left town without writing a goodbye note. He opened his email and began tapping out a letter.

My dearest Carol,

Forgive me for leaving you at the hospital. I know it was the wrong thing to do but I honestly thought I'd be off the course before you woke up. I called Dr. Sullivan on my way out of town and was happy to learn you're cancer free. What a good break, eh?

I'm guessing you're very angry with me right now and I don't blame you one bit. I don't know if I can make clear to you what I am trying to accomplish, but here goes. It turns out that I have a natural gift for this game of golf. I am very close to zeroing in on the perfect golf swing, something very few have ever achieved. After wrestling with this for a long, long time I have decided that it's necessary for me to shuck off the mantle of everyday, mundane responsibilities and venture deeper into the frontier of golf, to see where it might lead me. Carol, I think if you can imagine me on a kind of Lewis and Clark expedition, or as a lone astronaut soaring past the moon into the unknown, you'll have an inkling of how I feel or what I'm trying to do.

I am terrified at the thought of losing you, I hope you know that. At the same time I have never been so excited about what tomorrow may hold for me. Carol—I might even get good enough for the Senior Tour. Can you imagine? The way I see things right now, I will need

about six months of uninterrupted practice and
play to see if I have the stuff that makes a
professional golfer. After that, if you'll have me,
I will return. I don't promise to return the same
man as I am today. Success may change me, I
hope for the better. Wish me luck!
   Your devoted husband,
   Tom

The Hogan in him thought this last bit was a form of capitulation and he cursed Tom for surrendering before he had even started, and although Tom himself was not sure whether he had the stones to ever look Carol in the face again, implying a desire to return at some time in the future was probably the smart move.

The next day Tom got up early, took out the "Marty map" and drove to the next closest golf course circled in red. Playing it helped to wipe the distasteful memory of Lester's round from his mind. After the depressing encounter with Lester, Tom threw out the remainder of Marty's list of underground contacts and decided to strike out on his own. As the days passed he joyfully played —conquered is how it felt to him—each course in the Myrtle Beach area that he was meant to play, then he broke camp and headed further south.

He caught a few magical courses in and around Charleston and then leisurely swung his way down toward Hilton Head. He stayed away from the bigger resorts because they were too pricey for a man on a budget, but he did locate some well crafted and inexpensive layouts along the way. He continued to hug the coast until he came to the state line.

Sitting in a roadside eatery munching on a fried fish hero — a 'Po-boy' they called it —he pored over his map and it dawned on him that he was just a short drive from Augusta, Georgia. He decided on the spur of the moment to make a pilgrimage to the holy site.

Tom had no chance of playing Augusta or even being allowed to walk the grounds, but as he stood at the gated entrance staring down famed Magnolia Lane, he removed his hat in a salute to this most sacred temple of golf. Inside him the Hogan thing seethed.

"We're good enough, Tom," Hogan shouted in his head. "Bang on the gate if you have to, tell them you know me!"

A muscular uniformed guard at the entrance was giving Tom a hard stare. Tom offered a gentle smile in response, but Hogan snatched command of his face and turned it into a grimace and snarl instead. Tom tried to take a step back but the force within would not allow it. The guard was standing tall now, his hand drifting for the walkie-talkie strapped to his belt.

Hogan was becoming hysterical, beyond Tom's ability to control. The thing inside him overpowered the mechanics of Tom's lips and tongue and started speaking out of the corner of his mouth.

"What are you afraid of fella? He's not a policeman, for God's sake—he's not even armed."

To an onlooker I must look deranged, the Tom brain freaked. Hogan urged Tom's legs to move forward, Tom forced them back, and a real struggle erupted.

"I have two jackets in there!" Hogan roared, winning the battle for Tom's mouth. The guard brought the walkie-talkie to his lips and began speaking into it. Whatever the reason—perhaps worried about tarnishing his precious reputation—in this moment of real danger, possible arrest even, Tom felt the Hogan-thing shrink back a notch. It was just the edge he needed to shove the beast deep inside and take hold of himself. Tom smiled warmly at the guard…started whistling 'Camp Town Races' and walked quickly away.

Tapping his hands on the steering wheel, Tom drummed along to the twangy beat of a country song on the radio. He nodded and smiled warmly at any pedestrians he passed on the quiet streets of Augusta, and, making sure he ran no stop signs or exceeded the speed limit, was able to drive out of town without incident. A few miles out he pulled over and looked in the rearview mirror; Hogan was glaring back at him. "That's probably the only chance you'll ever get to play that course, Tom. Too bad you didn't have the guts."

"If we had taken just one step further I'd be in jail right now. Do you realize that? The moment I tried to explain that I have a golf legend living inside me, the great Mr. Hogan, and he wants to play Augusta, they'd put me in the loony bin. Then what, Ben?"

Tom caught himself. He was alone in his car, screaming with sweat pouring off him. For the first time since he'd begun his association with Hogan, Tom felt an unsettling sense of dread. Hogan had driven most of his golf decisions for years, and Tom had let him. Now, impossible as it seemed, here he was in the deep South on his own and far away from the bedrock of Carol's grounding presence.

"You could have done it," Hogan lit up a smoke in the mirror. "If you had walked through the gate like a man, with confidence, like you owned the place, you would have played Augusta."

Tom argued with Hogan over the incident all the way back into South Carolina, finally ending the spat by shouting at Hogan's reflection, "Fuck you, Ben! Barging into Augusta is something only an insane idiot like Lester would do."

After the scare in Augusta, Tom's bowels began to get weird on him. They were rumbling nonstop and he was having painful bouts of gas. He decided to go further inland and stay away from the more touristy areas. It was, Tom concluded, the food that was starting to get to him. First off he had to stop with all the donuts. There seemed to be a Krispy Kreme shop on almost every corner in the South and Hogan was crazy for them, he was eating three or four donuts a day. In the restaurants along the coast he found it very difficult to find anything on the menu that wasn't fried. They fried their chicken and their steaks and their fish. They fried their eggs and hot dogs too. Tom was pretty sure that if you asked, you could get a fried glass of milk with no trouble at all. He ended up landing in Columbia, a large enough metropolis with plenty of challenging public courses to play, along with moderately priced restaurants offering meals that occasionally had something green on the plate.

There were several layouts in the suburbs that particularly suited his eye. After asking around and reading bulletin boards, he found a little bungalow to rent for next to nothing and he set up house.

Tom had no trouble filling his days by playing new and exciting courses while meeting lots of interesting people who had come from all over the world to golf in South Carolina. It was the evenings that he found difficult to manage. Nursing a few beers and watching television at the local tavern got old fast, so at night, after he had practiced and played as much as he could handle, he'd eat his dinner while scanning the local papers looking for part-time work. He wasn't going to end up like Lester, that was for damn sure. He joined the local YMCA and got into a comfortable routine of doing a light workout and sauna before slipping, exhausted, into bed. Between rounds Tom found himself studying bulletin boards in the local pro shops for other nighttime activities, and finally found one that made him smile and think of Carol. A small poster had been tacked to a notice board at one of his favorite courses, advertising the services of a golf ashram. The poster pictured a middle-aged man wearing a turban, sitting in lotus position while suspended over a lush fairway. "Study with the Swami of Golf" it proclaimed, and although Tom had no idea what a golf ashram might be, he liked the sound of it. The lead line of their marketing spiel intrigued him. "Find the Sweetspot inside of you." It was taught by a former PGA Tour Pro, the poster bragged.

The ashram itself was located in an old Grange building on the wooded outskirts of town. When Tom first pulled up to the place he was a little put off by all the pickup trucks with gun racks. Several vehicles even had hound dogs sitting patiently in the back. *Good Lord*, he thought, *have I stumbled into some kind of Klan meeting?* But his fears lessened somewhat when he approached the front porch of the building and detected the familiar odor of burning incense, accented by the soft hum of New Age music.

He walked into a dimly lit arena, a kind of theater space with rows of raised seating facing a small stage in the center of the room. A man was standing center stage in front of a dozen men and women seated on bar stools arranged in a semicircle. Seeing Tom approach, the man pointed to a vacant stool while continuing to speak. This man, apparently the former tour Pro, looked like a tall version of Willie Nelson, with dual braided ponytails and a long gray beard. He spoke in a soothing tone, a whisper-like voice that, from Tom's experience with Carol's spiritual friends, seemed to be part and parcel of being a New Age guru. Tom sat and looked at the other golfers seated on stools around him and saw that they all had their eyes closed with their palms facing upward on their knees - some kind of meditation circle, he guessed. Being a few minutes late and sensing this was not the time to start asking questions, Tom assumed a meditative posture, closed his eyes and tuned in.

"I want you to visualize a golf course in your mind," the guru said. "This is the golf course that you see every night in your dreams; a course that is lush, with the greenest of fairways and smooth, undulating greens.

Wonderfully, there are no hackers and the play is not slow but always brisk and athletic. It is a clear and glorious day with the sounds of songbirds on a gentle breeze. You can smell cut grass in the air. You are holding a 5-iron in your hands. It is not a heavy, cumbersome thing that you are holding but light and balanced; in your core you are one with its purpose. Visualize the gentle swinging of the club back and forth until you can feel the exact weight of the club head in your fingertips. You perceive the nature of that swing as well as you know your own name."

Tom felt the edge of anxiety he'd carried since his altercation with Hogan at Augusta begin to ease with every minute of this relaxed meditation. He glowed inside knowing that Carol would think this was an ideal approach to the spiritual nature of one's golf game, but at the same time the cynic in him was getting snarky and he had to fight the urge to laugh.

"You are building a safe haven in your mind," the hipster continued, "and it is this place you will retreat to when things go awry during a round. An errant swing or an obnoxious player…they cannot touch you here. This is your private place and it is special."

Tom hadn't smoked marijuana since before he'd met Carol, but this guy was a weed man, no doubt about it. Hogan started chiming in with sarcasm. "That's just what you need Tom..," Hogan whispered in his ear, "…golf lessons with Timothy Leary."

Tom and the other golfers sat quietly meditating in the semi-darkness for a few minutes longer, listening to recorded sounds of an open meadow, the cry of a circling hawk, the buzzing of a bee - all of it accentuated by the occasional sound of a flush ball strike. While this was going on Tom sneaked an eye open and glimpsed the guru walking around the golfers, manipulating their posture with his hands, adjusting them into correct alignment. When the guru worked with the man seated next to him Tom peeked again, seeing that the guru had placed his hand on the man's abdomen. "This is your golf chakra," the guru said, "it is a yellow flame and your natural swing resides here."

Overall Tom found the experience soothing and peaceful, but inside he felt the Hogan part of him writhing. "Somebody should brain this guy with a gap wedge," he hissed.

After the meditation came a question and answer period. Each golfer was invited to talk about his habitual swing flaws. The guru asked the participants to assume their golf stance and then guided them through a meditative checklist to help eradicate the mental picture of the swing flaw from their minds. One fellow explained to the instructor that he experienced terrible anxiety on the first tee every time he played. He was so paralyzed by fear when standing in the tee box with other groups waiting and watching, that he could barely swing the club. The guru nodded with understanding, as he and all of those present had experienced that same fear to one degree or another. "Come out here and stand next to me," the guru told the man.

When the two were standing next to each other, the guru said, "Now strip your clothes off." There was a tense silence while everyone digested the command.

"What?" the startled golfer asked.

The guru nodded and offered the man his gentle smile. "If you really want to be cured, you'll do as I say."

After swallowing hard for a moment, the golfer began to undress until he was down to his skivvies. The man was overweight with a fantastic farmer tan. His head and forearms were a healthy bronze while his chest, fat belly and spindly legs were a milky, pale pink. The man was beginning to shake and on the verge of pulling down his underwear when the guru stopped him.

"That'll do."

A collective sigh of relief echoed in the room.

"First, hold your arms out like this," the Guru held out his arms like Jesus on the cross.

The near-naked man followed suit.

"Now, I want you to sing *Mary Had a Little Lamb*, at the top of your lungs."

"What?" the man asked again.

"*Mary Had a Little Lamb*, do you know it?"

The man nodded.

"Then sing it, my friend. Sing it out loud."

Sure enough the man sang, haltingly at first, but then louder and louder as he went. The man had no singing voice whatsoever and was so scared, his legs were shaking violently. The familiar tune came out less like a song and more like the rant of a madman. He got redder in the face as he bellowed, veins bulging in his neck, so that by the time he finished with, "…whose fleece was white as snow," it looked like his head might explode.

When he finished his last excruciating note, the guru smiled and led the group in a round of applause. "Now put your clothes back on. You're cured." he said.

Red-faced and gasping, the man quickly got dressed and as he was buttoning his shirt, managed to sputter out, "How the hell does that make me cured?"

The guru clapped his arm around the man's shoulder and beamed at the audience of golfers.

"Now that you've done something so foolhardy, so utterly ridiculous as singing that childish song at the top of your lungs, practically naked in front of a group of strangers, the risk of embarrassing yourself on the first tee should prove to be no problem at all."

The man stood there, still chagrined at what he had been made to endure, until everyone started clapping and laughing. He nodded and returned to his seat, laughing at himself while accepting hand-shakes and pats on the back by the rest of the group. "Don't you see?" the guru asked the group as a whole. "You can make the biggest ass of yourself here or out on the golf course, anywhere for that matter, and as long as your heart is in the right place, no one really cares. It has no meaning, none at all."

After the meeting broke for the evening Tom hung around to chat with some of the other attendees. He was reminded of some of Carol's psychic junkie friends he'd met, in that they all seemed a little lost. They were searching for something, maybe a better golf game, maybe a pathway to finding a spiritual interpretation to their swing. Whatever it was, Tom could tell by their faces that they hadn't found it yet. When the last attendee walked away from the guru, Tom went over and introduced himself. The former tour Pro greeted Tom hippy style, with a bear hug that almost lifted Tom off his feet. Pulling back, he regarded Tom intently for a moment.

"Your spirit guide is strong with you, very strong."

Tom's cheeks flushed. He was mortified that someone with elevated intuitive skills could sense the Hogan part of him leaking out.

"What brings you here?" the guru asked, continuing to eyeball Tom with keen interest.

Tom thought for a moment and then said what was foremost in his mind, had been for many years.

"I'm trying to find the Hogan swing."

The guru laughed quietly and nodded while scratching at his beard. He pointed toward the exit, signaling to Tom that he had to close up, and began to turn out the lights.

They stood out on the porch under the stars, surrounded by the sounds of the woods at night. With only a single lamp over the door for illumination, the guru took out a pouch of tobacco and cigarette papers and rolled himself a smoke with practiced dexterity. He lit it, took a deep drag, then leaned on the railing in front of them and turned his attention to Tom.

"There's no such thing as the Hogan swing."

"Bullshit!" roared the voice from within, but Tom wanted to hear what the man had to say and forced Hogan into silence.

"You can no more have Hogan's swing than I can have yours. Everyone's swing is different, just as we are all different from each other. You've got it a little backward, I'm afraid."

"How's that?"

"You think that the better your swing gets the better person you will become. In truth, it's the other way around."

Tom felt like laughing. Carol would have liked that.

"The important thing to do is try and find the swing that suits you best, then relax with it and see where it takes you." He puffed on his smoke in silence for a moment and then looked at Tom again. "You're from up north, I can tell."

Tom nodded. "I came down here to try and see if I could take my game to Hogan's…to another level."

"Yes," the old Pro smiled. "I've seen your kind before and I should warn you, it rarely ends well." He turned to Tom and looked into his eyes. "Your spirit guide tells you this is a good thing?" Tom thought for a moment, hesitant to admit to Hogan's existence, but then nodded. With that the guru crushed his butt underfoot and clapped a hand on Tom's shoulder. "Not all spirit guides have good intentions, my friend. You should go home, that would be my advice," he said with a friendly smile. "Try and learn to play the game the way you began."

"How is that?"

The guru turned and again wrapped Tom in his arms, this time whispering in his ear. "For fun," he said. Then he released Tom, stepped off the porch, got into his pickup truck and drove off into the night. Tom stood still, listening to the sound of his heart beating, matching time with the crickets.

Chapter Eighteen
Manhunt

A week after Tom had run off with his golf clubs Carol was attending a drum circle with a group of spiritual friends. It was here in a Harmonic Circle of Faith that she was finally able to put aside her incendiary rage at Tom's betrayal. The distraction of rhythmically beating her bongo drum with her group, attempting to raise the Spiritual Vibration of the Universe, allowed her to step outside herself and find the clarity she needed.

"It was the slap," she'd said, loud enough to momentarily disrupt the Energy Flow.

She suddenly grasped that when she had slapped Tom in the face those many months ago, he must have experienced some kind of mental breakdown. It took a monumental amount of courage for someone to abandon the family business and then walk away from a loving wife and family without so much as a farewell note. In all the years Carol had known him, Tom had never exhibited an inner fortitude like that. So who was this man who had betrayed and abandoned her so easily? Was there someone else behind Tom pulling the strings? Did someone have a gun to his head, forcing him to behave in such a dastardly manner? There were many, many questions to be answered before she could unravel his tangled web of lies. With every pulsating smack to the stretched skin of her bongo, Carol became more determined to find the truth of it.

That night, Carol went through every drawer in Tom's dresser and the pockets of his suits hanging in the closet, looking for some clue as to where he might have gone. She didn't really know what she was looking for, maybe a credit card receipt or a travel brochure, but other than several well-thumbed issues of old golf magazines hidden in his underwear drawer, she found nothing. Later, while standing at the kitchen counter sipping a glass of wine, her eyes fell on the door leading to the basement.

Staring at the padlocked door of the bunker in the dark quiet of an empty house, it was as if Carol was seeing it for the first time. Sinister, that's what it looked like. If she never understood the word *enabler* before, she understood it now. No sane wife would have allowed her husband to have a private room in the house and keep it under lock and key. That was just asking for trouble. All along she had suspected he might be hiding things in there but she had let him do it anyway. Over the past several years she had chided Tom occasionally about dismantling the bunker, but he was traveling so much…

…and now when she thought of him leaving the house every day of the work week for the last two years and staying away for two or three days at a clip, pretending to be at conventions or visiting potential warehouse sites, but instead joyfully playing golf all over the country, the rage she had disposed of came rushing back like a tsunami. In a flash, all she wanted was to put her hands around his throat and snap his stupid f—ing head off!

Carol pressed her palms to her diaphragm and counted slow inhalations through her nose, chanting "Sooo Humm," softly while she exhaled. After ten breaths she located her Center as her thoughts separated and became clear.

She shook her head and said aloud, "What a fool I've been."

The next morning Carol again stood in front of Tom's bunker door in the basement, but this time she had company. "Thanks for coming over, Tank, I didn't know who else to call. I don't know what we're going to find in here, but I'm hoping I can count on your discretion."

Tank nodded and approached the padlocked door with his bolt cutters, but paused just before snapping the lock. "Are you sure you want to go in there?" he asked, as if he was protecting her from a lurking danger within.

Bad energy is what she felt as soon as the door was open. Tom's little cubicle was rank with it, a hint of something dead behind the walls. She would need to have several of her spiritual friends over to perform a smudging, a ritual cleansing of the entire basement by wafting white sage smoke in every nook and cranny of the tainted space.

When Carol pulled the string on the overhead lamp she saw right away how far gone Tom really was. It wasn't the posters of his golf gods on the wall or the mangled golf clubs in the gun rack, although they were all clear indicators—it was the little things that broadcast so loudly. There were stacks of books about this Ben Hogan fellow. Instructional books by Hogan as well as biographies and magazine articles with headlines claiming they had found, "The Secret to Hogan's Swing". Tom had highlighted sections of the articles with comments in the margins. "*This is it!*" he had scribbled with arrows pointing to an underlined sentence or phrase. In one corner of his workbench she found a quart-sized spray bottle labeled, "Liquid Jesus." Carol picked it up and sprayed it so that a fine mist spread out over the bench.

"What on earth is this?"

Tank, who had taken one of the clubs off the rack and was examining it carefully, looked at the bottle. "Its holy water," Tank said with quiet reverence. "Tom sprays that on his balls," he added. "He thinks it gives

- 210 -

him an edge." The way Tank spoke those words, with such child-like sincerity, caught Carol off-guard. Was Tank mentally impaired? She made a note to send a blessing to Tank's deformed spirit.

She turned to the fat man and asked him flat out. "Tank, what is it about golf that can drive a man to this?" She waved her hand around the room at all the pictures and clubs...all of it. "I'm sorry, Tank, but I just don't get it." There was a bar stool in front of the bench and Carol sat on it and began massaging a knot of tension out of her forehead. Tank rested the club he was holding down on the table. It was the one with the aluminum wings in its head.

"I'm going to tell you what I told Connie years ago. She's never understood, but maybe you will." Tank took what appeared to be his version of a golf stance and clasped his hands together as if holding an imaginary golf club. "When you're out on the course, Carol," he began, "and you hit, say a 4-iron, flush, you know, right on the screws, the ball launches off the clubface in such a way it touches your core..." Tank's eyes got moist at the very thought of it, and when he went through the motion of completing the golf swing he stood there holding the pose while gently gyrating his hips, his enormous, furry navel popping out from under his tee shirt. His face went flush and his breaths came in short rasps.

Blessings would be wasted on Tank. He must have sinned profoundly in a Prior Incarnation to have been returned to such a low rung on the Ladder of Life.

"I see, Tank, yes. That's very helpful, thank you." As Tank's eyes regained focus, he picked up the driver again and began fingering the shaft while cradling the club head in his arms like a baby. Carol returned to inspecting the room.

Under the bench Carol found a small gray locked box and lifted it up to the bench top, placing it under the overhanging bulb. She pulled on the tiny lock but it wouldn't budge.

"Open that, would you please?" she asked the fat man.

With the slightest of snips from his cutters the tiny lock snapped and fell. Carol lifted the latch and opened the lid.

Tank peered over her shoulder and let out a cautionary grunt. "I think that's private, Carol."

Although it had become ingrained in Carol to impart compassion, not anger, to lesser beings, if Tank couldn't see the venom pouring out of her eyes he was blind as well as mentally challenged.

"Thanks for your help, Tank." Carol barely turned her head as she clutched the journal to her chest. "You can see yourself out, can't you?" Carol's dismissal was so curt, even the fat man picked up on her vibe. Carol went back to flipping pages in the journal and only looked up again when she heard Tank's car pull out of the driveway. When she glanced around she noticed he'd taken his bolt cutters and the air-foiled golf club as well as the spray bottle of holy water.

She put the journal on the bench under the light and began examining individual passages. At first she started to laugh; surely this was a joke of some kind, a gag. Within minutes though her mouth was hanging open and her breath was coming in rapid pants. Page after page were the uncensored ravings of a complete lunatic. Clearly Tom never meant for this to see the light of day.

Each entry was dated, going all the way back to the early days of his golfing experience and continuing right up to just a few days before his disappearance. Tom began most of the entries by addressing himself in one form or another. You could discern his mental state on each particular date just from his opening words. *Dear Asshole*, he had written to himself, or *Hey Shit for*

Brains!, many of the early entries began. As Carol read on she could see that he would occasionally feel good about himself and the entry would start with, *You are a God! Keep up the good work!* More than once she came across pages where Tom was anguishing over the state of his game, poor putting, or *'a case of the shanks'*, whatever that was, and saw what looked like water marks of some kind, droplets. *Tears*, she thought. *These are tear stains!* When it dawned on her what they were, she closed her eyes in despair. For the first time since waking up alone and terrified in the hospital, Carol felt a pang of sympathy for her husband.

About halfway through, she came upon an entry that must have been written after a heated exchange between her and Tom.

Carol said to me that I'm making a fool of myself obsessing over a stupid little game. STUPID LITTLE GAME! It's not a child's game, CAROL! It's a man game. It teaches me man lessons every time I pick up a club. It teaches me patience, CAROL, and by God that's what I need being married to you. It teaches me the value of persistence and practice. I have built something for the first time in my life; something from scratch, something that commands respect when I step up to the tee: my swing! Let me tell you something, little lady, hitting a high, crisp 5-iron and getting it to land softly on a dry, hard green is very, very fucking hard to do. It sets you apart from other men. It makes you special! NO, CHOSEN! Do you see? I have been CHOSEN!

Flipping through page after page of madness, Carol bit her lip, afraid of what might come next. She also noticed that his golf instructor's name was mentioned with more and more frequency in each entry. *Marty told me this…* and *Marty says that I should try that…*

and *Marty wants me to use a heavier putter… or, I loved the pants Marty was wearing today. Must find out where he got them.* Tom worshipped this Marty; that much was clear. These passages read like a love letter. God Almighty, Carol thought, Tom has a man-crush on this Marty.

All of the entries were disturbing to one degree or another but there were several that made Carol's face blanch. Some sections seemed to be written by two different people, a kind of back-and-forth between Tom and someone else. Tom seemed to be defending his practice habits while the other person, who referred to Tom in the first person, calling him 'fella,' berated him mercilessly. Weirder still, she recognized Tom's handwriting in these exchanges but the other entries, the ones written back to Tom, were clearly written in a different hand.

When she came to an entry dated sometime a few weeks after the slap, Carol froze. It was written in the unfamiliar hand and began ominously. *Something has to be done about Carol!*

Her hands were shaking; she could hear blood pulsing past her ears.

She's like a cat watching your every move. It's unnerving and it's beginning to affect your game! One of you has to go, fella. You decide.

Carol suddenly felt terribly claustrophobic in the bunker and a wave of goose bumps made the hair on the back of her neck stand to attention. In a panic, she yanked at the string hanging from the overhead lamp and backed out of the dark room before someone, something, closed the door on her and locked her in there forever.

Standing safely outside the bunker, clutching the journal and staring back into the little room, Carol shook her head. Oh, my poor, poor Tom. Something had happened to her beloved husband that day, another lifetime ago, when he'd first picked up a golf club, something diabolical; and by God, she was going to find out what it was.

Carol wouldn't have been sitting in the front pews in the Catholic Church waiting for Father Charlie if she hadn't been desperate. She'd hired a private detective, who after a few days and three hundred dollars of vaguely documented expenses came back to her empty handed. "He's not using his credit cards or his cell phone, ma'am, and he hasn't flashed his social security card anywhere either. Until he runs out of cash and buys a tank of gas on his Visa, he might has well have fallen off the earth." She left the man's disheveled one room basement office clutching the thin bone of hope he'd thrown at her back as she turned to leave empty handed. "Ask his friends where he is," the detective had shouted as the door closed behind her, "...one of them knows, you can bet on it."

The chance of getting any useful information out of Father Charlie was remote; the priest was just as lost to golf as Tom, but she had run out of options. Tank was useless and clearly on Tom's side in all of this, as was Silverstein, who hadn't even bothered to return her calls. In fact, Father Charlie had also refused to call her back until she contacted the Monsignor and asked him to intercede with the golfing priest on her behalf. Within minutes Father Charlie called her back, and couldn't have been more apologetic.

For some reason, a wave of nostalgia and loss passed through Carol and she started to quietly weep. Charlie appeared through a side entrance from the altar, spied Carol and came over and to sat next to her in the pew. He put his arm around her and did his best to comfort her. His touch was superficial, cautious even, like he was afraid she might bite.

"There, there, Carol, it'll be all right," he said.

"He's run away, Charlie, and I don't know where he's gone or if he's ever coming back."

Father Charlie raised an eyebrow and leaned in close. "Have you heard from Tom?"

Carol nodded and started fumbling in her purse. "Not long after he went missing he sent me an email. It was sort of a cross between a love letter and a mission statement. He said he loved me and that this wasn't about another woman, that he was on some kind of holy mission, an 'expedition' he said."

Charlie just nodded and continued to pet her shoulder. It dawned on her that Charlie's physical contact with living beings had probably been restricted to domestic animals, dogs and cats. Maybe he was hoping she'd purr.

"I wish it were another woman. Honest to God, I really do. If it were another woman, at least I'd know what I was up against. At least I'd have someone, some*thing* tangible to fight. But golf? How do I fight that? I'm trying to win my husband back from a game, a sensation, some ridiculous quest."

Charlie nodded, clucked his tongue. "I often counseled Tom that he needed to keep golf in perspective, in its proper place. He's had a difficult time with that, there's no question."

Carol sat up a little straighter and pointedly shrugged her shoulder in hopes that Charlie would stop the business with his hand, but he didn't take the hint. Finally, she had to lift Charlie's hand off her shoulder and then turned and looked at him full on.

"So what do I do now, Father?" Carol's switch to a confrontational demeanor shot Charlie to his feet. He stepped out of the pew, and with his hands clasped behind him, began to pace back and forth across the aisle.

"Are you thinking divorce, Carol?"

"I'm on the fence about it, Father. What do you think? Should I be?"

Charlie wagged a finger at her and shook his head as he continued his pacing. "The church allows for divorce Carol but only in the most extreme circumstances, and golf, while a weakness to be sure is not a sin."

Carol stood up and joined Charlie in the aisle. "What about abandonment? That's grounds for something, isn't it?" She reached into her purse again and this time found what she was looking for. She presented a dozen or so picture postcards and held them out as evidence. "What about affairs, Charlie? He's having affairs all over South Carolina."

Charlie snatched the postcards and started flipping through them, one by one.

"He sends me postcards of all the courses he's playing. It's like he's sending me pictures of his girlfriends. In one of them he tells me that even a non-golfer like me would take pleasure in a course like this, that I'd like it there. Like I might enjoy a threesome? Is that what he's suggesting? How sick is that?"

Charlie had gone mute and was standing stock-still. Carol watched him closely. As he looked at the colorful pictures of the courses on the postcards and read each of the lavish descriptions on the back, the hairline and temples of the priest began to sparkle with dots of perspiration. He was blinking his eyes and the tip of his tongue darted out of his mouth and wet his upper lip. She was reminded of when she was a young girl on dates with teenage boys. Just before they tried to kiss her in the back seat of a car they would get the same greedy look.

"Goodness gracious," Charlie whispered as he fingered through the glossy cards a second time. "He's playing a lot, isn't he?"

Watching this supposed holy man shift from a show of paternal concern to overt lust in thirty seconds made Carol feel uneasy. *What is wrong with these people?* she thought. A middle-aged man could look at a beautiful girl of twenty with no more interest than coming upon a dead mackerel washed up on the beach, but the smart layout of a lush golf course could bring him to the point of fevered arousal. She sat back down as she felt the strength drain from her legs.

Charlie started to rock back and forth on the balls of his feet, flipping through the postcards again as if he'd missed something.

"What are you looking for?" Carol asked.

Charlie, jolted from his reverie, jerked his head up and looked at Carol as if he'd forgotten she was there.

"He doesn't say how he's hitting them," he said. "Is he posting his scores, do you know?"

Carol shot out of the pew and snatched the cards from Charlie's hands, bringing her face to within an inch of Charlie's nose. Charlie froze and his childlike eyes went wide, as if caught in the act of doing something despicable.

"Where is he, Charlie? Can you at least tell me that?" Carol had yelled the last bit and her words echoed in the empty church. Charlie flinched, then pulled a hanky out of his pocket and began wiping the damp from his brow.

When Charlie said nothing, Carol barked out one last volley. "Don't make me call the Monsignor out here, Charlie."

"I have no idea Carol. Honest, I don't." Charlie's eyes did a quick scan of their surroundings, making sure they were alone. "Tom stopped confiding in me a long time ago. I'll tell you who would know, Marty, the golf Pro." A look of regret or resentment, she wasn't sure which, flashed across Charlie's face and he added, "Yes, that's right, go ask Marty. Tom tells Marty everything."

Chapter Nineteen
So Long Fella

Three months had flown by and Tom had played almost every course on Marty's hit parade. Playing seven days a week, often twice a day, Tom could feel his swing becoming more consistent, more reliable than ever before. His confidence was such that he rarely felt the need to hit a warm-up bucket before going out. After a few minutes stretching, he was good to go. Unfortunately, with each passing day, with each greens fee he shelled out and restaurant meal he consumed, he watched with alarm at how fast his 'wedge accounts' were shrinking. He tried to keep financial considerations from interfering with his play, but found himself looking for cheaper twilight rates more often, and like his old friend Silverstein, he was beginning to irritate his playing partners by wandering deeper into the brush looking for lost balls. Soon he would need to find a way to make some cash.

Lester had been right about one thing—the Southerners were happy as hell to take your money and have you as a guest, but when it came to hiring anyone from north of the Mason-Dixon Line, they were none too generous. After several weeks checking the want-ads and asking around, Tom finally got a part-time job chasing Canadian geese off one of the courses he frequented. Freckles, the border collie who normally performed that function, was out of commission with a fractured leg after being hit by a wayward tee shot. The job paid no salary, but when he wasn't wrangling geese he was allowed to play the course for free. It wasn't much, but it slowed the steady drain on his wallet.

Growing up, Tom had discovered a simple truth in life. It was that even with the simplest tasks like changing a tire or fixing a leaky faucet, there was always a learning curve to overcome. His first job in the golf industry was no different. They gave Tom a shotgun, a bag of blank shells and a beat-up old golf cart to drive around the course while hunting down flocks of geese that had settled on the fairways and greens. The geese were so accustomed to humans, however, that Tom could drive right into the middle of an enormous flock and the damn birds would barely move to make way for him. Once situated in the midst of the geese he would load the shotgun, point it skyward and fire.

When he first fired the shotgun the cacophony of noise generated by the sudden flapping of thousands of wings along with the crescendo of honking from the terrified geese was deafening. Tom had more or less expected this and barely flinched as the enormous flock rose as one and took flight. What he had not expected, was that in their anxiety of being rousted by the loud bang of the gun, the geese would relieve themselves in unison just as they flew over Tom's head, pelting him with thousands of gobs of warm, wet goose shit. At the end of his shift he returned the golf cart to the clubhouse where he was met with hoots of laughter and pointing fingers. On his second day on the job as goose warden, he showed up dressed in a sailor's bright yellow rain suit and hat. By week two he hated the wild fowl so much that he spent a little of his own money and replaced the blank shells with live ammo.

Although Tom was still playing solid golf and had won the admiration of many of the locals he played with, and even though he had a job (however lowly), he was occasionally plagued by doubt. Now and then he would play with a fellow Northerner who had done what he had - chucked everything in pursuit of a more consistent swing. Whenever he found himself winding his way around a golf course with one of his fellow deserters, he occasionally heard things that set off tremors of anxiety; things that made him afraid that embarking on this whole adventure might have been…rash.

One guy a decade younger than Tom, a lefty named Roger, told Tom that he had been a successful Wall Street trader with a nice home and family.

"One day on my lunch break," Roger said with genuine surprise, "I was hitting a bucket of balls at Chelsea Piers, a driving range on the Hudson River in New York City, and the next thing I remember, I was waking up in a sleeping bag on a beach in South Carolina with my arms wrapped around my golf clubs and no memory of how I got there."

By the time he read what had happened to Lester, the wonderful sheen of confidence that Tom first exuded when Hogan first entered him had begun to lose its luster.

While scanning the bulletin board at his regular course one day he came across a news article pinned to the board. Written in the margin above the article someone had penned in magic marker:

"Attention golfers. When you hear the siren, come off the course!"

NORTHERNER FOUND DEAD ON FAIRWAY

Powerful thunderstorms passed through the state last Tuesday afternoon and in the aftermath, the body of a man was found on the sixth fairway of Weasels Run Golf Club. According to police reports, the man, whose true identity was not released by the authorities, but who was known locally as Lester the Yankee, was indigent and living out of his car, in which a suicide note was found. Apparently depressed over his vagabond existence, coupled with a persistent case of the shanks, a debilitating golf ailment, the man had stripped himself naked and run onto the grounds of the golf course during the height of the storm while holding a 4-iron aloft in his hands. Witnesses who had sought shelter in the greens keeper's barn say he was heard shouting, "I surrender, I surrender!" The police went on to report that when recovered, his remains were still steaming from the force of the lightning strike, which was so intense it melted the shaft of the iron he was holding onto his hands, and in the end the man's remains had to be shipped north with it still attached.

Police Chief Sammy Ray Perkins went on to say that this is a perfect example of the dangers of lightning and warned that caution be used at all times when storms like this pass our way. "Find cover immediately......"

Perhaps it was just loneliness, or an increasing sense of isolation, but Tom had gotten into the habit of sending picture postcards to Carol from the various courses he played. He was careful not to put a return address on the cards, so, as much as he desperately wanted to hear back from Carol—news about the twins would certainly lift his spirits—it was out of the question. One night, after a couple of beers, he dialed Tank's number and got Connie's version of a warm hello.

"Tank can't come to the phone right now you bastard."

"Good to hear your voice too, Connie," Tom shot back. "What's wrong with him now?" Over the phone came a growling sound, the kind a cornered animal makes.

"Hey," Tom asked trying to keep it light, "Did you guys get a dog?"

"He's in the hospital because of you." She screamed that last part and slammed down the phone. Tom knew that Tank's health was not the best but that was mostly due to his bad habits and excessive weight, so why Connie had snarled at him, he couldn't fathom. Tom wrote it off to Connie's drinking and let it go at that.

A week later Tom sat at the tiny kitchen table of his bungalow, shirtless and sweating. Usually he'd put his feet up, read a novel and chip away at the better part of a six-pack at the end of a hard day of play, but lately he'd found that alcohol left him depressed and weepy, so he'd given it up. Out of a bottomless sense of boredom he'd focused his attentions this evening on an aggravating water stain in the sink. When he'd scoured and bleached the stain away he'd gotten on his hands and knees and scrubbed what little linoleum flooring there was until it shined. He'd taken his beautiful Breitling sports watch off to keep it from getting ruined in the soapy water. When he was through with the floor he slipped the watch back on his wrist. He caught himself staring at the second hand, each revolution driving home a terrible sense of isolation and loneliness. *It's so fucking quiet!* The watch had been on Larry's wrist for twenty years before he died, and then Carol had given it to Tom. *Twenty three years we've been married*, he thought. *How can that be? What about our boys? I wonder what they're doing tonight. My God, they're in college now. They're as good as gone. How did that happen?* At that moment, Tom wanted nothing more than to talk to his sons and explain to them what he was trying to accomplish. *Would they understand? Did they even love him anymore?* Before he could stop himself he grabbed his phone and dialed home. After a couple of rings a man's voice came on the line.

"Hello?"

"Who's this?" Tom asked.

"Dad?" said the voice.

"Zach? Oh my God, is that you?"

"Yes, Dad, it's me." Zach's tone was flat, cold.

"Zach, what are you doing home from school? Is there something wrong?"

"It's Easter, Dad. Max and I are home for Easter break." Zach punctuated each statement with a sigh.

Tom couldn't believe how deep his son's voice had gotten. "Hey, how's school going…" he started to ask but heard Zachary shout instead.

"Mom, it's your lame husband."

Tom was flabbergasted that his son would dare to talk about his father like that and when Zach got back on the line he was going to give him a piece of his mind... but then he checked himself. Having abandoned his family and run off with his golf clubs didn't give him the necessary moral authority. He heard the clunk of the phone being put down and then some hurried whispering. After a few tense moments, he heard Carol's voice.

"Hello?"

Well, she sounded calm, he thought, that's a good sign. "Hello Carol, its Tom."

After an uncomfortable pause, Carol said, "Yes, I recognize the voice." A long impatient sigh and then, "But which Tom is calling? Is it Tom my husband, who claims I'm the only woman he ever loved, or is it Tom the insane golfer who lies to his wife and cheats and steals? Is this the Tom I married, the father of two wonderful boys—who by the way think their father has completely lost his mind—or is this the other Tom who handed over my father's company to strangers without so much as a conversation about it?" Tom had expected as much from Carol, but was surprised at how even-keeled her voice was. He suspected she had spent many, many hours in her meditation sanctuary honing a sharp edge to her spiritual center.

"We still own the company, Carol; I just hired a firm to run it for us. You're still getting my salary checks right?"

"Yes, Tom," Carol sighed.

"There, you see." Tom said, trying to put a positive spin on it. "If the new management doesn't run it into the ground, we should be very comfortable. I'll pick up the reins when I get back."

"And if they do run the company into the ground? What then, Tom?"

"We'll still be all right, Carol, we'll just have to watch our pennies, that's all."

"Oh yes, that's how I imagined we'd spend our final years, Tom, staring at a pile of pennies inside some f—ing coin jar."

Her patience snapped with that last line and he waited a moment for her to calm down. In an attempt to steer the conversation away from the business and money in general, Tom took a different tack. "Hey, what happened to my old friend Tank? Do you know? Connie said he was in the hospital."

The steely calm returned to Carol's voice and she became almost blithe as she relayed the next part.

"In my attempt to find out what happened to you, I asked Tank to come over with some bolt cutters and take the lock off your workshop in the basement."

Tom's heart sank. That meant Carol had been in the bunker and seen everything—the golf posters, the vast number of Ben Hogan photos and books he had collected (which at a glance would shout *fixation*), as well as his collection of experimental clubs. Then there was the dreadful possibility that she'd come across the insane ravings in his golf journal. Tom felt his tongue go dry at the thought and struggled to keep his voice in check. "Oh?"

"I was so absorbed by what I found in there, all those pictures of Ben Hogan and especially that fascinating golf journal of yours, Tom, which was a real eye-opener by the way, that by the time I looked up, Tank had gone and snuck off with one of your homemade clubs."

Tom did not have to ask which one it was. Tank had constantly been bugging Tom to take the air foiled Devil Stick, the driver with the CO_2 cartridge in the club head, out to the driving range for a test run. Tom had wanted to try it himself but he was embarrassed to be seen publicly with such a monstrosity. He'd also been afraid that it might prove to be dangerous. It turned out he'd been right.

"The idiot took the club to the driving range that very day and damn near killed himself. Apparently he was starting his downswing when he pressed the button you put on the grip to release the CO_2 and the sudden gush of gas made the club head go so fast that Tank lost control of it and impaled himself with the metal fins during his follow-through. The fins were stuck so deeply in his back that the EMS people had to cut the shaft with a hack saw in order to fit him in the back of the ambulance."

"What a jackass!" Tom said. At the same time he couldn't help noticing Carol's comfortable use of the words "golf grip" and "downswing" and "follow-through." Living with him over the years had certainly given her a working knowledge of the lingo. "I told him over and over again that it was experimental," Tom yelled into the phone.

"I always knew there was something wrong with him," Carol said. Then her voice seemed to soften. "What are you up to, Tom?"

Tom proceeded to tell her all about his ashram experience and then, trying to end the conversation on an up note, he told her about his work as the goose wrangler.

"So," he boasted, "I got my first job in the golf industry."

Carol must have dropped the phone, because Tom heard it bang repeatedly on what he assumed was the kitchen counter. After a moments silence, Carol came back on the line. "Oh, for God's sake, Tom, you're doing a job that a dog used to do." Carol let out an extended heavy breath and then claimed she had to get off the line; that she had just come home and was in the middle of putting something together for the boys to eat. When Tom asked to speak with his sons, Carol's tone went flat.

"I don't think so, Tom. That's a privilege reserved for family. When you come home you can talk to the boys. When that happens, if they want to talk to you…well, that'll be up to them." Click.

Tom felt a gloomy emptiness wash over him. All his self-righteousness and sense of clarity that he had at the beginning of his Southern campaign evaporated in an instant. For the first time since he had arrived in South Carolina and begun his quest for an exact understanding of the mechanics of the swing, he harbored thoughts of giving the whole thing up and heading home. He thought of Carol's smile and the sound of her laughter, suddenly wishing he'd brought a piece of her clothing so he could bring it to his nose and maybe get a hint of her scent. He thought of the simple joy of holding her hand, the raucous times chasing her around the kitchen for a little grab-ass. Sitting at the wobbly-legged card table in the kitchenette of his tiny rented cabin with his head in his hands, he was overcome by the notion that neither of his sons would talk to him on the phone. A lump came up in his throat and he choked out a sob. His eyes began to flood with tears. "What am I doing?" he wailed.

The lit cigarette butt hit Tom squarely on the crown of his balding head and rained a shower of sparks down past his eyes and into his lap. Tom knew instantly what had happened and a terrible sense of loss gutted him like just finding out an old friend had died. Across the room the great man stood, Mr. Ben Hogan in all his manly glory, leaning against the door frame that led into what passed for a living room in the shabby bungalow. He was posing in a devil-may-care posture with his legs crossed, arms folded across his chest, wearing a maroon cardigan and silky smooth white slacks, twin plumes of smoke pumping from his nostrils.

"You are the weakest example of a man I have ever met," Hogan hissed at him. "At the very sound of your wife's voice, the merest hint that your precious twin brats might be angry with you, you fold like a tent and want to go running wee, wee, wee, all the way home."

Tom clenched his fists at the insulting words, the arrogant tone. He wanted to argue with Hogan, to list the sacrifices he had made to be with him, the years he had put in, but he lacked the strength. He felt sapped, drained. He understood that no matter what he laid at this creature's feet, it would never be satisfied. The Hogan beast would consume all Tom had to offer: friends, family, money, all of it. Very soon, Tom realized, he would end up broken and desperate, surrendering just like Lester.

"I don't lend myself to just anyone, you know," Hogan said, a sneer of contempt stamped on his face. "I look for men and women with character, with guts. You have neither." Tom stood up and braced himself, his hand drifted to his neck, suddenly wishing he wore a crucifix. *It's going to attack me now,* Tom thought, *just like it did in my basement.* A phrase that his boys used to yell at him when he tried to get them to clean up their rooms or pick up their toys popped into his head.

"You're not the boss of me!" he screamed.

Hogan calmly pulled one of his wretched cigarettes from his pocket, put it in the corner of his mouth and lit it. He regarded Tom for a moment, letting out an extended exhale that blurred Tom's view of him with a veil of blue smoke.

"I can't imagine what I was thinking when I took you on," Hogan sneered. "You're such...a hacker." With that, Hogan turned towards the unlit living room and over his shoulder he offered Tom a final curse.

"By the way," he said, "your swing blows!" Tom never heard the front door open or close but he knew by the vast emptiness he felt inside that his Spirit Guide was gone.

Chapter Twenty
It's a Zen Thing

Getting some private time with Marty was more difficult than Carol could possibly have imagined. Making an appointment when spring was in full bloom was worse than trying to get a doctor's appointment. Marty's availability was limited. She was welcome to leave him a voice mail, but that would give away her one advantage, the element of surprise. The only way to get a face-to-face was to book a private lesson with him for the hefty price of $100 an hour, paid in advance. She didn't need a calculator to figure out they could easily have put a third child through college with the fortune that Tom must have dropped over the years. *I swear to God, I'll kill him!* Despite reservations about spending the money, Carol made the appointment under her maiden name.

Marty's teaching schedule was so packed, Carol had to wait a week before she was allowed into the presence of the Magnificent one, which gave her plenty of time to bring her Spiritual Clarity to peak level, as well as cement her plan of attack. She started the week with a colon cleansing to rid her body of toxins. When she wasn't at work or showing homes, she spent all of her free time meditating and realigning her chakras. At night she pulled out all the spring and summer clothes she had and put together an outfit for the lesson that she thought would allow her a wide array of physical movement but at the same time be provocative enough to distract the lecherous Marty. She picked a light sleeveless blouse (a loose cotton weave a blind man could see through), and a black lace push-up bra. After some consideration she settled on a short sports-skirt that accentuated her trim backside and showed off her shapely legs. She'd put her hair in pig-tails and arrive for the lesson dressed like a high school cheerleader if she thought it would help her cause.

Carol was told by an attractive young woman behind the counter in the pro shop that she did not need her own clubs for her first lesson with Marty; used clubs would be provided. However, after a couple of lessons, if she decided to take the game seriously, she would need to start thinking about purchasing a set of her own. The young woman directed Carol to Marty's secluded teaching area adjacent to the public driving range. She had to walk to the far end of the parking lot and then follow a narrow path through a stand of blooming dogwood trees that came out to a small, well-manicured practice tee.

On the range was a middle aged man of average height who, by his splashy colored, tight fitting Polo shirt and smartly tailored slacks appeared to be in excellent shape. His head and eyes were protected by a blond straw fedora and a pair of dark reflector sunglasses. Carol stood to the side and watched him hit a few golf balls. Although she didn't know the first thing about it, she was athletically aware enough to see that his motions were smooth and exuded great confidence. She watched as he lined up a shot, took a flowing, yet forceful swing and then held his finishing pose as he watched the ball in flight.

Then he did a little thing that she recognized from the thousands of practice swings she'd seen Tom take in the yard and in the house. While holding his finish pose, he spun the shaft of the club in his finger tips, and then let it slip through his hands until the club head dropped to the level of his face. He blew at the club head like a gunslinger would do with a smoking pistol barrel and then finished with a slight pelvic thrust in the direction of the ball. *How strange*, Carol thought, then coughed into her hand. The man turned sharply, no doubt startled to be caught in such an intimate moment.

"Are you Marty, the golf Pro?"

Marty strode toward Carol extending his hand and breaking into a wide, toothy smile.

"Head Pro," he said, making sure she got the distinction. "You must be Carol, my three- o'clock."

Marty took Carol's hand and held it a second or two longer than she felt was necessary. His dark glasses prevented Carol from seeing Marty's eyes but from the subtle up and down motion of his head she could tell he was weighing the material he had to work with.

"I understand this is your first lesson. I hope you're as excited as I am."

Marty came in close on the last line and spoke in a low breathy tone, creating an unwelcome feeling of intimacy. She smelled mouthwash and a fresh application of cologne. Although she remembered Tom laughing as he regaled her with tales of Marty's antics with his female students, she was still taken aback that anyone would dare flirt so shamelessly, during introductions no less. What made it all the more maddening was that she found herself blushing anyway.

"So you're the famous Marty," she gushed while taking a step back, doing her best to appear vulnerable and awestruck.

Marty rested both of his hands on the top of the shaft of his golf club and struck a bashful pose. "Oh, you've heard of me," he said. It was a statement, not a question.

"Oh, yes," she said, playing the innocent farm girl, "I've heard an awful lot about you. You've been teaching my husband for years."

Marty nodded and put his arm around her, guiding her to the center of the range like she was family. "No kidding? Who's that?"

She formed the 'T' of Tom's name with her tongue but caught herself. "Can I ask you a question?" she said.

Marty noted the conversational pivot with a tilt of his head and removed his arm, but his made-for-TV smile stayed intact.

"You certainly may."

Carol noticed a picnic table and bench behind the hitting area, protected from the blazing sun under the shade of a few ancient chestnut trees. There was an array of golf clubs resting against it. She walked over to the table, sat on the bench and patted the seat next to her with her hand. Marty followed but sat on the table itself, positioning himself just above her. Carol bit her lip and looked up at Marty with an expression of concern. "You see, I've come to believe that my husband is, for lack of a better word, addicted to golf."

"I see," Marty said, his smile morphing into an impish grin.

"We still have children at home," Carol lied, "and if I were to become equally addicted, I can't imagine what our home life would turn into. I'm sure it won't happen to me, but the very idea of both of us falling under golf's spell has made me...." Carol searched for the appropriate word.

Marty helped her out. "Anxious?"

Carol feared she was overplaying it as she fanned her face with her hand, her best Scarlett O'Hara to Marty's irascible Rhett Butler. "Why yes, that's it exactly!"

Marty's farm boy character disappeared and was instantly replaced by a smooth and confident salesman. "And yet, you've decided to give it a try anyway. Good for you. If you're serious about it, I'm willing to bet it will improve your marriage."

Carol coughed, almost choking on the laugh in her throat. "But first I need some assurance from you, the professional, that I won't become obsessed with it like my husband."

Marty nodded and slapped his knee. "Yes, well, once you lose your soul to golf, it's gone for good."

Carol sat speechless, unsure of how to respond, and as the moment came and went, Marty laughed under his breath. There was something lurid about his laugh, something sinister in the easy grin beneath those sunglasses that made Carol feel like she was having a conversation with a lowlife, a criminal. As charming as Marty presented himself, that little laugh, not directed at Carol but more like an inside joke, confirmed her dark appraisal of him.

"But how does that happen?" she asked. "I mean, it's just…golf."

Marty stood up from his perch and took a few idle half swings with the iron in his hands. Then he stopped and turning to Carol said, "I honestly don't know how to answer that, Carol. It's said that we're made in God's image, so I'm thinking maybe….," and Marty pointed the shaft of his golf club directly to the sky above, "…just maybe…God is a golfer. I bet he's a low handicapper too."

Was he serious? Carol did not know what to make of it, but then Marty pointed at her and grinned. She waved her hand at him for being silly and then they were both laughing. Marty reached for Carol's hand and she gave it to him. With the grace of a ballroom dancer, he gently pulled her off the bench and walked her to the hitting area.

"You're all a little nuts," she said, as Marty deftly slipped a club into her hands while making a show of glancing at his watch.

"Let's get started, shall we?"

For the next few minutes Marty went over the basics. Carol understood it was a speech he'd given a million times before, but he passed the information on to her with an extraordinary level of zeal and charm. He described the various parts of the club and talked a little about balance, the importance of trying to stay relaxed, and how important it was to hold the club in such a way as to be able to feel the weight of the club head in your fingertips. "You're not a lefty, are you? I have a hard time with lefties."

Carol was surprised that Marty would admit to a weakness of any kind. "What's wrong with lefties?"

Marty shrugged. "They're difficult to teach because everything they do is from the opposite side and…from my experience, they're all a little weird."

"How do you mean?"

"Most midgets are left-handed, did you know that? It's the same with carnival workers and dwarfs and Hobbits."

Carol stared at Marty as if he'd lost his mind.

Marty stepped in close, his lips cinched to one side in a smirk. "I'm kidding, Carol. My goodness, we're going to have to get you up to speed on golf humor."

"Yes…clever stuff, that," Carol said, "I'll have to toughen my skin a little."

Marty had her by the elbow now and began using his hands to get her posture into a proper stance position.

"Well, not too tough," Marty grinned and gave her elbow a gentle squeeze.

When she had a basic idea of the stance, Marty had Carol hold the iron, a 7-iron he told her, with just her left hand. He placed her hand in the correct position on the grip of the club and then gently slipped her right hand underneath. "When you place your right hand on the club, you want to make sure that you cover your left thumb completely with the palm of your right hand. We call that 'putting the hot dog in the bun,' " Marty said, while making made a kind of purring sound with his tongue.

Oh my God, Carol thought, *hot dog in bun, if that's not a sexual reference...*

"If your fingertips are turning white like yours are now, you're holding the club too tightly. You don't want to strangle it." Marty pried Carol's fingers off the club and then gently put them back on. "Lighter, that's it, lighter still. I want you to imagine you're holding a small bird in your hand. You don't want to crush the bird and at the same time you don't want to let it get away from you." Carol felt the tendons in her forearms tighten each time she grasped the grip of the club. "My God, you've got a strong grip," Marty exclaimed. "You don't squeeze your husband like that, do you?"

"He's never complained about it."

"Really?" Marty said, "Grab hold of me like that and I'd let out a squeal." Marty howled like a wounded animal and then laughed at his performance.

Good Lord, he thinks we're dating.

"All right, now," Marty continued, snapping back into teacher mode. "Let's start swinging." Marty proceeded to teach Carol the swing technique by guiding her through small, timid swings at first. As Carol grew more at ease the swings became longer and more fluid.

Carol did as she was told, with Marty frequently repositioning her swing stance in preparation for her first full swipe at the ball.

"Make sure you're bending forward at the hips, not the waist," Marty insisted. He put one hand on her hip, another on her back and tilted her slightly forward.

Carol tried to follow his lead but she just wasn't getting it.

"Not from the waist, Carol, bend lower, from the hips. Try sticking your butt out a little bit." Carol leaned slightly forward and pushed her backside a little to the rear and in doing so she bumped into Marty's thigh.

"Hello, hello," Marty said, using a cheesy British accent.

"Now, just a minute," Carol shouted and stood up out of her stance.

"What?" Marty held his hands out from his sides, all boyish and innocent.

"Are we having a golf lesson or sex? I feel like I'm about to get pregnant!"

Marty raised his eyebrows at Carol, the sparkle in his eyes coming right through his tinted glasses. "Not to worry," he said while guiding her back into the golf stance. "I've had my tubes tied."

Good God, she thought. "Lucky me," she said. When she was able to clear her head of Marty's dirty innuendos, she refocused her attention on her stance over the ball, making a point of sticking her backside out to attain the correct posture.

"That's very nice," Marty said lightly from somewhere behind her. "I think you've got it now. Let's try a full swing shall we?"

Carol stood over the ball and focused harder than she had on anything she could remember. She summoned all of the relaxation techniques she had acquired over the years and when she felt she had found her center, she swung as hard as she could.

She swung so hard and so fast that on her follow-through the club went over her left shoulder and spun her completely around in a pirouette. The last thing Carol expected was to miss the ball entirely. She regained her balance and looked down at the ball, her eyes wide with exasperation. Glancing behind her she saw Marty standing with arms folded across his chest, a hand over his mouth barely smothering a laugh.

"You think that was funny?" Carol spat out.

"You know why the golf Pro stands behind the student? It's so that they can't see him giggling," he said, then laughed at his own joke. "Relax, Carol,"

Marty shrugged and held his hands up meaning no offense. "I want this lesson to be fun for you, nothing more."

"So what happened?" Carol said, furious that she'd looked foolish in front of this man.

"Good news, bad news," Marty said, walking toward her. "The bad news is you missed the ball. The good news is that your swing looked pretty darn good. Let's try again, shall we?"

Marty guided Carol back into the proper stance, again with the touching. He put his hands on either side of her head to get it centered just behind the ball and then pulled her backside out by tugging on one of the belt loops at the rear of her sports-skirt. What surprised Carol the most was that she let him. Once in position, Carol took a few slow and easy practice swings.

She stepped up to the ball and settled. This time she gave it very little thought and concentrated on simply staying loose and relaxed. She breathed a few cleansing breaths and let her mind go blank, then made a deliberate slow turn with her body, cocked her wrists and swung forcefully at the ball.

The ball left the club face with a smart slap and soared into the air. Carol stayed in her finish pose as she had seen Marty do and watched the flight of the ball. For that one moment she felt such a surprising and satisfying sense of physical harmony that she forgot to breathe. The sensation that flashed through her body at impact felt so perfectly coordinated that her arms and hands continued to hum for several seconds afterward. In that one remarkable moment she realized what Tom and Tank and the others had been chasing after all these years. It wasn't about putting a ball in a hole at all. It was the physical rush that came with solid contact. It was the swing.

"Son of a gun," Marty said under his breath as the ball landed well out onto the range and came to a stop.

Carol turned and saw that her instructor was truly astonished. He snapped off his sunglasses and stared at Carol.

"Is that it?" Carol shrieked. "Is that how you do it?" Carol wanted to jump for joy. She suddenly wished that others had seen it. She wished she had videotaped it so she could watch it again and again. She wanted to show it to people, to the boys, to Tom. She wanted to own it.

Marty slipped his glasses back on and flashed his impeccable grin. "Carol," he gushed, "I've seen that maybe ten times in my teaching career. You have what's referred to as a natural swing. How did that feel?"

Carol searched for the words but they wouldn't come. How did you describe an orgasm? She finally settled on a phrase she had heard now and then used by people of her sons' generation, but had never spoken herself, until now. "It felt so....righteous."

There was a man, she suddenly noticed, an older gentleman in a cardigan sweater sitting at the picnic table behind Marty.

"Who's that?" Carol asked Marty as she acknowledged the man with a little wave, thrilled that someone had witnessed her accomplishment. The gentleman lifted a casual finger in Carol's direction and puffed on a cigarette just as Marty turned to see where Carol was looking.

"Who's who?"

Carol glanced at Marty as if he'd gone blind, but when she turned back toward the picnic table the man was gone.

"Oh," Carol shook her head, dismissing the vision of the man. "Never mind, I thought I saw someone." Resuming her swing motion she tried to reassemble the action that Marty had shown her, again clearing her mind with easy breaths. A thought occurred to her and it rang in her head like a bell. "It's a Zen thing, isn't it?"

Marty shrugged. "Sure."

While Carol rehearsed her swing move for her next attempt, Marty spoke from behind her. "I believe that the golf swing is a window into a person's soul and you, Carol, have a beautiful soul."

"Shut up," Carol said and gave Marty a playful punch in the shoulder. This was fun, Carol thought, and deep inside she felt something soften, then give way. It was the hard, frozen block of ice she had built up around the idea of golf over years of disgust, and it was melting. "Can I hit another one?"

"Absolutely," Marty said and once again molded Carol into the proper address position. He had one his hand on her upper arm as he tugged on her belt loop with the other to get her to bend at the hips by sticking out her butt. Marty gave her arm a little squeeze. "You work out, I can tell you do." Carol stood up out of her stance and gave him an exasperated look.

"Are you going to do this every time I hit a ball?"

Marty raised his eyebrows with glee. "I may have to."

The boldness of his flat-out flirtation astounded her. "And you get paid for this?"

Marty now had one hand in the middle of Carol's lower back and the other on her shoulder in an attempt to mold her torso into the proper spine angle, but at the same time it had the unsettling effect of forcing her chest to stick out. He was so close to her, all he had to do was whisper.

"Sometimes life isn't about the money, Carol."

Carol stiffened and then slowly dropped the club to her side and stood up out of her stance. All emotion fell from her face and she glared at Marty as if he had said something deeply offensive, profane. "Sometimes life isn't about the money," she repeated, "so that's where Tom got it."

Carol began to circle Marty, a lioness taking measure of her prey. All of the pleasure of the lesson and the magical memory of hitting the golf ball were gone. She remembered now that this man, this thing, was her enemy. Oh, how clever he is, this enemy of mine, how seductive, she thought. She was seeing him clearly now, with his nifty little hat and his immaculate two-tone golf shoes. "You're just a cad, is what you are. I can see why my husband would admire you, in a childish, infantile way. Look at you, all handsome, charming and athletic, every immature teenage boy's fantasy man. Tom tells me you've been married three times. I'm not surprised. There's just no room in your life for golf and a relationship."

While Carol spoke, Marty took off his sunglasses, and producing a handkerchief from his pocket, slowly wiped the lenses. When Carol was finished with her rant, he slipped the glasses back on and grinned that impish smile of his. "So, you're Tom's wife?"

Carol's silence was answer enough.

"Carol. Of course I should have guessed; the fear of golf, the tight grip. How is Tom?"

Carol's veins were pumping fresh ice as she glared at Marty. This was the bastard that had seduced her Tom away from her like some cheap man-whore. She did her best to remain calm. "He's run away with his golf clubs. I assume you knew about his travel plans."

Marty became aloof. "Can't talk about that I'm afraid, it's kind of a doctor/patient thing, confidential. The golf student looks to his instructor much like a parish priest."

Carol snorted. "You can't be serious. Like a priest?"

Marty shrugged. "Or a Rabbi."

Carol forced herself to stay in the moment, to remain calm and keep the conversation rolling. Marty might slip up and give out some crumb of information. "Tom's running away, leaving his family, you don't seem surprised." she said.

Marty gently pried the golf club from Carol's hands, pulled a golf ball out of his pocket and dropped it. With the slightest flick of his wrist he caught the golf ball with the club face and started bouncing it off the face over and over. Carol understood that he was demonstrating that he was unfazed by her presence or her questions, which was maddening to her, but even still she was impressed by his remarkable display of dexterity. Marty kept bouncing the ball higher and higher until, like a carnival act, he gave the club head one last flick sending the ball to shoulder height, at which point Marty pulled his side pocket open and the ball dropped right into it. He smiled at his performance and looked back at Carol. "These things happen. Tom has taken a little time off from life, that's all."

 Carol closed her eyes and began rubbing her temples. "Will he come back?"

Marty laughed and took the ball out of his pocket and tossed it on the ground. While Marty talked he stepped to the ball, took a stance, and hit a beautiful, high arcing shot deep into the range. "Of course he'll come back. He's probably thinking about it right now. You see, he's like a lot of golfers who get a great swing going and then end up trying to make it even better by tinkering with it. In a few months he'll be so lost he'll be crying like a baby." Marty held an imaginary cell phone to his ear and pointed to it, indicating he had a client on the line. He began imitating the weepy whine of a golfer in distress. "Oh, Marty, I'm slicing the ball again. What should I do?" As Marty mimicked he pretended to wipe imaginary tears from his eyes. "Oh, Marty, I'm hooking something awful. What should I do? Oh, Marty. Oh, Marty. I can't get the ball up in the air. I can't get it up."

Carol could hear real anger creeping into Marty's voice and she understood that these types of phone calls were anathema to him. Marty snapped the imaginary phone shut, then headed back towards the picnic table and started to gather the clubs they had not used.

Carol followed Marty and clutched at his elbow. "He'll come back for you, but will he come back for me?"

She was certain he was going to end the conversation and storm off but instead he turned, sat on the edge of the table, and held her gaze.

"You put him in a difficult position Carol. You tried to make him give up golf. You tried to make him choose. 'It's either me or golf,' you said. And so he chose. Did he choose wisely? That's not for me to say. All I can tell you is that by the time he came to me he was just looking for a map."

Clubs in hand, Marty hopped off the table and turned to go when Carol glanced at her watch. "I've still got fifteen minutes," she said.

Marty stopped and looked over his shoulder at her. "I'll stay and continue the lesson if you like, but if you ask me about Tom again I'll have to go. I'll answer any questions you have about your husband, but only in the presence of my attorney."

As much as Carol desired to get away from Marty, some voice, instinct perhaps, told her not to burn this bridge. There was more to learn from this creature and the last thing she wanted was to make him go running behind the protective shield of some shyster lawyer— but there was more to it than just that. There was another part of Carol's brain that was talking to her as well. The idea that the golf lesson might be ending made this part of her brain come alive and it was tugging at her. "Take a few more swings," it said. "Maybe you'll hit a good one." Carol looked at the clubs Marty was holding and pointed to one with a longer shaft and a large club head. "Can you show me how to hit that club?"

It was as if Carol had flipped a switch in Marty's head and that juvenile smile leapt back onto his face. He separated the club Carol had pointed to from the others, took hold of her elbow and marched her back to the hitting area. "This is a 3-wood," he said, slipping effortlessly back into instructor mode. "You're not really ready to swing a big stick like this, but what the hell." Over the next forty-five minutes Marty joyfully took Carol through the differences between the set-up and stance of the iron she had been swinging before and the 3-wood she held now, and within minutes he'd gone right back to feeling her up.

Chapter Twenty-One
A Native Embrace

The night that Hogan left him, Tom slept fitfully and woke the next day feeling jittery and small. He spent the morning dawdling over a local paper at a donut shop, working up the courage to grab a tee time and try to sail around a course without his Spirit Guide's hand on the tiller.

That afternoon, Tom stood on the first tee of one of his favorite courses. Although he was in the company of men he'd played with before, three excellent competitors, he felt alone and naked. For the first time in a long while he felt the swing-killing tension of nerves creep back into his arms and he promptly hit a snap hook out of bounds. All the strength and confidence he'd experienced when Hogan was inside him shriveled into a knot of fear and doubt. From that moment his most valuable asset, what he had spent twenty years of his life creating, his beloved swing, deserted him. His reaction was to do what Marty had warned him against many times: he stopped trusting the feel of the club in his hands and began *thinking* about it. He started tinkering. "Dance with the girl you came with," was Marty's refrain, meaning don't try and change your swing in the middle of a round; but Tom could not help himself. First he changed his grip and then his tempo—the clubface position at the top became shrouded in mystery—and before he knew it he had mangled everything that Marty had ingrained in him over the years and he fell into a sickening slump.

His first impulse was to call Carol and beg her to read to him the passages in his golf journal, thoughts he'd written down that captured his understanding of the swing—his eureka moments—with the hope that maybe he could piece it back together that way. He argued with himself for a week about it, actually dialing home a number of times but then hanging up before he heard it ring. He might have had the fortitude to call Carol for a favor like that if Hogan were still inside him, but not now.

He phoned and emailed Marty several times, leaving messages about his dilemma, and was broken-hearted when Marty never returned his calls. He'd thought they were closer than that. Marty did finally answer one of his emails but his response was curt.

Hey, Tom, my lawyer advises me that by responding to your calls I may be inadvertently admitting that I am in knowledge of your whereabouts, thus putting myself in legal jeopardy. When you return to the area I will be able to stitch your swing back together for you. Keep your head down, Marty.
   P.S. I met Carol. She's something else!

Tom blinked at the message on his lap-top, unable at first to fully comprehend it. What the hell did that mean? *"I met Carol. She's something else."* It was after receiving that message that Tom began to consider abandoning his Southern campaign and heading home. If it was true that Marty had somehow met Carol, there was no telling what might happen.

More than once Tom had been in the back room of the golf shop, a privilege granted to only the most intimate of Marty's associates, and watched with a blend of awe and envy as The Man prepared himself for a golf lesson he was about to give to a beautiful divorcée or a lovely and vulnerable woman whose husband traveled a lot. The few times he'd seen Marty ready himself reminded Tom of a top rated matador he'd seen on PBS, performing an intricate spiritual rite before an important bullfight. Just outside his cramped office Marty had installed a vanity table with a well-lit mirror where he'd lay out what he needed. First he would remove his golf shirt, apply a fresh coat of deodorant and then put on a new shirt, cleaned and pressed. He would undo his belt and tuck the shirt in, fussing with it until it hung just right and then buckle his belt, grunting like a samurai tightening his sash. After that Marty would sit in a halo of light and using the mirror, he'd floss his teeth, then finish with a mouthwash and gargle. Leaning in close to the mirror he'd inspect his nostrils, clip away any runaway nose hairs, and then dribble a few drops of Visine into each eye. The final touch was the passing of an electric shaver over his face, whether he needed it or not, topped off with a healthy dose of aftershave. Whenever Tom wandered into the pro shop looking for Marty and caught the aroma of that cologne, he knew exactly what Marty was up to and did not need to be told that the golf Pro was not, under any circumstances, to be disturbed.

The only thing that kept Tom from jumping in his car and racing pell-mell back home was that as well as he knew Marty, he knew Carol even better. Carol's sense of decency and her belief in the family bond was so strong that even a Don Juan like Marty would face tremendous challenges breaking through. The only way Carol's fidelity might be compromised was if she started taking golf lessons with Marty. The golf pro/student relationship was Marty's stage, the arena where he was at his most powerful. Occasionally Tom had blundered onto Marty's teaching area hoping to hit a bucket in private, and caught him in the act. Marty was so close to his female students he looked like a writhing boa constrictor confounding a helpless bit of prey. This public display of intimacy, the muted voices and quiet laughter, made Tom feel like an unwelcome voyeur. It was enough to make Tom avert his eyes and slink quietly away. Thankfully, given Carol's absolute, almost visceral hatred of golf, the idea of her taking lessons was laughable.

When he could no longer endure the humiliation of his ghastly play in front of talented golfers, he'd abandoned his favorite courses and chose instead to play more far-flung places where he didn't know anyone, where the embarrassing sting of playing like the hacker he'd become wasn't quite so painful. Most of the courses he ferreted out were not the marquee tracks found on the Marty map. They were easy layouts; flat, executive-type courses often of the nine-hole variety where Tom found himself playing with retirees, some of them so old they appeared just hours from death. They were so aged and infirm that the game they played resembled a form of croquet more than golf. Usually he could hold his own with this crowd, but as his swing deteriorated, even these ancients were taking him for the last of his pocket change.

He was a vagabond now, wandering from county to county, looking for the cheapest greens fees. He'd been sleeping in his car for the better part of a month and even though he took special care to park off the road in dense wood lots where he was unlikely to be bothered by the local police, or worse, harassed by tattooed roughnecks thrilled at the prospect of roughing up a homeless Yankee, he was in constant fear of being rousted. This night time vulnerability was taking a toll, because with every hoot of an owl or rustle of a branch his eyes snapped open with a surge of panic. Maybe that was his problem… if he could just get a decent night's rest…

One day he found himself in Oconee County, a desolate part of the state, an area more secluded and rural than anyplace he'd come across. There were few paved two-lane roads in the county and if you left them for any reason, you drove on dirt. While passing a settlement of rundown trailer homes or a cinder block ramshackle residence he noticed that power lines and telephone wires had yet to reach this part of the world. The likelihood of finding a course in this neck of the woods was nil, but in his desire to find someplace where he could wrestle his demons in private, he decided to explore. By midday he was on the verge of giving up and heading back toward some semblance of civilization when, driving up a small backwoods lane he glimpsed a sign almost invisible from the road. He had to stop and back up to get a closer look. Sure enough, nailed to a tree adjacent to a turnoff was a small wooden sign that read, "Snigglers Hollow Golf Club." The lettering of the sign seemed to have been accomplished with holes bored into the wood with a drill, but when he got out of his car to examine the sign more closely he noticed that the holes forming the letters were erratic and crudely done. *Had the artwork been done with a rifle?*

He turned onto the path and drove a bumpy half mile through dense forest until he came to a clearing. There was no clubhouse to speak of, no parking lot either, but instead what looked like someone's home, with a poorly manicured putting green in the front yard and a derelict tee box just off to the side. The house was tobacco juice brown, a shingled, two-story wreck that hadn't seen wet paint in a decade. There was a leaf littered porch with a few rocking chairs at the front, kept in shadows by the roof above it which tilted severely to the right. The cause of the tilt was due to one of the support beams, a quick-fix length of PVC pipe cut two feet short. The only sign of life was a barely visible wisp of smoke curling out of the chimney.

Tom got out of his car and slammed the door. He froze and farted in fear when two ferocious looking dogs the same color as the house jumped up from the porch and started barking. They were hunting dogs, or what they called coon dogs down here, and as he approached the steps they greeted him with lots of sniffing and snarling. He knocked on the screen door and a nervous minute passed between Tom and the dogs, their hackles up and tails not wagging, before a man appeared out of the darkness from within and peered through the screen at him.

At first glance Tom couldn't help but think of the old sixties television show, *The Beverly Hillbillies*. This man could easily have passed for an inbred brother Jed Clampett would have rightly left behind. He had a shock of unkempt gray hair that had never seen a comb and a smoldering corncob pipe was planted between his puckered lips. The man was wearing a grimy tee shirt under a pair of equally filthy overalls. By contrast, Tom was dressed golf-ready. Living out of his car had taken a toll on his appearance; he desperately needed a shave and a haircut, but he still had some fairly clean clothes left.

Today he was sporting a wrinkled short-sleeve Tommy Bahama silk shirt and a pair of stain-hiding dark colored khakis held up with a tarnished, silver-buckled alligator skin belt. Even attired in the bottom layer of golf clothes from a box he kept in the trunk of his car, he felt fantastically overdressed. At Sniggler's Hollow, if he walked out to the first tee in a sweat stained wife-beater tee-shirt, cut-off jeans and a pair of flip flops, he'd still have to roll in the mud to fit in with the specter standing before him.

Tom stepped through the door the old man held open for him and immediately felt transported back in time. He entered what looked like some kind of general store...*someone had changed the channel because now he was in The Twilight Zone*. In the middle of the room was a large potbelly wood-burning stove with a pile of cut wood stacked next to it. There was no television or radio and the silent room smelled of a mixture of smoke, wet dog hair and body odor. There were a couple of similarly dressed middle-aged country boys sitting around the stove staring up at Tom, slack-jawed, as if an alien from another world had just walked into their midst. The man who held open the door for him went behind a counter situated in front of a side wall dragging a crippled foot as he went. On one side of the counter were general-store-type sundries, jars of mayonnaise, cans of soup and snacks like potato chips and popcorn. On the other side was a sparse selection of golf supplies. What caught Tom's eye were the dust covered sleeves of golf balls in the glass case. Tom recognized the brand names of the balls they were selling but he also knew that none of these particular items had been on the market in over a decade. If he'd had the money he'd have bought some. Silverstein would wet his pants if Tom were to hand him a mint condition sleeve of vintage Titleist Balatas, still in the original box.

No one spoke, so Tom cleared his throat and broke the ice. "I saw your sign on the road and thought I'd come take a look." Tom's Yankee accent sounded like the harsh blast of a car alarm in the quiet room and the three men exchanged furtive glances as he spoke. "I don't suppose I might get out for a few holes?" The man behind the counter peeled a slip of paper off a pad in front of him, pulled a pencil from behind his ear, then scribbled something on the slip and held it out to Tom. It was a ticket to play the course, Tom guessed.

The man moved his lips and a moist, lip smacking jingle-jangle of sounds came out. Between the brutally thick country accent and the missing teeth it was almost impossible to interpret, but, "That'll be eight dollars," was in the neighborhood. Tom gave the man his last ten dollar bill and got a vintage two dollar silver certificate in exchange, so there it was.

The continued silence was unnerving but Tom refused to let these mountain men get the best of him. He coughed into his hand. "Do you have a scorecard?" The counterman didn't so much as blink but the two men by the stove swiveled their heads back and forth, following the simple conversation as if their exchange was riveting.

"S' on the ticket," the man behind the counter mumbled. Sure enough, the numbers 1 through 18 were printed on the ticket with the par markings below each number. Tom asked for a pencil and the old man shook his head.

"Really?" Tom laughed, "No pencil?" The old man continued to stare blankly and gummed the stem of his pipe. Then one of the fellows, a red haired beast with a lisp by the stove spoke up.

"Don' you worry 'bout no pencil, you wone be keepin' no score by the third hole."

All three of the yahoos smiled, exposing slick pink gums and nodding to one another at that bit of hilarity and sparkling wit. They were having a good time at his expense and Tom felt himself getting a little pissed off. He wanted to show them how a man behaves on a golf course and maybe even rub in what a shit hole this place was.

"I know I'm going way out on a limb here," he leaned into the old man across the counter, assuming an air of bravado, with just a hint of intimidation, "but I don't suppose you have a map of the layout?" His tone was more juvenile and snide than he had intended and instantly he wished he could take it back.

The three hillbillies shared a silent glance among themselves and then the red head by the stove grasped the arms of his chair and heaved himself to his feet. The spectacle of this creature suddenly rising out of his chair startled Tom, partly because the man looked like he'd been born in it, and when he finally unfolded himself and stuck his thumbs behind the straps of his coveralls, he looked about six-and-a-half-feet tall. His appearance was so cartoonish that Tom had to bite the inside of his cheek to keep from laughing out loud. Besides the thick mass of unruly red hair the giant had enormous wide set eyes and a spray of freckles across his face. Fully erect and grinning, he resembled a monster version of Howdy Doody.

"T'aint no map, mister, but tell you what. Why don' you let me come wid y'all and I'll show you the way?"

"You... play?"

"Oh, I hack it round some."

With that he turned and ducked through a doorway that led into a back room, returning with a set of clubs hoisted over his shoulder. He stuck out his enormous hand. "I'm Jimmy John," he said.

Tom shook his hand, feeling the lizard-like roughness of it. The golf bag Jimmy John held was a filthy, canvas thing and when Tom looked into the bag itself, he once again found himself struggling to keep a straight face. Jimmy John had a vintage set of clubs that looked like they might have been new when Tom was still in elementary school. They were an old set of blade irons that must have weighed five pounds apiece and the grooves on the club faces were worn to the nub. He had one 3-wood in his bag, a battered old persimmon head, and the putter blade was all banged up and dented with a hickory shaft. This yokel was going out with his grandfather's clubs.

Well, what the hell, Tom thought and grinned back up into the big man's face. "I'm Tom. Let's rock and roll."

What passed for a first tee at the Hollow, a lopsided rise in the earth, looked out over a steep gully filled with scrub brush and an ocean of poison ivy. Across the canyon Tom could just make out a narrow, tree-lined fairway carved out of the forest, about a hundred-and-eighty yards on the other side. Tom turned his gaze to the tee box itself.

"No markers, I see," Tom sighed. "Where do you tee up?"

Jimmy John just waved his hand over the tee box and flashed his two brown teeth. "Oh, we 'taint dat formal," he chuckled. "Anywheres you like."

Tom shrugged and teed up on the only semi-level piece of ground he could find. He took a few practice swings to get the kinks out and then let it rip. To his relief he hit a decent shot that landed over the gully onto the left side of the fairway. Jimmy John hummed a sing-song moan of appreciation, then reached into his pocket and tossed a filthy, nicked ball onto the ground. From his bag he pulled out the old persimmon 3-wood, then twisted his body back and forth with a furious wrenching motion a couple of times to loosen up. It sounded like every joint in his body cracked as he shook himself violently to and fro. When he finished he went to his ball and took his stance. Tom glanced at Jimmy John's feet and smiled. *Work boots,* Tom thought, *he's wearing fucking work boots.*

Jimmy John seemed on the verge of taking a swing when he stepped away from his ball and gave the crack of his ass a deep and thorough scratching. *How magical,* Tom thought, and then watched in amazement as Jimmy John stepped back into his stance and without even bothering to tee it up, swung at the ball right off the deck.

It was by far the most fucked-up swing motion Tom had ever seen. As Jimmy John swung he let out a loud, animal sounding grunt. The entire swing was an uncontrolled spasm of motion that looked vaguely like a baseball swing but he also twisted his body around as if he were performing a hammer throw. The sudden jerk of the downswing was so violent in nature that Tom pictured a per-historic museum diorama he'd seen as a kid; a Neanderthal clubbing a small animal to death. Still, the monster managed to hit the ball flush, dead straight over the gully and into the fairway beyond. "Nice shot," Tom said as he pulled his bag over his shoulder, and *lucky as hell*, he thought.

By the end of the front nine Tom was playing his usual game of one decent hole followed by two disastrous ones, but he was still outplaying the goofy-looking country boy by more than a few shots. The guy could actually drive the ball fairly straight and he occasionally was able to get his iron shots in the air, which was quite an accomplishment, given his caveman swing and the ancient set of sticks he used, but his putting was horrendous. Upon closer inspection Tom could see that Jimmy John's putter had an old hickory shaft that was terribly bent. He wouldn't be able to hit a straight putt with that thing under any circumstances. Not ever.

Because Jimmy John's form was such a jerking spasm of movement, each swing accompanied by a roaring grunt, it became physically disturbing for Tom to watch. He winced and averted his eyes at every shot. Yet, impossible as it seemed, Jimmy John managed to advance the ball.

The course itself was a joke. The bunkers had no sand in them whatsoever, just hard packed dirt and rocks. If there was a decent spot to hit from when you landed in the crabgrass these yokels were passing off as fairways, Tom had yet to see it. The only aspect of the place that resembled a real course was the greens. They were in fairly decent condition and seemed to be well looked after. There was no design to the layout that Tom could see. At times it seemed that several fairways intersected and leaving a green to find the next tee box involved walking long, unmarked paths through dense forest. The entire experience was disorienting and Tom felt certain that without Jimmy John as a guide he'd have been completely lost. It wouldn't have surprised him at all if they came across an abandoned set of golf clubs with the skeletal remains of a long forgotten duffer lying crumpled alongside.

At one point Jimmy John hacked a tee shot that bled to the right and when it landed it took a bad bounce off a wide expanse of hard-pan, flying into some dense underbrush. While retrieving the ball, Tom noticed the mountain man delicately reach into the tall weeds and bushes with an iron and after a long process of tentative prodding, finally pluck the ball out. Tom wondered why a country boy was so cautious and hadn't just stomped into the woods and picked up his ball. "What's the matter?" Tom taunted, "Afraid of a few prickers'?"

"Copperheads," Jimmy John hollered. "Don't bend over in the tall grasses whatever youse do; they'll fang ya right in the face."

Tom felt his loins contract as a twinge of fear shuddered through him and he gave his partner a grim nod. "Thanks for the heads-up."

Every golf course Tom ever played had water dispensers of some kind at intervals of three or four holes, but not at the Hollow. Looking around after finishing the 9th hole, it became clear that there was no refreshment to be had until they walked off the 18th hole back at the club house... but then his heart lightened. Just off the tenth tee box Tom could see a small shack masked by a clump of trees and brush. A plume of gray smoke billowed out of a tin pipe in the roof. "What's that place?" Tom nodded in the direction of the shack. "I can't believe you have a half-way house here."

Jimmy John looked at the shack and then back at Tom. "Y'all 'taint no federal agent, is ya?"

Tom had to think for a second but then the penny dropped. "Moonshine, eh? Is it any good?"

Jimmy John shot Tom a gummy grin. "Best in the county," he said. "Would you like to buy a pint?"

"I'm a little light on cash today," Tom said, "In fact I was lucky your greens fees were so low or I'd never have seen this lovely...." and he trailed off, not knowing how to finish. Tom tried to imagine what a brochure for this place might look like. Most advertisements for golf resorts touted villa-lined fairways or a dramatic course design with glossy photos of swimming pools and dew-covered greens. He'd amused himself with a little copywriting in his head as he hacked his way around the front. "A Stumblebum's Paradise!" was one line he came up with. "Test your skills by playing out of our gravel filled bunkers" was another, and the clincher, "Let the charm of the locals wash over you!"

"I tell you what," Jimmy John suggested, "why don't we play the back nine for a bottle of that shine?"

Tom thought it over. He'd never tasted real white lightning before and a free bottle of that hooch might be just the thing to break the dark spell he'd been under.

"Actually, I'd love to but as I said, I don't have any cash to wager with." Jimmy John stepped a bit closer to Tom and with one of his alligator textured hands reached out and stroked the sleeve of his silk golf shirt.

"Tho thoft," Jimmy John lisped, his eyes widening at the touch of it, "Youse a medium?"

Tom felt his pulse quicken. Excellent, he thought. This bumpkin with the primeval swing and ancient golf clubs thinks he's going to take the shirt right off my back. Tom's fantasy brain snapped into action. Instantly he envisioned himself rattling around the countryside with cases of moonshine that he was winning off these hillbillies and selling it out of the trunk of his car. Tom looked at Jimmy John who was an extra-large at least, wondering what he wanted with a medium golf shirt to begin with, but then realized he must have a banjo-playing son around somewhere, probably inside the shack, working the still.

"Yes," Tom stretched a smile the big man's way, "that's exactly what I am, a medium."

An hour later Tom was thinking back to his childhood and could hear his mother's voice chiding him. "Always put on a clean pair of underwear in the morning, just in case." Back then he'd always answered her inane advice with, "In case of what?" Now he knew.

He was standing barefoot, wearing only his last clean pair of underwear on the eighteenth tee. The rest of his clothes—shirt, pants, belt, socks and golf shoes—were stuffed somewhere inside Jimmy John's bulging golf bag. Tom had been taken for a ride; sandbagged by this caveman for every stitch he had on. By the fifteenth hole he had already lost his shirt, shoes and socks and guessing how it was going to end he'd covertly slipped his wallet and watch into his own bag, removing them from the wager. Jimmy John still had the swing coordination of a gorilla, but he had been holding back with his putter. What he could do with that bent, fucked-up stick was amazing. On the tenth hole the mountain man chunked a chip onto the edge of the green, leaving himself a thirty-foot, three-break putt for par, which he then drained without so much as a practice stroke. At that point only the smallest glimmer of hope remained. Even with his C-game, Tom had the advantage off the tee and most approach shots, but Jimmy John knew the greens like the back of his hand. They were his babies.

It was late spring but the sky was overcast, making it cooler than normal. As hard as he tried Tom could not stop shivering as he stood on the tee, embarrassed that his pale torso and legs were covered in goose bumps. He wouldn't allow himself to think about that. Not now. This situation required total focus, the kind that Hogan had instilled in him. The final hole was a fairly short par five with a right-turning dogleg. If he could bang his drive over the corner trees he'd have an easy pitch in and at least get his pants back. Jimmy John threw him a bit of Southern largess in his lispy drawl. "Leth's jus play this one for fun."

Tom smelled weakness and threw his last chip on the table. "Fuck you, mister. I'm not leaving here without my pants." Jimmy John shrugged and dropped his ball on the ground. He hit a low, weak shot down the middle of the fairway well short of the turn and Tom did the math. It would take Jimmy John three more shots at least to make it to the green and with his trademark one putt, the best he could do was par the hole. The worst Tom could do was tie. He teed up his ball, confident he'd walk away with a shred of his pride. He closed his eyes for a moment and tried to go to the golf sanctuary in his mind, the one that the Golf Guru had suggested, a place that was peaceful, friendly and warm. When he thought he'd caught a glimpse of his golfers' Valhalla, he took his club back, then promptly snap-hooked his ball deep into the woods on the left. After the two men watched the ball fly into the forest, hearing it clatter off the trees in the distance as it disappeared, Jimmy John reached over and snapped the waist band of Tom's briefs.

"A thirty-four waist...am I clothe?"

Tom was butt naked as he rounded the dogleg and, to his horror, the other two hillbillies were standing on the porch quietly watching them approach the green. "Oh, sweet Jesus," Tom said under his breath as they got closer. They had a camera. *Click.* Tom's head was swirling. He was in the middle of a nightmare from which he could not wake up and in his ears all he could hear was the terrifying acoustic soundtrack from the movie *Deliverance*. Jimmy John putted out by sinking an impossible downhill breaking putt from twenty-five feet. Tom didn't even bother. He gave a cursory handshake to the red-haired goliath, *Click*, and headed straight for his car. Unfortunately he had to perform a nightmarish walk of shame past the front porch where Jimmy John's camera-happy pals were standing, slapping their sides in amusement and clicking away, the coon dogs at their feet. Tom's mind was racing. *Should he cover his genitals with his hands or would that be interpreted as a sign of weakness?*

"Found your way round all right?" the counter man sniggered. Jimmy John thumped his dusty boots up the steps of the porch and tossed Tom's underwear to the hounds. The animals sniffed a few times, poking the underwear with their noses and then began to snarl and fight over the grimy shorts, ripping them apart in seconds.

With his clubs dangling from one shoulder, Tom made his way to the car, the whole way his brain shouting at him. *"Don't run, don't run."* He opened the trunk and started yanking clothes out of his golf attire box. He'd managed to slip into a pair of shorts and a wrinkled polo golf shirt before Jimmy John came out of the house and approached the car. In his hand he was holding a large Mason jar filled with a clear liquid. A plain white label was taped to the jar with the words "Nipple Twister" written in blue marker. He clapped

Tom on the shoulder like they were old friends and handed him the jar.

"Don't want youse leaving here empty-handed," he said. Tom took the moonshine as Jimmy John peered into the trunk of Tom's car, eyeing the box of clothes. "Come back tomorrow and I'll play you for the rest." he said, flashing the pink wet of his mouth at Tom.

"Yeah, sure, that's a great idea." Tom replied. He opened the jar and sniffed at the contents. The fumes were so strong they made the membranes of his nose sting and his eyes water.

"Careful with that, now," Jimmy John cautioned and then leaned in close. "You go on home and drink about half a-that there and when you wake up you won't even remember how you lost your panties." With that he tipped his massive Howdy Doody head in Tom's direction and ambled back up to the house, scratching deeply at his hindquarters in a parting gesture of farewell.

That evening Tom sat in the front seat of his car, exhausted, depressed and anxious; on the verge of tears. He'd parked off the road in a quiet spot, hopefully hidden from view behind a thick stand of pines. In his lap was an open box of fried chicken he'd picked up on his return trip from golf hell and he began to morosely gulp it down, not bothering to wipe the grease as it dribbled down his chin. He'd gotten an iced soft drink with his meal, which rested on the dash in a small puddle of condensation, but his eyes kept drifting over to the bottle of moonshine on the seat next to him. "It'll help you forget..." Jimmy John had said. Tom reached for the Mason jar and unscrewed the cap. He wouldn't forget walking down that eighteenth fairway naked as a jaybird or the sniggering of those photo snapping halfwits if a surgeon cut open his skull and removed his entire brain. That kind of memory was seared so deeply into Tom's DNA that a thousand years from now his descendants would dream about it and wonder why. He put the rim of the jar to his lips and took a baby sip.

Chapter Twenty-Two
A New Girl in Town

When Carol got home from that first lesson with Marty, she felt elated and dirty at the same time. Elated because Marty had spent an extra forty-five minutes with her once they got off the topic of Tom and down to the business of hitting golf balls. Dirty because in the process of teaching the basics of golf, Marty had found a way to touch almost every square inch of her body from her ankles to her forehead. It was so off-putting that at one point she turned, and holding her club over her head like an axe, threatened to hit him with it.

"Just cut it out!" she screamed. "Do you do that with all your female students?"

Marty didn't even blush. Instead he shrugged, "It's genetic," his impish grin smeared across his face, "I have a little Italian blood from my mother's side."

He was incorrigible, but when it came to the golf swing, he knew his stuff. To both their astonishment, Carol had a fantastic natural proclivity toward the physical action required to swing a golf club correctly. In an excited rush they went back and forth between hitting the 7-iron and the 3-wood; in both cases she would frequently hit one "right on the screws," as Marty kept saying.

She'd heard Tom use that same expression a thousand times over the years and had only the vaguest idea of what the hell he was talking about, but she understood it now. She understood completely.

Marty was ecstatic over her natural abilities and taught her as much as he could in the short time they had together. He reviewed the grip and the stance again and again, making sure she understood that learning the two concepts was critical and that they needed to become second nature to her. Marty explained that he was taking her far beyond what he normally showed a student in a first lesson, but there was no sense holding back since she was taking to it so quickly. When they ran out of balls, Marty pulled out his cell phone, called the pro shop and had another basket brought down to them, *"Pronto."* At one point she noticed Marty glancing at his watch. Fearing that he would stop the lesson, she covertly undid the top two buttons of her blouse. When she was in her golf stance again, she caught Marty's eyes peering over the tops of his sun glasses, glued to her cleavage. Two swings later he took out his cell phone and cancelled his next lesson.

Before she knew it, the lesson was over. Walking back to the pro shop, the two of them arm and arm, she promised him she'd sign up for a series of private lessons and join a beginner group clinic as well. Once in the shop, Marty gave her a used ladies' 7-iron with a lightweight graphite shaft and some golf-ball-size wiffle balls to practice with at home.

While fitting her for the iron he noticed a small blister on Carol's left thumb and offered her a golf glove, "free of charge," he had said, giving her a wink. *What a sport.*

A few hours after she got home, the almost tactile swell of elation bubbling up inside her began to fizzle, and while showering off the Marty smell, doubts crept into her mind. *Jesus Christ, Carol*, she thought, w*hat the hell are you doing?* The expense alone was enough to back her away from all those lessons she had signed up for. And golf, of all things. This was Tom's undoing, his opium, and here she was racing toward it like a silly high school girl running into the arms of some jerk with a muscle car. She decided that after dinner she would call the golf shop, cancel all the lessons and tomorrow she would return the practice club.

*   *   *

That evening, as darkness fell, one of the neighbors was taking his wife's dachshund for an after dinner stroll when he stopped at the end of Carol's driveway. He listened to the sounds coming from behind the garage and smiled. It was a sound that had been familiar in the neighborhood for as long as he could remember. *Whack!* A plastic golf ball sailed over the garage and landed on the side lawn where a few other balls lay in the grass. The dog walker had been under the impression that Carol and Tom were having marital troubles and that Tom had moved out, at least that's what his wife had told him. *Whack!* Another ball hit the peak of the garage roof and rolled down the other side. The little dog circled a patch of Tom and Carol's lawn, then squatted and relieved itself. *Whack!* Hearing the sound of Tom working on his swing made him smile again. "Good," he said, tugging the dog towards home. "I hope they work things out."

*   *   *

Over the years Carol had come across many wonderful expressions in her spiritual exploration. One expression she liked the most said, "There are no coincidences. Everything happens for a reason." She was pretty sure that if Tom had called her right after he'd left, or even within the first several weeks of his disappearance, she would have told him she was getting a divorce and then slammed the phone down. But he had put it off, probably due to shame and fear, so by the time he did call, Carol was already weeks into the adult intermediate golf clinic and had heroically fended off Marty's advances through her third private lesson with the lecherous Pro. Her golf skills were advancing

- 266 -

rapidly and every time she hit one of those really wonderful flush shots, her wrath toward Tom would ease just a little. Not that she had dismissed his behavior as acceptable or reasonable or fair—she hadn't—she did not condone his behavior one bit, but she was beginning to see the path, the arc of it, how it just might possibly happen.

With every passing week Carol found herself drawn more deeply into the universe that was golf. She'd met some of the other female golfers who frequented the clubhouse and was quickly invited to join the ladies' nine-hole league, something she did without a moment's hesitation. In addition to being a lot of fun, it was excellent networking for her growing real-estate career. When the boys came home from college for the summer she put a word in with Marty and he gave both of them jobs working in the golf shop.

On top of everything else, her luck turned when it came to selling real estate. When showing clients around town she saved the town park and Rocky Shores for last. While driving them through the facility, giving her practiced tour guide's speech, her deep affection for the place came through loud and clear. Perhaps it was due to this newfound enthusiasm for the facilities that the town had to offer—who can say—but she sold two properties during this period and Linda brought her on as a full-time agent. By the time Tom had been gone four months, Carol was an entirely new woman with a life all her own, surrounded by her job and her sons and golf.

Now and again she found herself missing her husband and hoping he would return. If he came back, that would be great, she thought. If he didn't, well, even though she still rolled over some nights and found herself stroking the empty place beside her, she knew she could survive that too. Besides, Marty said Tom would definitely come back when he got it out of his system, so there was no point in worrying about it. Her spiritual friends had advised her along similar lines. Tom was on his own personal journey and it would take him where it was supposed to take him.

*   *   *

He heard birdsong, then the sound of a car passing close by as his eyes fluttered open. The sting of the morning light was blinding so he clamped his lids shut. He jerked his head away from the glare and his brain exploded. In an instant he was hyperventilating, full panic mode. *Oh dear God in heaven, I've been shot.* That was the only thing that might explain the incomprehensible pain in his head. He was shot and bleeding. Even worse, he could feel a weighty lump of dampness on his chest. What in God's name was that?

Had his worst fear come true? Had he been discovered while sleeping and attacked? He'd suffered a calamitous injury to his head, there could be no doubt. It explained why he was unable to focus his thoughts or why he heard a terrible ringing in his ears—or was it a buzzing? He couldn't tell. Was he paralyzed? He tried moving a big toe. It felt like it moved, but his damaged brain could be playing tricks on him. If he had been shot in the head—then what was that heavy wet on his chest? Was it the remnants of his blasted face? If he survived, would he be forced to wear some kind of ghastly prosthetic mask for the rest of his life? Would his wife and children ever again be able to look him in the eyes without stoically fighting to hide their revulsion? Oh dear Jesus. Would he ever be able to hold a club? Even swing one?

Frozen in panic, Tom held his eyes shut. He lay still, listening, until he was sure that he was alone, that his attacker had gone. While he played dead, another sensation penetrated the wall of pain in his head. What was that putrid smell? He had the acrid taste of vomit in his mouth, but there was something darker in the foul miasma he breathed. Had he dirtied his pants? Yes, he decided, if he'd been shot, then probably, yes.

He tried taking a deep breath but the overpowering stink made him retch. Now there was no air at all, stars, suffocation, darkness. He dreamed briefly of lying in bed with his wife, Carol. They were reading the same book together, kind of a contest, with hot mugs of tea on their bedside tables. A cool breeze teased the curtains, giving the linens a fresh, clean smell. They were laughing, he was sure of it.

The euphoria of the vision made him sigh out loud, but his throat felt full of phlegm and he coughed, wrenching himself back to the surface again. There was a hard gob of something stuck on the back of his tongue. He coughed forcefully this time in an attempt to dislodge the lump and his frontal lobes mushroomed, pounding nails against his eyeballs. The pain was so intense that he sobbed, but the sobbing constricted his facial muscles and made it worse, so he forced himself into absolute stillness. When the jackhammer of agony dulled to a rhythmic pounding in his temples, he spread his hands out like a blind man feeling the space in front of him. Touching the headrest of the front seat of his car he immediately understood where he was. He was partially reclining in the back seat with his head jammed against the rear door window. He tried to adjust his position, but the stabbing thrust of pain in his cranium was so intense that his entire torso cringed in an attempt to distance itself from his head. Along with the agony came a gut-wrenching nausea that bubbled acid up in his throat. *Vomit now*, he told himself, *and you'll have a fucking stroke.* He decided to remain perfectly still and wait it out. An hour later he dared to open his eyes.

Drifting his filmy eyes over several items in the back seat, Tom pieced together his recent past. Next to him on the seat, flies were feasting on the greasy bones of a fried chicken meal. Beside that was the Mason jar that had contained the moonshine he'd been given by that hillbilly piece of shit Jimmy John. The cap was off, and the jar lay on its side; a tomb for dead flies but otherwise empty. He remembered Jimmy John warning him that just three or four swallows would be enough to erase Tom's humiliating defeat from his memory. The shame of what had occurred at the end of that match had induced Tom to drink the whole of it.

Tom gently moved his head an inch to each side and when his forehead did not explode, he held his breath and looked down. He had barfed his chicken meal—tater-tots and biscuit included—directly onto his chest where it sat in a wet, fly infested lump. With superhuman focus, he turned his left wrist toward his face and looked at his watch. It was the thirtieth. *My God*, he thought, *I've been sitting in my own filth for two entire days.* "Fuck me!" he moaned. The Nipple Twister was so powerful it had put him in a forty-eight-hour coma.

An hour and a half ticked by before Tom was finally able to stumble out of his car and collapse face first onto the ground. He pulled himself up to all fours, his torso convulsing with spasms as he dry-heaved repeatedly into the dirt. With each heave he felt as if someone was sledge-hammering a railroad spike into the back of his skull. Still, it was an improvement over the ghastly stench in the car. When his stomach gave a final twist, he pulled himself to his feet. He was quivering and weeping, but managed to fumble the Volvo's trunk open and lift out the gallon jug of potable water he kept there. He took a sip and rinsed barf residue out of his mouth. The second sip he tried to swallow, but his stomach was not receiving and it came spewing back up. Stripping off his soiled clothes—and gagging a final time while disposing of the mess he'd made in his pants—he gave himself a makeshift shower by pouring the remaining water over his head. He stood there, naked and shivering while rubbing at the crusty places. He felt a warm splattering at his feet and looking down, noticed that he was pissing uncontrollably. When the shaking stopped and the spurts of urine slowed to an intermittent dribble, he went back to the trunk and took a moldy towel from his laundry bag. Tom finished drying himself, and with two fingers he carried the towel and soiled clothing away from the car and dropped them behind a tree, kicking dirt and leaves over the pile.

After taking some shorts and a golf shirt from the box in the trunk, he went about the business of cleaning out the car. He moved like a frightened ninety-year-old on slippery ground, groaning with every breath. As he inspected the rear seat he was grateful that the entirety of his spew had landed on his chest and not the beige leather interior. *First decent shot I've had in a month*, he thought. When the car was cleaned, he slumped down in the front seat and started to pray. As his hand reached for the glove compartment, he was praying just the way he had as a little boy when he begged God for the five-speed Raleigh bike or the pump-action BB gun to be under the tree on Christmas. *Please Jesus, please, let it be there.* The bottle of Advil spilled out and when he heard the rattle of pills inside, he clutched the bottle to his chest and mouthed the words, *thank you, Jesus.* Only after tossing four tablets into his mouth did he realize he had used all of his water. He grabbed the plastic soda cup, decorated with cartoon caricatures of famous Confederate heroes that had come with the take-out meal, and sucked a gulp of tepid soft drink into his mouth. The mixture of pills and sweetness made it halfway down, then he felt his stomach and esophagus clench and it all shot up and exploded back into his mouth. Tom gripped the steering wheel hard with both hands and forced himself to re-swallow, fighting the gag urge for a full minute until he was able to keep it down. Perspiration and tears ran in mixed streams down his face as he stared out the bug splattered windshield. For a long time he sat still, numbly watching from the shade of his hideaway, as the sun flickered past the trees into the late afternoon. When the owls began to hoot and twilight settled in, he lay down flat on his back on the front seat of the car. The only way he could stretch his legs straight was to stick his feet through the passenger window.

Back in the day, before Carol, Tom had partied hard with his friends. He found that when he had gotten sick from it—not emergency-room sick like this, but close enough—he was able to get the terrible banging in his head to retreat by lying flat and concentrating on deliberate, slow breathing. It was his secret hangover remedy. He would place his hands over his chest like a dead man in a coffin and breathe very slowly, very deeply, for as long as he could until the throbbing in his head began to slip away - meditation breathing, Carol called it, to cleanse the mind. In Tom's case his mind was already blank; he was just trying to keep it alive.

It took another hour of this breathing technique along with the double dose of Advil melting into the cells of his poisoned flesh before his brain switched on and an actual thought began to form. The thought kept repeating itself like an SOS signal until he started to mouth the words, and then like a mantra in one of Carol's meditation circles, he heard himself vocalizing the sounds: "What have I done?" Outside, night was closing in on the Volvo and just under the rising chorus of bull frogs and crickets was the sound of Tom's breathy wail. "What have I done? My God, what have I done?"

The following morning Tom found himself standing next to his car. He had no memory of getting there. His head felt light, hollow. As if the mantra he'd been chanting all night had wiped his slate clean. He had no hopes, no desires, not even regrets or excuses. Like a grandfather clock whose spring has wound down, his brain stopped dead and everything went still. Squinting up into the splintered sunlight filtering through the tops of the trees he turned and leaned his hands on the hood of his car, peering at his warped-carnival-mirror reflection in the windshield. He thought he could hear an old Joni Mitchell lyric that he had liked in college, and though he couldn't remember the melody, he spoke the line out loud. "You don't know what you got...'til it's gone." He repeated the line several times. He didn't know whether to laugh or cry. Gazing at the distorted version of himself, he finally spoke the thought that had been fighting for weeks to come to the surface. "It's time to go home, asshole."

Chapter Twenty-Three
Home

When Tom called announcing that he had 'bottomed out' and was coming home, he'd caught Carol a little off balance. She was in the middle of a round with a threesome she played with regularly, and although her partners had strict rules about cell phone use on the course, she felt compelled to take it.

"Yes, Tom," she said in a low tone, trying to be discreet, "What's that? You're coming home? Oh, well, that's nice." She gestured to her friends that she was sorry about the call and doing her best to get the annoying person off the phone. "Oh dear, you've lost your swing. Well that's just tragic, dear. I am very sorry, but I really can't stay on the line, you caught me with a client. Yes, that's right I'm working. Why don't you tell me all this when you get home. Yes, I have strong feelings for you too. Okay, bye now." Carol snapped the phone shut and put it back in her bag.

"Sorry, boys, it won't happen again," Carol apologized and continued her march down the fairway. One of the group sidled up to Carol as she came to her ball, and checked to see that the green ahead was clear. The man grinned at Carol and shook his head.

"You know, Carol," he said, "When Tom sees how you're hitting the ball he's going to have a heart attack." Carol checked her distance from the green and pulled a 5-iron from her bag.

"Well, Father," Carol replied while settling into her stance and sticking out her butt just like Marty had taught her, "if he does, I'll give you a call and you can zip on over and give him his last rites."

And now he's finally coming home, Carol thought as she lay in bed that night. *He's in for a rude awakening, that's for damn sure.* Carol had come to the conclusion over the past several weeks that she did want Tom to come home and that yes, she still loved him. Was it the fiery love like they had when they were young? No, it was not. She had worked as hard as she could over the years to keep the children happy and the home neat and clean. Every night supper was on the table, the laundry was done, folded and put away, the beds were made. She worked out regularly at the gym to keep herself attractive for her husband, but even with all that effort, Tom had left her for a deeper love. He'd snuck around behind her back for years and then, the moment she'd discovered his treachery, he ran off to fulfill some insane notion that he might find a new life in golf. What a jerk.

But, she remembered the good times too. She could still draw from memory the passion of their young love and when she thought of the sparks of laughter they'd shared over the years, it always put her feelings in touch with the old Tom. That was the man she'd married. Now, just maybe, now that she had discovered how wonderful golf could be, maybe there was a future for them.

As she lay still in the darkness she saw the two of them walking down a fairway, holding hands and laughing with the afternoon sun warming their backs, perhaps engaged in a little friendly competition. Who knows, they might even gamble for sexual favors. Like a skins game...only different.

But Carol was through looking after Tom. If he thought he was playing golf every day with the boys, he had another thing coming. Let him do the shopping and the laundry and make the beds and hump that God-forsaken vacuum up and down the stairs all day; and when he was done with all that, if he still had the energy, he could come out and play the back nine with her. It was going to be Carol's turn now. Let's see how Mr. Premeditated Mid-Life Crisis liked that.

* * *

Every couple of miles or so, as Tom wove his way through the back roads of South Carolina and then on to the interstate that would take him back home, he would look at his face in the rearview mirror and then sink back into the seat of the car, shaken by his appearance. "Jesus Christ," he muttered. "I was supposed to be down here on a life-changing adventure and I look like I've aged ten years in six months." He was talking aloud to himself as he drove and he slapped his hand against the steering wheel each time he caught himself doing it. Dread filled his heart as it dawned on him that he'd been doing it for years. *Had he done it in front of Carol?* The thought of it made him cringe. *In front of his boys?*

Another glance in the mirror and this time his focus drifted to his shaggy beard and greasy shoulder length hair. He grimaced at his reflection and was jarred by something new. Maybe it was the light in the car but he'd be damned if his teeth hadn't turned an unsightly gray/brown color. "Oh my God," he yelped, then turned on the overhead light to get a better look, "I have old man's teeth."

Part of the problem had been money, of course. He'd pretty much run out of cash a month back and was forced to give up his bungalow. On top of that the damn goose-chasing dog's leg had healed so Tom lost his job and the free golf that came with it. Since then he'd been living out of his car. His last razor had gone dull weeks ago and, not wanting to waste precious dollars on a new blade, he'd let his beard grow out. To his shock it came in with just a tinge of red around the lips, the rest was snow white. He'd clearly lost weight, his face was positively gaunt. The weight loss was a natural side effect of not eating three square meals a day—a further effort to economize—and the last few weeks he'd been getting by on one fast food meal a day and whatever clubhouse coffee and doughnuts he could scrounge. Yes, he looked much older, and maybe that was to be expected, but the dirty tinge to his teeth really jangled his nerves.

What worried him most was his smell. He had to keep the windows all the way down as he drove because he was farting nonstop and the stench coming out of him smelled like death itself. Part of him was terrified he'd gone and contracted stomach or bowel cancer from all the cheap fried food and barbecue he'd been consuming. He couldn't remember the last time a vegetable had passed his lips. A few weeks back he'd stopped at a roadside barbecue stand—it was just a shanty, really—and ordered their "famous" two dollar rib sandwich. He'd asked the woman who served him, a slow moving ancient with a mountain of gray dreadlocks piled on her head, what was in it. After working a finger into her explosion of hair and scratching for a moment she said, "pork." The taste and texture were so foreign to him that he pressed her further as to what other ingredients it might contain.

"Like I said, pork…and some other stuff," she'd mumbled. The meat had a strange gooey consistency and a weird tangy after taste that triggered his gag reflex but he was hungry so he ate it anyway. He thought he could trace the death farts back to that awful meal but whatever it was he'd better be over it before he got home. Carol might take a decrepit old man back into the house, but not one that was generating that kind of stink all day. No sir, she would not sit still for that at all.

Pulling into the driveway of his home in Westwater, Tom almost burst into tears. If there had been neighbors on the street he would have hugged them. Never in his whole life had he been more grateful to be anywhere. All he could think of as he got off the highway and wound his way through the streets of his glorious hometown was a hot shower—maybe two. Clean clothes and fresh sheets. *Oh, my Christ*, he thought, almost weeping at the prospect, *my own toilet.* Tom had been using public restrooms and port-o-potties for so long, the very idea of sitting on the john in a sparkling clean bathroom made him quiver with anticipation. He got out of the car and it was all he could do to keep from dropping to his knees on the front lawn and kissing the ground. He took his suitcase out of the back seat and, with shaking hands, fumbled with his keys until he was able to open the front door and stumble in.

There was no one home but on the kitchen table was an envelope with his name written in Carol's hand. There was some kind of note inside but he wasn't ready for The Gospel According to Carol yet. First he needed to use the toilet, then shave followed by a long, hot shower.

After washing his hair (twice) and standing under the hot spray for ten minutes, he started to tremble and get weak in the knees. Stopping up the drain, he lay down in the tub with his eyes closed, letting the water rain down on him. When the water rose to his chin he turned it off and just lay there, soaking.

He was thrilled to be home at last, but at the same time he lay there mourning the loss of his dream, his quest. He understood that for him a perfect golf swing was unattainable, always had been probably. All the way home he'd wrestled this notion around in his mind. He plotted the trajectory of his passion for golf from his early days on the driving range and tried to pinpoint the moment when he'd gone from being a regular Joe who pursued golf as a hobby, to a compulsive fool who'd put his career and family on the line just for the opportunity to crack the sky with a high lofted four-iron. He thought of Gary and the roomful of hopeless golfers he'd felt contempt for. Was he really one of them? He pictured himself pushing coin after coin into the ball machine behind Marty's shop, dripping sweat and cursing himself, knowing full well he should be home with his family instead. Yes, he decided, that is exactly who I am.

Then an idea passed through him that made him sit upright. He couldn't believe he hadn't thought of this before. That a perfect golf swing, total control of a golf ball's flight at all times, would ruin the game, take the joy out of it and make it boring. That's what the guru at the golf ashram had been trying to get through to him. We don't play for perfection, we play *around the imperfections*. We play golf for the *fun* of it.

It came to him what a great relief it would be to be rid of the rampant desire to tee one up, to crush one, to be free, but he was not fooling himself. He was hooked. Hooked like a fish following the tug of the fisherman's reel. The urge to slip on a velvety leather glove and savage a bucket of balls with the sweet spot of a five-iron, would be with him forever. The trick, it occurred to him, would be to not let his obsession define him. If he couldn't do that and learn to approach the game like a responsible human being, he might as well throw up on himself, get back in the car, return to South Carolina and wait for a thunderstorm.

Standing at the kitchen counter in a fresh set of clothes, so crisp and clean, it felt like he was wearing a tuxedo, he inhaled the magical aroma of fresh brewed coffee and stared at Carol's envelope. He had called Carol to tell her he was coming home and had been surprised at her response. She hadn't told him to go to hell as he'd thought she might, nor had she sounded relieved. In fact, if he had to describe her tone over the phone he would say it had been ambivalent. She had sounded distracted as if she were only half-listening to his heart-felt apologies and promises of a new life. When he'd sworn to her that he would make it up to her and told her he had learned just how ungrateful he had been over the years, all she'd said in response was, "It's about time." Then she'd begged off the phone, claiming she was in the middle of something and that their talk would have to wait until he got home. She had been dispassionate, remote - not the Carol he knew at all.

Tom poured himself a cup from the coffeemaker. He held the ceramic mug in both hands, relishing the weight of it. After drinking half the cup, he took a deep breath and opened the letter.

Dear Tom,

Glad you have come to your senses. Also glad that you have decided to embark on a new life. Growing up is hard to do and as my father used to tell me (you remember him, don't you?) when you finally take on the mantle of adulthood you also earn your own self-respect, and "What's not to like about that?"

I have embarked on a new life myself, and in order for me to reach my goal, I'm going to need your help and cooperation. You can begin by doing the load of laundry I left for you in the wash room and then prepare the steaks I left in the fridge. Don't make a mess!

After dinner we will discuss how we are going to play the "back nine" of our lives.
Carol
P.S. We can make this work!

Tom read the letter again and then flipped it over to see if there was more. He couldn't believe that was all she had to say. The damn thing read like a telegram. She hadn't put *love, Carol* at the end and that added to the coldness of it, but after his behavior what could he expect? And that business of the "back nine of our lives" was unnerving. Was the golf reference an attempt at humor? That could be a good sign, but maybe it was a hint that she was going to beat him over the head with his asinine behavior for the rest of his life, which was a bad sign.

Tom folded the note back up and tapped it on the counter top for several confused minutes. He concluded that this was one of those times in life where no amount of planning or scheming would help. He would embrace one of Carol's spiritual lessons, one that she was forever preaching to him and the boys, and just take life one moment at a time, *live in the now*.

He salted and peppered the steaks, then rubbed the meat with olive oil, the way Carol liked it. After finding the laundry Carol had left he added his own sack of filthy clothes and saw that he had an afternoon's worth of work cut out for him. It was all he could do not to worry about what would happen when Carol got home from work—he found himself checking his watch every five minutes—so he was happy for the distraction of separating the clothes by color and loading the washer. He was humming a new tune he'd heard on the way home in the car. It was an upbeat and happy melody that he couldn't get out of his head, sung by someone named Patty Griffin, a folk singer he'd never heard of. While sorting the jumble of clothes he suddenly went silent when he noticed grass stains around the ankles on a pair of Carol's slacks. He pictured Carol mowing the lawn while he was away and imagined her tugging over and over on the pull-start of the mower. How long had it taken her to figure out you had to prime the carburetor before it would start? The vision of her huffing and puffing across the yard, pushing the mower ahead of her, made him laugh out loud. His eyes misted and he felt a warm pulse of love for her, until his fingers slipped into the front pocket of the slacks.

He was checking her pockets for gum or loose change when his hand closed around something that brought him up short. It was a ball marker of some kind; it was pink and plastic but there was no mistaking what it was. Moments later, in the pocket of a pair of shorts he came across, of all things, some golf tees and in a rear pocket, a golf scorecard. A queasy sensation clenched his stomach and he was hit with a disorientating sensation, like he was in the wrong house, which made his intestines cramp and gurgle. Not daring to foul the house with the dead animal stink that was leaking out of him, Tom burst from the laundry room, raced through the kitchen, opened the sliding glass doors and leapt out on the patio.

Standing outside, waiting for the air to clear, his mind ran wild. What was she doing with a scorecard? And golf tees? What the hell was going on? Examining the scorecard more closely, he saw that it had Carol's name on it and that the score had been attested to by another player's signature at the bottom. The scorecard showed that Carol had played 18 holes of golf at the town course and shot an 89. Tom stared at the score for a full minute trying to comprehend its meaning until it hit him and he laughed out loud. It was a joke. She was playing a trick on him. It had taken Tom five solid years of persistent practice to break into the 80s. *Ha, ha,* he thought, *very funny.* Still, it took half an hour for his bowels to settle down before he could safely bring himself back into the house.

While the first load was washing, Tom went upstairs and scrubbed the slimy, gray-brown layer of crud that ringed the tub. *"Don't make a mess!"* When the washer had cycled through, he put the load of whites in the dryer and then loaded the washer with the darks. As he was placing a navy-colored blouse in the load, he took a moment and sniffed it, hoping for a whiff of Carol's aroma. He caught the slightest reminder of her scent, and then mashed the blouse against his nose, inhaling deeply. He could smell Carol's heavenly scent on the blouse all right, but there was something else, a startling mixture of other aromas underneath. Moving the blouse around in his hands, he sniffed again, and then again. There was the familiar smell of sunscreen, no mistaking that, but as he continued to sniff and sniff, he detected a hint—more than a hint if he was being honest—of the rank aroma of a man's cheap cologne.

"Where's Marty?" Tom looked straight into the assistant Pro's eyes and leaned heavily on the glass countertop, despite the sign on the counter expressly asking customers not to do so. The assistant Pro reached for his cell phone, which rested on the register, but Tom got to it first and snatched it. "Just tell me where he is."

The assistant stared coolly at Tom and was about to say something when Tom waved his hand in front of the man's face, aborting the lie before it began. "I know he's here, I saw his car in the parking lot." Tom turned and strode toward the door that led to the storage area and to Marty's private office, knocking over several new golf bags on display. He threw open the door to Marty's office only to find it empty, but his nostril's filled with the masculine scent of Marty's cologne. "God damn it!" Tom ran back into the shop and shouted, "He's either teaching down below or he's out on the course. Which is it?" When the assistant just stared back Tom fled through the front door with the assistant's phone still in his hand. He didn't want Marty and his student to be given a heads-up. He started to run down to Marty's private teaching area when he glanced into the barn where the golf carts were stored. Marty's sky-blue sports-car golf cart was not among them. Marty thought he looked like hot shit tooling around the course in it. Tom got back in his car and drove completely around the perimeter of the course trying to spot the snazzy blue cart.

On his second lap he saw it. The cart was perched up on the sixteenth tee and even from the distance of several fairway widths he could see there were two people in it. Parking his car, he got out and walked behind the sixteenth green, adjacent to the tenth green, exactly where Carol and Connie had bushwhacked Tom and his companion's years back. Tom walked down the side of the fairway and stopped adjacent to the white plastic 150-yard marker embedded in the middle of the fairway. From this vantage point he could watch Marty and his student tee off in his direction.

Marty got out of the cart and after his signature practice swing, teed off hitting a beautiful drive that split the center of the fairway. He got back in the blue golf cart and drove up to the ladies' tee. Tom couldn't be sure from a distance of over three hundred yards, but thought it could very well be Carol getting out of the cart to tee up. The woman took a couple of graceful practice swings and then addressed the ball. Whoever the lady was, her form was flawless. She hit the ball with a tremendous swipe and a second later Tom heard the sharp crack of flush contact and watched with envy as the soaring drive landed just thirty yards behind Marty's. He walked to the center of the fairway in the direction of the balls and then waited as the cart left the tee and raced toward him.

Marty and his student could not miss Tom standing where he was, with his hands on his hips like a traffic cop in the middle of the fairway. Marty brought the golf cart over and stopped. He hopped out, extending his hand.

"Well, well, look who's back," he said, smiling genially as if Tom had only been gone for a week. Tom ignored Marty's hand and instead stared over his instructor's shoulder at Carol, who remained seated in the cart. She gave a little wave at Tom, as if she was Marty's date, waiting patiently waiting for the two men to finish their business so she could get back to her lesson.

"Would someone tell me what the hell's going on?" Tom said.

Marty walked to the back of the golf cart and began removing Carol's clubs. "Why don't you two walk in the last couple of holes? I have to get back for another lesson anyway."

Carol frowned, then sighed, surrendering to Marty's decision. She took her bag from Marty who jumped back behind the wheel.

"I understand you're having trouble with your swing, Tom." Marty said as he slipped on his sunglasses. "Give me a call and we'll straighten you right out." He tipped his hat to Carol, and then turned back to Tom. "You've got quite a gal here. I wouldn't let her get away if I were you."

Carol and Tom stood in the fading light of the afternoon, watching Marty drive across the fairway, down behind the 16th green and out of sight. When he was gone they turned toward each other. "So, you're back," Carol said.

"Yes," Tom said. "I'm back." For a moment, gazing into Carol's beautiful eyes, Tom thought he might burst into tears. Instead, after a few awkward moments of silence, Tom knelt on one knee and bowed his head. He held his arms out in supplication. "If you'll take me back, I'm here for you now. I want you to know that." When Carol did not respond Tom looked up and watched her take him in. Did she see that he was haggard and nervous and sad? Could she tell that for all of his faults, his stupidity and selfishness, that he still believed that she was the only one for him? She was taking her time, deriving enjoyment from seeing him kneel before her. *Why not*, Tom thought, *she'd earned it*. Finally, Carol bent down and gave him a little kiss on the forehead. She pulled back and wrinkled her nose.

"You smell weird," she said.

A golf ball thumped the fairway a few feet away. They turned to the tee box behind them to see a foursome standing there shrugging their shoulders and holding their arms up in the air in outraged impatience. Carol waved at them and pulled an 8-iron out of her bag, nodding to Tom. "Caddie for me, will you?" Silently, Tom stood up and shouldered her bag, following her to where her ball lay. Carol stood behind her ball, lined up her shot to the pin, took her stance and swung a couple of practice swings.

Tom had always found the athletic golf stance of a pretty female a real turn-on and it was no different as he watched Carol set up. When she stood over the ball with her feet spread apart and her pert butt jutting out behind, she had his full attention. At the same time, he took great satisfaction that this was his wife and he was leering at her like a teenage boy.

There was a crisp thud when Carol hit the ball; she took a good sized divot and the ball soared up in the air. Tom thought the arc of the ball a little low, but it landed just behind the pin on the green, and from Tom's vantage point it appeared to bite and spin back toward the hole. Tom's eyes widened and his jaw dropped as low as it would go. With just the slightest of grins, Carol handed the iron back to Tom, who wiped it clean and replaced it into the bag as Carol started off towards the green.

"What's happening?" Tom panted as he struggled to catch up to Carol's quick march. "Who are you? Where did you learn to do that?" Carol said nothing but instead held out her hand. It took Tom a moment to realize she was waiting to be handed her putter. He was so completely unsettled by what was happening, not to mention the 180-degree change in the dynamics of their relationship, that his stomach fluttered and he began a machine-gun string of farting. He handed Carol her putter, then backed away, keeping his distance while fanning his backside as he went.

As he retreated past the pin, Tom pulled it out and watched awestruck as Carol marked her ball and deftly repaired her pitch mark. Carol replaced her ball and lined up her putt, then with a confident stroke promptly hit the back of the cup as if she'd been doing it all her life. She pulled her ball out of the hole and handed her putter back to Tom.

"The first hole you watch me play and I birdied it!" she almost screamed, then gave a little fist pump as Tom replaced the flag and followed her off the green.

As they strode briskly toward the seventeenth tee, Carol brought Tom up to speed. "I was desperate to find out where you had run off to and it seemed Marty was the only one who knew exactly what had happened and where you were. The only way I could get an appointment to see him was to book a lesson, so that's what I did." There was a defiant rebuke in Carol's tone and Tom knew that the blame for whatever may or may not have happened between Carol and Marty was being laid at his doorstep.

"You've been taking lessons from Marty?" he wheezed, finding it difficult to keep up. When Carol nodded and raised her eyebrows in obvious glee, Tom stopped. "Oh my God, you're not pregnant, are you?"

Carol laughed and then waved at Tom, signaling for him to keep moving forward. Once at the tee box they looked down the fairway where they could see a twosome just getting off their second shots. They had a minute to wait before she could hit, so Carol sat on the bench adjacent to the tee.

"He thinks he's such a ladies' man with his corny jokes and smarmy ways, it's almost laughable. Most of the women in the league think he's a hottie, but those of us under the age of seventy know better. He's so hands-on with his teaching I can't tell whether I'm getting a lesson or a massage. But he sure can teach golf, I'll give him that."

Tom stared at Carol and while she talked an electrical synapse flashed across his brain. It occurred to him while looking at her in the soft light of late afternoon, with her sports-skirt and sleeveless blouse, not to mention the healthy tan she'd acquired, that she was more beautiful than he'd remembered. His eyes misted up at the joy of being in her presence. He cleared his throat, about to confess his feelings when the fairway cleared and Carol stood up, walked to her bag and pulled out her driver. It had a fire engine red club head with a bright pink shaft.

Tom watched as she teed up her ball and took a few practice swings with a physical grace most golfers would envy. "How far are you hitting your woods?" he asked.

"I make a lot of mistakes and I'm very erratic, but when I really tag one I can get up to two hundred yards with a little wind behind me."

Tom's eyes popped open wide but he said nothing. When Carol set up for her drive, Tom became transfixed. The way she stood over the ball, determined focus on her face, her sexy stance, Tom felt blood rush to his loins for the first time in months. Carol's shot went a little right but still she'd put plenty of smack on the ball and it landed in a decent lie in the first cut of rough.

"If I'm making you nervous I can wait in the parking lot," Tom said.

"Not at all," She handed the driver to Tom, then started walking down the fairway. "I've never had a caddie before. I love it." Tom shouldered Carol's bag and shuffled behind her, trying to keep up.

Several months later, after Tom's anti-depressant medication had kicked in and his therapy for Traumatic Stress Disorder was well underway, Tom and Carol played their first 18 holes together. Their play was competitive for the front nine but Tom's nerve was shattered on the tenth tee when they were joined by a single. The newcomer opened his mouth to offer a respectful greeting and his words came out flavored from the deep South. "Mind if I join y'all on the back?" he drawled. Tom never found a fairway the rest of the way home.

Not only did Carol beat Tom by seven strokes but for the first time in her golfer's life she shot an even 80. After the round they were joined by Marty in the clubhouse for drinks. "Congratulations Carol," Marty said, hoisting a frosty mug in her direction. "Your growth as a golfer is nothing short of meteoric. When you break 80, which I have no doubt will be very soon, you will join the ranks of the exalted few."

Carol looked across the table at Tom then back at Marty. "When I do break 80 I believe I get a little envelope of some kind from you, Marty, isn't that so?"

Marty shot a cold stare in Tom's direction. "We've never had a female member of the break 80 club." Marty swallowed hard and for the first time ever Carol saw him stammer. "Uh, we'd have to make...some...uh, accommodations in that eventuality."

"Oh, I shouldn't think it would take much," Carol grinned at both men, "they're sprucing up the ladies rooms at Augusta I hear."

"Yes," Marty said while waving the waitress over for another round. "That's what I hear."

"The only change I can think of offhand that we ladies would insist on," Carol reached across the table and patted the hand of each of the men, "is that you'd have to get rid of that stupid pole."

"Soooo…..Hummmm. Soooo….Hummm." Tom's mind was just drifting into a pleasant quietness, a level of serenity he was finding easier to achieve with each passing day, when in the near darkness of Carol's sanctuary Carol slipped her hand into his pajama bottoms. "Hey," Tom protested, shocked to be pulled to the surface so rudely."

"What?" Carol whispered, then sucked on one of Tom's earlobes.

"Come on Carol, I was just getting into my zone."

"Really, in the zone were you?"

"Not tonight darling, I'm pooped." Staying in the lotus position while a one handed wrestling match was taking place in his underwear was a losing effort. It had become their habit at night, after the dishes were cleared and if the weather permitted and they'd taken their evening walk, to climb up to Carol's sanctuary, light a few candles and meditate together.

"Stop it," he said when she persisted. "Both of us worked this morning then played eighteen holes, came home, talked to our sons, ate a big dinner. I'm cooked, done. Show's over."

Carol began to withdraw her hand but then stopped as one side of her mouth slipped into a grin. In the candlelight her eyes sparkled a gentle maroon.

"When do you think we can get out again?" she whispered, leaning close and sticking her tongue in his ear. "I don't know about you but I'm dying to spank one." Tom sat still and said nothing. With her free hand

Carol pushed Tom on his back and purred some more. "Putting that stiff shaft on your 3-wood was the smart move. You're really hitting it deep."

"You stop that right now," Tom said, but there was no fight in him.

Carol nibbled on Tom's lower lip. "Marty was right about that shaft," she moaned. "Stiff is the one for you."

They kissed for a long time and when Tom came up for air, he gasped, "Marty was right about another thing too."

"What's that?"

Tom panted over her open mouth. "You do have a tight grip."

John O'Hern's initial foray into writing was *A Rooster in the Henhouse*, an acerbic memoir based on his wife's first pregnancy experience seen through a man's eyes. It was this attempt at memoir that evolved into his highly praised one-man off-Broadway show of the same name. John's next writing project was his two person play, *Sweetspot, Confessions of a Golfaholic. Sweetspot* the novel is the off-spring of that play. John lives with his wife and children in Connecticut.

Author's note: *I discovered the secret to the golf swing this past winter and promptly lost it as soon as the course opened. It came back to me in full the day I finished this book. Coincidence...I think not.*

www.sweetspotthebook.com

www.sweetspotthecomedy.com